SIDE EFFECTS

OTHER BOOKS BY PATTY FRIEDMANN

Too Smart to Be Rich

The Exact Image of Mother

Eleanor Rushing

Odds

Secondhand Smoke

SIDE EFFECTS

A New Orleans Love Story

PATTY FRIEDMANN

Shoemaker & Hoard

Library of Congress Cataloging-in-Publication Data
Friedmann, Patty.
Side effects : a New Orleans love story / Patty Friedmann.
p. cm.
ISBN-13: 978-1-59376-096-0 (alk. paper)
ISBN-10: 1-59376-096-5 (alk. paper)
1. Drugstore employees—Fiction.
2. New Orleans (La.)—Fiction. I. Title.
PS3556.R538S53 2006
813'.54-DC22 2005027472

Book design by Mark McGarry | Texas Type & Book Works
Set in Plantin

Printed in the United States of America

Shoemaker S&H Hoard
An Imprint of Avalon Publishing Group, Inc.
Distributed by Publishers Group West

10 9 8 7 6 5 4 3 2 1

I did it all for
The Esme and The Werner.

If I didn't have the genius Susan Glade to thank, I'd have a bartender. Susan fine-tunes and off-labels my meds so I can write. One day the pharmaceutical companies will give her the means so I also can feel.

Even though everyone in the Riverbend Walgreens can attest that I know a lot, I had to scrounge for much information for this book. Thanks to Cherie Amedio, Bryan Moody, Richard Ochs, Susan Rosenthal, Margot Stander, and especially Ruby Tremont for educating me.

As always, it's friends and family who are the magical elixir. My mind reader agent Rolph Blythe. My dream-come-true-forever publishers Jack Shoemaker and Trish Hoard. Jane: in my house, that's it, Jane. Jane Vandenburgh, the source of *everything*. Roxy Font, Matt Kaye, Julie Wrinn, Heather McLeod, Elaine English, Courtney Eiswirth: amazing handholders. Debbie Davis and Leslie Hollingsworth, who are my image of Ciana and Lennon. Rebecca Stilling, who cures without chemistry. Ed, who gave me policy number 838721014, son Andrew, and Muchmore. And family, dwindled to a small, but finally completely loving circle of all the same name. Tommy Friedmann. Lynda Friedmann. Esme Friedmann. And Werner Friedmann II, at long last.

I

LENNON sees Errol Nash, out in the waiting area, reach over and squeeze the bulbs on all the sphygmomanometers, and the cuffs are jumping in the boxes like toy frogs. Lennon cannot concentrate on what he is doing because he is sure that if Ciana doesn't take care of Errol soon, all those cuffs are going to pop out of their boxes and fly off the shelf. They'll be all over the floor near Pick-up, which is not the most sanitary place, and Lennon chose this profession because, among other reasons, he likes enforced cleanliness. He trusts Ciana will bump Errol up the queue. But he won't believe she will until she does.

Right now five people are waiting, and they all look sick. Not sick in the way that makes Lennon's hands tingle because the people are sneezing into used-up Kleenexes, but the kind of genuine sick that doesn't show on the surface. Except the woman waiting with the baby in the Pepto-Bismol pink jacket that's almost raspberry down the front from mucus and saliva. Lennon knows the mother will be back in three days, feeling so sick she wishes she were dead. That seems to be the way it is with children. Nobody goes near the two of them.

The sickest evidently is Errol, or at least he is the one who has made himself the sickest. Errol's Medicaid won't pay for his two-milligram alprazolam tablet until today, and according to Lennon's watch Errol has about fifteen minutes to get that pill into his system or he will be a complete wreck. Nine times out of ten his mother is the one who comes in asking for "my boy nerve pill," because nine times out of ten somebody in that house has overslept, and Errol can't drag his agitated every-which-way skinny body four blocks over to the store. Ciana once said to Errol, "You know, if you didn't live with your mother, you wouldn't need this," and Errol said back, "Uh, uh, my mama very good to me," and that had been the end of that for the time being. So Lennon had thought he would give tending Errol's soul a try, and he had said to Errol a while later, "You know, I really enjoy having my own apartment," a variation on the theme, he thought. Errol had said, "Who you think you is?" and stormed out, and his mother had come in for the medicine for several weeks after that.

Ciana brings Errol's prescription up to the counter just

moments before Lennon is convinced that there is going to be a race of blood pressure cuffs down the cosmetics aisle. "Bless you, Miss Ciana," Errol says, knowing full well that he arrived after the baby and her mother. The baby lets out a pitiful wheeze.

Ciana says she likes Errol because he pronounces her name right even though he only knows it from the tag she wears. It's *She-ah-na.* Not *Shah-nah.* Her real name is Luciana, and for reasons not clear to Lennon she made sure when they first met that he knew she was very lucky as a child to get the right nickname. She told him flat out that she weighed a hundred pounds in fourth grade at Holy Name of Jesus School and if she'd had a name that could downgrade to Shamu she'd have had to kill herself. Lennon had known white girls slightly growing up, but he never had known white women up close, and he couldn't quite figure out why Ciana was telling him this. Ciana was a big woman, probably two hundred pounds, but a quite beautiful two hundred pounds, with a face like Michelle Pfeiffer. He thought, but didn't say, *Well, you're no Shamu now,* and afterward decided that maybe that was her purpose. Lennon spends an inordinate amount of time looking at Ciana's face. He also owns a videotape of *Dangerous Minds*, and not for the reason his sister says he does.

Of the people in the waiting area, one has not turned in her prescription. She has seen others come and go, and Lennon suspects she is not coming forward until no one else is around. The girl is a Tulane student, he would guess from her clothes, even though she is as bedraggled as it is possible to be in mismatched sweats that must have cost over a hundred dollars. He is wishing that more customers were self-selecting in turn-taking this way when Vendetta calls out to the girl, "I could help you?" The girl pulls herself up with a like-I've-got-a-choice-*now* expression, approaches the counter, points at Ciana, and says, "I think maybe *she's* the one I ought to talk to."

"Mmm, hmm," Vendetta says. Vendetta is the tech, but Vendetta is on a par with Ciana and Lennon, and all three of them know it. N.O. Drugstore sits at the improbable intersection of South Claiborne and South Carrollton, separating nothing from nothing and everything from everything, black Pigeontown from white Tulane, and Vendetta can pick up a snub much faster than Lennon can. Lennon looks at the girl, perplexed, and she says, "I mean, like, it's *her* picture on the wall." It's true. In the waiting area, for reasons that fascinate Lennon, someone has hung framed photos of Ciana and Maureen, who alternate days, even and odd, as pharmacy manager. The photos surely are graduation photos, and Ciana's is, to Lennon, simply breathtaking. She was his age then.

"You got a question or a prescription?" Vendetta says. "Not that it make no different. We all the same back here. What you need?"

"I think I need to talk to *her*," the girl says, pointing at Ciana. She is still slouching in her seat. Definitely Tulane. Lennon has been at Xavier long enough to recognize the affect. Xavier is turning into a Tulane for black kids, but it's still got the décor, if not the full decorum, of having been founded by a recently canonized saint, so it's not there yet. If this girl wants to get her way, she ought to consider standing up, he thinks. Though she's probably been led to believe the exact opposite. The girl drags herself peevishly up to the counter

"Ci*an*a," Vendetta says, audible only within the pharmacy but possibly to the girl, "I think you got somebody with a scrip for EC." With that Vendetta scoots off to the computer at the other side of the drop-off window, leaving Lennon standing at the counter. "How'd she know that?" the girl says.

"She's been here a very long time," Lennon says neutrally. Emergency contraception is not a business he wants to be caught up in. Ethically he agrees one hundred percent with Ciana's stance on EC. Emotionally he worships her over it. But purely pragmatically, he is not going to touch it until he has his license. Luciana comes to the counter, and Lennon can back off a few feet, grateful and just the slightest bit aroused. "Yes?" Ciana says.

"Like, my friends say *one* of you does these, and the other one doesn't," the girl says, pointing in the direction of the photos on the wall. "She says the pretty one."

Lennon only has laid eyes on Maureen once, and he has to admit that the photo does her far too much justice, that she is religiously plain, that this girl actually is telling the truth. Maureen may weigh eighty pounds less than Ciana, but there is no comparison. Maureen has an apologetic posture about her job, visible even in the head shot. But Ciana knows that she wields many powers, one of which is the ability to dispense Schedule II drugs and pills that end pregnancies before they begin. That makes Ciana sexy, probably even to women.

Ciana takes the prescription right over the pick-up counter, even though the girl ought to be back at Drop-off, handing it to Vendetta. "Next time, just turn it in like a regular prescription," Ciana says.

In the voice of someone who has stayed up all of at least one night, the girl says, too loudly, "There's not going to be a next time," and that is the moment when Mr. Walker chooses to cruise past the pharmacy during one of his finest, most idle moments. Seeing the blood-red vest and large brass manager's nametag, the girl bursts into sleep-starved tears. "People shouldn't have to go through this crap," she says to the uniform.

Mr. Walker eases up to the counter as if he has say-so in the operation of the pharmacy. He may be the manager of the store, but the pharmacy is autonomous. Lennon steers clear of him only because he never can tell what sort of letters of recommendation he is going to need when it's all over with. Mr. Walker has mistaken him for a stock clerk twice since he has been here.

"Miss Jambon, would you like to tell me what this is all about?" he says to Ciana. Mr. Walker never has called anyone by his or her last name in as long as Lennon has worked here. But Mr. Walker did not go to college, and

Tulane students make him nervous. Technically, Ciana has a doctoral degree—*Dr.* Jambon—but Lennon is not going to mention that. And he certainly is not going to mention that in the spring he will have one, too.

"I don't think you want to know," Ciana says. Her voice is kind, sweet, taking in both Mr. Walker and the girl, both of whom should let it go at that.

But the girl says, "My friends have gone to about *every* drugstore in all of uptown, and they all know everything, and they tell me, come here, there's a lady that won't give you a hard time, and she'll give you the pill. So, I, like, can't come yesterday, when I *need* to come yesterday, because the other one's working here, and I come today, and what happens? She acts like I'm some kind of slut."

Mr. Walker still doesn't understand, so Ciana says, "I do emergency contraception, and it's my choice, all right?"

Mr. Walker tells Ciana that he needs to see her in his office, and Ciana puts the prescription up on the rack in front of the computer, absentmindedly wipes her hands on her smock, and walks right out the security door into the drugstore. Mr. Walker is still standing in the waiting area, stunned by the sound of his own voice, when Ciana comes up to him and says, "I'm ready." Ciana is the same height as Mr. Walker, and Ciana is not a tall woman. She starts to move toward the front of the store, and Lennon is sure she is going to have to give Mr. Walker a little tug if he doesn't unfreeze soon. The Tulane girl says, "Hey, what's going on?" and that is what it takes for Mr. Walker to become masterful, straightening up to his best posture as he aims himself toward his office. Though scurrying ahead of Ciana, marking double time, he looks very much as if he is in for a scolding.

The prescription is sitting where Ciana left it, and Lennon knows it will do no good to fill it until he finds out whether Ciana is going to sign off on it or not. He notices that Vendetta has edged her way up to where he is despite the fact that she has nothing to do there. With a half dozen phone-ins pending, Lennon can ease himself back to the dispensing station, but evidently Vendetta is in the mood to fiddle around with the Prilosec-sample display so she can be front and center when something happens. It doesn't take long enough for her to get even one stack of Prilosec packets lined up with a geometric precision that would please Lennon before the Tulane girl says, "So, I need that right now, you know."

Lennon can practically feel Vendetta filling up with air. "You *know* Miss Jambon the only one can give that stuff to you," and her voice carries the acknowledgment of every racial insult she's ever heard in her entire life.

"Aw, come on," the girl says, and then she looks to Lennon as if she has something he wants badly enough to violate local, state, and federal codes, no problem; she's a rich white girl, and he's a black boy with a *job.*

"You got to wait for her, and when she go in his office, she sometime don't come out for *hours,*" Vendetta tells the girl.

In all the time Lennon has worked at N.O., Ciana never has been summoned into Mr. Walker's office. Never.

"Probably, you better off going someplace else," Vendetta says to the girl. "I *know* you got a car."

Lennon knows very well that Vendetta knows no Tulane student ever has seen any part of New Orleans besides the university section and the French Quarter, not even the chasm that lies between the two, except during Mardi Gras week of freshman year. Lennon also knows that the only other pharmacists who fill prescriptions for EC work in precisely that purgatory, those city wards where Planned Parenthood doctors do a lot of business.

The girl asks where she can go. "Baby, I don't know what to tell you," Vendetta says.

After the girl has left the store with nothing in hand except that slip of paper, Vendetta says to Lennon, "Aw, don't be all upsetted. She *ain't* pregnant. I think she pregnant, I fill that scrip myself."

IF ASKED, Ciana couldn't quite pinpoint the time in her life when she quit walking into her mother's house unannounced. She keeps the key and uses it only if she has called ahead and rung the bell upon arrival, and she has respected her mother's privacy that way for as long as she can remember. Today she forgets *all* formality, *all* adult civility. Ciana got out of bed this morning, threw on her clothes without any thoughts of personal hygiene, and drove over here thinking about the same thing that kept her awake all last night. "Mama!" she says as she throws herself through the front door and plants herself in the middle of the foyer.

She expects her mother to come out of the kitchen because the alarm is off, but instead Mrs. Jambon shambles slowly down the stairs. She is going as fast as she can, but for a tiny bird of a woman who is not yet seventy, her best speed isn't going to save any lives. Ciana has been uncomfortable being seen in public with this sincere, delicate woman ever since Geoffrey said that together they looked like Baby Huey and his mother.

And that was probably when Ciana was *twelve*. Geoffrey is two years older than she is, but he has tormented her since her parents brought her home from the hospital. If a stranger eyes her and her mother when they are shopping, Ciana will say in a stage whisper, "Yes, she's my mother. It was a hell of a delivery." She doesn't let Geoffrey win, even when he's not around.

"Honey, are you all right?"

This is why Ciana adores her mother. A breach of good behavior gets sympathy, not annoyance. "No," she says. "No, I don't think I'm all right."

Silently she follows her mother into the kitchen. She watches to see whether her mother is going to do all she needs to soothe her, and when she sees the measuring cups and griddle come out, Ciana posts herself at the cooking island and begins talking to her mother's moving head. "She really came after me this time." Mrs. Jambon breaks eggs into the bowl. "Get this." And so Ciana tells her mother as she makes pecan pancakes with extra vanilla that Corinne, the sister-in-law who lives to get Mrs. Jambon completely in her thrall, once again has tried to make Ciana's life miserable. "She told the manager that I was dispensing *abortion* pills, and that if I didn't stop she'd have every Catholic she knows boycott the store. As if she knows more than a dozen *people* altogether."

This kitchen is Ciana's psychiatrist's office. It has a certain neutrality to it because it has changed so little over decades; eventually she has come to see nothing in detail. Her mother has bought every new appliance on the market, but most are in cabinets, so whatever Ciana wants to say bounces off safe, familiar surfaces. In this room, Ciana learned to think that eating beyond reason was fine, that a fat girl would be loved unconditionally, and she never dieted as a child because her mother was dismissive of the idea. Since then she has considered dieting because it seems no one shares her mother's opinion, including possibly her mother. But Ciana's never quite gotten over loving herself. She never has figured out exactly what to do about food, but she knows one thing absolutely, that she always eats to happy excess in this kitchen, and she is comfortable.

"Well, are you?" Her mother doesn't even turn around to speak. To her credit, though, it is time to flip the pancakes, and Ciana respects that.

"No," Ciana says. Bill Clinton pops into her head, and she knows she's going to have to get good and semantic with her mother right now, but she also knows her mother isn't going to be as dumb as Corinne hopes she is.

"No, I don't dispense abortion pills. Yes, I dispense birth control pills."

"I know that."

"Okay, so these are sort of birth control pills you take right after you might be pregnant."

The pancakes are now viable, and Mrs. Jambon focuses fully on Ciana. Bores in on her, really. Ciana's sense of smell leaves her completely open. "Abortion is birth control you do after you're pregnant, sweetie."

"Well, all right," Ciana says. So much for being nuanced.

Her mother serves Ciana two pancakes, sets two aside for herself, pours out four more, and says, "I can't take sides, you know that."

"You're pro-choice, Mama, it's not like it's any big secret."

"You didn't come over here to fight *Roe v. Wade*, Ciana. I swear, for all I know, if you and your brother weren't so hell-bent on being at war with each other, you'd probably agree on *everything*."

"That's an insult," Ciana says, and then she laughs. "Yeah, if he didn't live to destroy me, he'd have to admit I was right."

"Sometimes *he's* got the answers."

Ciana considers saying, *Name one*, but she is strictly not in the mood for an examination of her lifestyle. Geoffrey and Corinne are married with three children who go to Catholic school and church, and Ciana can't even claim to go to church herself. Her mother doesn't exactly condemn the way she lives, but Ciana knows that, as far as her mother can see, it is an embryonic stage at best, and whenever Ciana implies that it's not temporary she knows she's being judged wrong. Of course, if she's honest, she judges herself wrong, too. Ciana wants to get married and have children, too.

"Ciana," her mother says, "you know you're my favorite. That's why I give them preferential treatment."

She has no answer to that one except to remember it forever. And to change the subject quickly so her mother won't know how well she heard her. "Where's Nookie?" Ciana says softly.

"Oh, no!" her mother says. "I came downstairs so fast I forgot." She casts around frantically trying to figure out how she is going to succeed with her next batch of pancakes and run immediately up to fetch her dog, who is too small to go down steps on his own. He is not too small, however, to pee significantly all over her bedroom if he doesn't go outdoors fairly soon after he has been lowered off the bed.

Ciana takes the steps two at a time, a feat she mastered when she was in grade school and never has lost the ability to perform, no matter how heavy she has become. It always has involved a lot of leverage with the banister, but so far the banister has not detached from its wall anchor. Nookie is waiting at the top of the stairs, whimpering accusatorily, and every bit of comical affection oozes through Ciana. He is a toy dachshund with the most delightful mutation of being largely yapless, and Ciana scoops him up and cradles him to her breast, noticing that his little weenie is not wet; he is holding it in. "He's being good," she calls down the steps, and she goes straight out the front door and places him on the grass; Nookie doesn't even bother to lift a stubby leg, squatting and peeing for a good half minute.

"Why'd she do it?" Ciana says as she eats her second serving of pancakes with Nookie on her lap. Nookie does not lunge at her plate. Nookie is close to perfect. Nookie was named by Ciana's smarty-pants niece, Caroline, who told her grandmother that there was a song called "I Did It All for the Nookie." Caroline's church-going parents did not say a word.

"I assume Corinne was acting out of conviction," her mother says. Ciana hears no conviction in her tone.

"When she comes over here, what do you talk about, church doctrine? Supreme Court decisions? How she and Geoffrey have kept from having any more kids since Lucien?"

"Calm down, Ciana."

"She tried to get me in trouble at work," Ciana says. She can hear her childhood voice echoing in this kitchen, and she doesn't mind too much. Usually as a child she complained about insults, but the effect was the same. It feels sweetly familiar, sort of like hearing the theme music to "The Price Is Right." "She *thinks* Mr. Walker's my boss."

"He's not?"

Ciana's mouth is full, happily full, and she shakes her head, no, her loose pale hair coming perilously close to a pool of syrup at the side of her plate. "Mama, I earn twice his salary."

"Money isn't everything," says a woman who never has had a job but always has had four figures in her checking account.

"It is in a drugstore chain," Ciana says. "That's why he hates me."

"Well, if he's not going to fire you, I don't see why you're so mad at poor Corinne."

"I guarantee you *poor* Corinne didn't go to any other drugstore. This was about me. I don't know where she got the idea anyway. Corinne isn't exactly in any pipelines, you know."

"There was an article in *Gambit*," her mother says. She gets up and slides another pancake onto Ciana's plate, even though Ciana has quite a large number of perfectly cut pieces that are perfectly saturated with syrup already there. Ciana sits back and folds her arms across her chest, feeling the isometric strain necessary to keep Nookie on her lap.

"You knew," Ciana says.

Her mother takes on the testy tone of a parent caught in crossfire. "I know where she got the idea, Ciana."

"Mama, I got called into that man's office like I was an embezzler or something. I am sure Lennon thinks I'm a criminal. For all I know he would never do this kind of thing."

"And would you want a man who disagrees with you on something like that?"

"I'm not getting into this today." Her mother believes that every marriage can be like Geoffrey and Corinne's, forged in childhood and built on full agreement on every subject. Her mother also believes that every marriage must be like Geoffrey and Corinne's, founded on idealization. And as she has reminded Ciana as delicately as possible on numerous occasions, Ciana cannot be idealized. *Even a black man* is the way her mother opens every explanation of why no man adores Ciana enough to take care of her forever. Even a black man would only fall in love with a woman who's not fat. Men fall in love with me all the time, Ciana counters. For Saturday night, her mother says back, sadly. "Lennon wears Romance for Men every day," she said the last time the subject came up. Her mother had no answer, so she said, "And he didn't when he first came to work at N.O."

Someone opens the front door with a key, and Ciana looks at her mother for an explanation. Her mother has had a doorbell-ringing maid service ever since her housekeeper retired five years ago. "Something the matter?" Corinne calls from the foyer. "I saw Ciana's car out there." She's still not in the kitchen.

Ciana gently deposits Nookie on the floor, hands him one tiny cube of pancake, and picks up her car keys.

"Don't leave," her mother says.

"I'll talk to you before your trip," Ciana says. Corinne is in the kitchen now. Corinne, who has wangled her mother into a trip to New York. "Trust me," Ciana says, "I'll talk to you before." She doesn't let Corinne catch her eye on her way out.

VENDETTA knows that if even one finger emerges from the covers and moves toward that phone, Jaquilica will come in from the kitchen and force her out of this bed. That includes any rustling she might do peeking at the Caller ID. Though she has a good idea of who it is, calling her at this hour. Only one person knows her work schedule perfectly, and that person has the same schedule. Luciana Marie Jambon. Vendetta's best friend. In spite of what her sisters say. Or maybe because of it.

Jaquilica has no business being over here in her side of the house, but it doesn't seem to matter. The deal they all made ten years ago was, Vendetta would live with Mama, and Jaquilica and Frieda could share the other half of the shotgun double with their kids. The brothers were shit out of luck because Mama said so, in so many words. Vendetta figured everybody knew what the deal meant: *she* would take Mama to dialysis and watch her die up close, and when it was all over, *she* got her own half. That was fine for a while, as long as Vendetta had a husband. But as soon as she didn't have Robert anymore, they might as well have broken through the separating wall. Jaquilica and Frieda come and go as they please; all they lack is an entry point anywhere except at the front and the back doors. Jaquilica is in the kitchen at the back. Vendetta knows this for a fact because Jaquilica is always in the kitchen at the back.

It occurs to Vendetta that if she doesn't pick up, her sister is going to hear Ciana's message as she leaves it on the answering machine. Vendetta is going to have to get voice mail. She hates the idea of voice mail. It's not right out there where she can *see* it. Ciana knows Jaquilica hangs around the house, but Ciana probably doesn't know all the details about Vendetta's answering system. For close friends, they don't know many specifics. Ciana's only been over maybe four times. And always for a reason.

"You need to get your ass back out that bed," Jaquilica calls through the house, and Vendetta reaches for the phone before the machine can pick up. "Yeh," she says sleepily, hoping at least to make Ciana feel a little guilty since guilt is impossible with her sister.

"I'm sorry," Ciana says, "but you know I wouldn't do this if I weren't losing my mind." Ciana always says she understands how hard it is for Vendetta to get up every morning and get a child out for school, but Ciana never has plaited hair, and that's just for *starts*. "Let me pee," Vendetta says.

Going to the bathroom is risky because in a shotgun the bathroom is behind the kitchen, but Vendetta holds up the portable phone at Jaquilica like a cross at a vampire, and her passage is safe. She figures Jaquilica checked the Caller ID in the kitchen. Jaquilica talks a big game about Ciana, but in the long run she doesn't want to mess with her.

Ciana can't fool Vendetta, even over the phone. In public both of them are scary women, and they know it, making people look them in the eye when they hand over antipsychotics and suppositories and swipe the bar code like they're handing over carrots in the grocery. Their best week was the one when everyone had to sign the HIPAA form. "Confidentiality!" Ciana would whisper to her. "Confidentiality!"

In private Ciana tries to act like she doesn't care, but Vendetta knows exactly what she's going to ask. Not what Mr. Walker thinks. What Lennon thinks. Everything has to be right for Lennon. And Lennon has a very high standard of right. He likes the pens in the holder all to touch bottom. Ciana always wants to impress Lennon, who is no older than Vendetta herself. Ciana one time said that some sun spot must have flared the year Lennon and Vendetta were born, given the wackiness of their names. Lennon had been miffed, since his name came from a specific event, not a moment when his not-yet-born-again mother was crazed. "Mine come from a specific event, too," Vendetta had said back. "Something happen, on the front of the Metro section.

That where my mama got *my* name. In a *headline*." Ciana had been very quiet for several days after that.

"Before you start up, baby," Vendetta says, "I'm here to tell you nobody said nothing." She gets back in the bed and pulls the cover over her head because it is her best chance not to be heard by Jaquilica. Of course it is also her best chance for Jaquilica to sneak into the room and eavesdrop without being seen.

"I know you didn't hear actual words," Ciana says. "But people don't need to talk for *you* to know what they're thinking."

Ciana thinks Vendetta is wise beyond her years, but Vendetta *ought* to be wise beyond her years. Unlike Ciana, she did not go straight from high school into college and graduate school, and then scuttle like a scared cockroach behind that counter. Being a mother when she was eighteen made Vendetta wise up fast. Even if she was married. Especially if she was married. Being able to read a boy like Lennon ought to be very easy for someone like her. Trouble is, it's not. "How many time I have to tell you, I got no earthly idea what that boy thinking?" she says to Ciana. "Jaquilica boy a flat-out sissy, but he don't act like Lennon. I got Everett totally figured out, but Lennon something else."

"He's not a sissy," Ciana says.

"You show me a boy keep his dreads neat as I keep Patricia's plaits, I got to wonder about him."

"He *has* to look like that if he's working with the public."

"Then he ought to get hisself a bald head like everybody else," Vendetta says.

Ciana falls silent, and Vendetta knows she hasn't called to talk hair. Vendetta isn't staying awake to talk hair. "You know, Ciana, you the one supposed to give him a grade. He not here judging you. I didn't know you better, I be thinking you got a crush for that fool, and he not much older than me. I won't even mention he not much darker or manlier than me, neither."

Vendetta has a feeling Jaquilica is in the room. Jaquilica lives on disability because she drinks, and Jaquilica feels obligated to the government to keep drinking so they get their money's worth. Vendetta can smell her through the sheets. Maybe tomorrow Jaquilica won't be sure that she's heard her accusing Ciana of being hot for Lennon, but maybe she will. Vendetta throws the sheet off herself. Sure enough, Jaquilica is standing by her bed. And sure enough, Jaquilica is too crunked up to be startled. "Get out of here!" Vendetta says right into the phone.

Ciana says she is going to hang up now. "Ah, ah, don't do that," Vendetta says.

"Who that is?" Jaquilica says.

"You know damn well who that is," Vendetta says. Jaquilica doesn't have memory problems. She can remember what she saw on Caller ID two minutes ago.

"I *know* you not telling no white woman about fucking no black man," Jaquilica says, filling up Vendetta's free left ear. In her right ear, pressed to the phone, she hears Ciana say, "Okay, now I'm not hanging up. Go lock yourself in the bathroom with this phone." Vendetta is still in the bed, and she can't imagine ever going back to sleep.

Her foot is sheathed in bedclothes, and Vendetta gently starts pushing at her sister's thigh. It is the sort of thing she will feel entitled to do to any of her six siblings for the rest of her life. She will see nothing wrong with punching one of her brothers in the stomach when she is eighty. It's natural. "Move, Quilica."

"All right," Jaquilica says, bored, and she shambles off to the kitchen. "You want some eggs?"

"Where we was at?" Vendetta says.

"We were talking about Lennon," Ciana says. "But I don't want to talk about Lennon."

Vendetta takes this as a signal to go right ahead and talk about Lennon. "Girl, Frieda *and* Quilica, they both telling me go after him, never mind he a little too girlish for his own good, that man gonna make some good money. But what I'm telling you that for? He be making same money you making, right? So what you want him for? He probably gonna live on the down low, and you know you can do better than that."

"All I asked you was how he reacted to that crap with Walker."

"Ciana."

"Vendetta."

"I tell you what I think he think. He see you walking behind that man, acting like it some kind of pretend thing, you know, like you letting the poor little bastard let hisself look all important for that Tulane girl, and he got to respect that. Leastways that's how I figure he taken it. Lennon no Republican. Lennon going out there and selling RU-486 soon as he get his license. Lennon getting even with his mama. That's why he like he is. Don't you ever talk with him?"

As soon as it's all out, Vendetta wonders whether somebody's going to be in trouble because she has a big mouth. She has learned over her lifetime that the person who gets in trouble is hardly ever herself.

Ciana's quiet. "I guess not. When do you find time for all this deep political and psychological probing?"

"Ask me about anybody in the store," Vendetta says. "I know the same shit about them."

"Boy, does that not answer my question," Ciana says.

"Tell you what. Here's all you need to know. You got to chill. When it come to Lennon, we all got to chill. Three people in that little space, only one of them a man, the rest got to pretend he not hardly there. Elsewise he gonna get very tired of at least one of us."

Jaquilica toddles in from the kitchen wielding a spatula, which announces to Vendetta that being fried is the only destiny for the eggs. "How you want these eggs?" she says. Vendetta covers the receiver. "They ain't already broke and lying in the skillet?" "Yeah, but you could change your mind," Jaquilica says. "You gonna bring it to me in the bed?" "Shoot, what you ever done for me?" Jaquilica says. "I'm a eat those eggs, that's what I'm a do for you," Vendetta says, and Jaquilica toddles back out. "Tell me what Walker say," she says into the phone.

Ciana tells her the one important fact, that there has been a complaint lodged, and the complaint lodger is F.B.'s wife. Vendetta started calling Ciana's brother F.B. about six years ago when his wife had her last baby and he called the pharmacy six times a day during the confinement. Not for professional help, but for unpaid drudge help. He wanted Ciana to drop everything and go get his two girls. Never mind that she had a job.

"It's your fucking brother," Vendetta said after the third time, and that wound down politely to "It's your F.B.," after the fourth.

"So Walker doesn't care if I'm *performing* abortions on top of the checkout counter as long as people still come in the store," Ciana says.

"Yeah, but," Vendetta says. If nothing else, she's sure F.B.'s wife, Corinne, knows where to put the stick in the shitpile.

"Yeah, but what," Ciana says. "The woman tells him she's telling every Catholic she knows not to come into N.O. Well, I've done her carpool at Holy Name, and I promise you this: if there's more than one Catholic who even recognizes Corinne, she wouldn't give her the time of day. And I'll tell you what I told Mr. Walker. I've known Corinne my entire life, and I'd bet my last nickel her call to him was the only call she'll make. Know why?"

"Hmm?"

"Corinne is the laziest woman alive."

Jaquilica walks in with a plate bearing four runny over-easy fried eggs. She has a closed bag of Bunny bread in her other hand. Vendetta can't one-up Ciana. Today.

IF LENNON were not a man of science and pure reason he would swear that something karmically strange is going on among the women he knows, and only among the women he knows. But Lennon spent too much of his growing-up years at Bellevue Baptist in Memphis to believe anything fuzzy anymore, so he has to figure that he is the constant at the center of all this; he just has to sort out the variables. Logic *should* tie it all together. But these are four *women*, and two of them are linked to his sister, who is linked to his mother, and if he has learned nothing else from his mother, he has learned that logic never will do him any good.

For the past week Ciana and Vendetta have been very cool, and Antonia and Andrea have been very hot, which makes him a nervous wreck. He doesn't know why the two of them are in New Orleans except to torment him: it doesn't seem as if they are using their time to do anything else.

The Hollingsworth twins are freshmen at Tulane, and they ought to be alternately drunk and panicky like all young people who choose to come to New Orleans for college. Antonia and Andrea grew up three houses down from Lennon, and they worshipped his sister, Diana. They should have had a crush on him, but they never did. If anything, they had a crush on *Diana*. Diana is barely a year younger than Lennon, named in 1981 for a news story the same as Lennon was named in 1980, and even Lennon admits Diana was worth having a crush on. Model-thin and fine-featured, she wears her hair in untamed dreads and looks uncannily like him. The twins copied every item of clothing they saw on her in the daytime, and when Diana bought a Chihuahua, each of them had to have one, too. Lennon is certain that they came to school in New Orleans because Diana told them to. And he is certain that they are poking at him every waking moment of his day because Diana has told them to do that, too. He just doesn't know why.

The shift ends at seven instead of nine because it is Saturday, and Lennon has been watching the security mirror since five. He is sure the twins will make good on the threat Antonia made on the phone last night. "If you don't tell me right now that you're taking us out, just watch what walks into your store." They think they're going to make him nervous about his job; they haven't come into N.O. since they arrived in town, as if it's the big artillery he knows they have. But it's not the job that makes him nervous; it's Ciana. These girls are tall and thin and brown and glossy, and they move like identical sidewinders who will strike any prey in their path. Female, too, probably. Ciana would be in their path, stricken without a direct attack. Lennon doesn't want Ciana injured, even if she is punishing him for something he didn't do. It helps that Vendetta's doing it, too.

The curve of the security mirror magnifies all the wrong parts of the store; without his knowledge the twins are at the counter like happy little snakes who've made it all the way across the yard without terrorizing anyone. By pure instinct, Vendetta takes it upon herself to step up to the counter and say to them, "I could help you?"

"No," Andrea says in a flirty voice, "*Lennon* could help us."

Lennon can tell them apart, but it's not a trick he's proud of, especially now. He's certainly not going to address her by name. That much familiarity with the Hollingsworths will never do him any good in New Orleans. "This is where I *work*," he says to her.

"And this is where we said we were coming to get you," Andrea says, almost singsong. Lennon feels doomed. Andrea is the more reasonable of the two. He tells her he doesn't get off for another hour. "Good! We'll shop!" Andrea says. A nested stack of blue plastic shopping baskets stands next to the pick-up counter, and each takes one, slings the metal handle over her arm, and looks as menacing as she can without actually being a signatory on Lennon's credit card. He doesn't want to, but he turns to an incredulous Ciana and says, "I need ten minutes." This has been a no-bathroom day; the pace has been that frantic. Ciana is never going to forgive him for whatever it is he already didn't do.

He takes Antonia's smooth pipestem arm and leads her out of the store, knowing Andrea will follow. "You two aren't funny," he says when the glass door closes tightly behind him.

"We're just playing with you, Lennon," Antonia says.

"Trying to get me fired isn't playing."

"Who's going to fire you? I only saw two other people back there, and we are talking about two serious *losers*," Antonia says. "You could probably fire them."

If ever there were a time for Lennon to switch allegiance, it would be now, when he is being ganged up on by Ciana and Vendetta, but instead his feelings are hurt. For Ciana in some measure, but oddly in greater measure for Vendetta. "Those are my friends," he says.

"Boy, you are in worse trouble than we thought," Andrea says. "You need to check out right now. And take off that coat."

He thinks he gets it. "Please don't tell me your daddy is paying full tuition for the two of you to come down here and get me a social life."

The girls shoot dares at each other. At least that's what it looks like to Lennon. It's possible that a ream of information has been transmitted in a single glance between the two of them. "Don't you like us?" Andrea says. The question also is very full.

"I babysat you."

"No, you did not."

"Well, you're still babies. Look, I'll take you to dinner one Sunday, how about it?"

"Right," Antonia says. "And then what? Church?"

Andrea's cell phone rings, and she turns her back to answer it. Whoever is calling has a better offer than tormenting Lennon, because when she hangs up she says, "We'll be back," and both girls grin with a shared pleasure as they sidewind away.

It's not rational, but Lennon is certain they have gone across the street to the park to hide in the grass with more snakes and regroup, and he's jumpy until enough time passes and they haven't returned. Maybe he has succeeded in pacifying the wrong women. Ciana and Vendetta aren't twins. They should be easier, but he knows that's not the case, not at all.

Just as he's stopped being so vigilant, an air of commotion accompanies a person entering the store. Through the open door has come the sound of something like a car alarm going off in the parking lot, except the rhythm is uneven. Lennon gets an adrenal rush before he sees that it's just Les, scurrying in the direction of the pharmacy. It figures that if something is going on in the parking lot, Les would be running deep into the store. As a security guard, Les prefers to police people he already knows. "Ciana!" he says through the Patient Consultation window. "United Cab, got some womens in it, want you to come outside, say you giving them your cell phone." Lennon trusts this is not the twins. He hopes they're not that clever yet.

Ciana is on the phone with both hands busy, and Lennon aches to reach out and relieve her of one responsibility. He jockeys into her line of vision, raises his eyebrows, sees what she'll do. If he is forever on her shit list, she'll turn away, but she nods vigorously, and Lennon takes the phone from her and finds himself on hold, Muzak playing. He wonders what will come onto the line, but he's sure he can wing it. Ciana gestures at the computer, and he sees she's waiting for a doctor's approval. He winks, and she gives him a qualified little smile. "Tell her if she wants my cell she can come get it," Ciana says to Les. "She wasn't shy about coming in the last time. Tell her that."

"Which one?" Les says. "They's two of them."

"The mean one," Ciana says.

A minute later a woman who doesn't seem to have a mean bone in her body comes up to the checkout counter by herself. Ciana rushes over to her as if she can keep everyone from noticing the woman if she's fast enough. "Corinne should've come in," Ciana says to the woman.

"Sweetie, you're the one who thinks I need the cell phone," the woman says.

Sweetie. Lennon knows who this has to be. He studies her from the fine vantage point of a man on hold with a doctor's office. Mrs. Jambon is dressed for a colder climate, but even through her clothes he can see that she is breakably thin. And a head shorter than Ciana. He can imagine them together, how gentle Ciana must be.

Ciana cocks her head to the side. "You don't mind the idea of having it," she says to her mother.

"I'll be all right," her mother says.

"And I want to know it every five minutes."

The horn is audible in one steady blast through the door as a customer walks in, as if someone besides the driver is leaning on it. Mrs. Jambon shrugs. "I don't know why Corinne's so worried," she says. "*I'm* paying the meter."

Ciana leans across the counter and kisses her, and Lennon looks away politely because he knows he could easily see all the way up Ciana's skirt if he tries, and because he knows Vendetta could see him doing so; he doesn't need to be caught. Ciana whispers "I love you" to her mother in a way that means she doesn't care who hears; she sounds as if she thinks she's never going to see her again. "Call me every five minutes," she says, and hands her the cell phone in a little Burberry travel pouch that holds the charger, too.

Her mother walks away, and Ciana turns with her head held up in that way women have of making sure tears don't fall. When she sees that Vendetta is over by Patient Consultation berating Robitussin off the record and Lennon is off the phone, she looks right at Lennon through watery eyes and in the saddest voice he's ever heard come out of her says, "Aw, shit." Lennon cannot recall a more romantic moment.

"Is Vendetta angry at me?" he suddenly has the brilliance to ask.

Ciana looks confused, and then she gets it. "Oh, we're trying to be more professional," she says. "I guess we should have told you."

He gives her a that's-okay grin so she'll never know he noticed that she, too, was being stiff and professional and downright cold.

"I guess we didn't tell you about Corinne, either," Ciana says to Lennon, and she sniffles delicately. "But never mind."

"Okay," Lennon says.

"So she's taking Mama to New York. And Mama doesn't want to go to New York."

"Okay," Lennon says. The woman who just came in *seemed* ready to travel. But people who come into the drugstore always seem ready to do whatever is necessary for their own good.

He's trying desperately to figure out from contextual clues who Corinne is.

"She told my mother her trouble was that she was bored." Ciana breaks into a nasal uptown voice. "'You need culture, Mother Jambon. Real *thee-tur*. And, ooo, shopping, maybe we've got Saks Fifth Avenue, maybe we've got Macy's, but New York's got the real stores. You'll talk about it for months.' I wanted to say, *Then what? Keel over?* She wants my mother dead. I just know she's waiting to get my mother's money."

"She's not going to kill her."

Lennon has not even had time to hear his own insane words when the person who must be Corinne comes running up to the counter, clacking on three-inch heels that do not seem to be the footwear of choice for a woman who will be walking all over New York in a few hours. She has the frantic look of someone whose travel partner just has had a heart attack in the taxi.

"See?" Ciana says, as if her mother already is dead.

"Where're the instructions?" Corinne hollers.

Vendetta moves in front of Lennon and Ciana. "Excuse me?"

Corinne angles around her, but she seriously has underestimated Vendetta. Vendetta knows how to block a customer's view of Ciana or Lennon without knowing where either one is behind her. "You not talking about no cell phone, I *know*," she says.

"Ciana!" Corinne says.

Ciana suddenly manages to see something very important on the computer. Vendetta says, "Shoot, a five-year-old *child* know how to operate a cell phone. You turn it on. You use it. You push the buttons 'til you figure it out."

"Well," Corinne says, "tell Ciana not everybody has the kind of money *she* has to throw around on every contraption that comes on the market. Her brother and I can't afford a cell phone."

"Baby, people out there on welfare got cell phones," Vendetta says.

Corinne turns to leave, and Vendetta calls after her. "Oh,

and might be a bad idea, practicing while you up in the airplane. Leastways that what all my friends on welfare tell me."

The next time the Hollingsworth twins come into the store, Lennon trusts that Vendetta will be the one to talk to them. She is very cool and professional.

5

CIANA'S head is so swollen from the presence of Lennon that sound doesn't reverberate past her eardrums, so she doesn't hear the private phone ring. At least that's how she explains it to herself when Vendetta loops her way through the shelving with a coil that must be twenty feet long when it's not stretched. Vendetta doesn't cover the receiver when she says, "It's F.B." Ciana bonks her on her soft wooly head with the receiver, the mouthpiece still uncovered. She can hear a ducky version of Geoffrey's voice coming out of the receiver as she scurries off. "What's F.B.?"

"You," Ciana says, "and the B stands for brother. What." She's stretched the cord all the way back to the bottles for colonoscopy prep and leans against a shelf, thinking for a second how deceptively appealing the lemon-lime and cherry labels look.

Geoffrey never has called her in the middle of the day before, but then Geoffrey and Ciana never have been the only two adults in town before. If one can define adults as the two of them and Corinne and their mother. An emergency with one of the kids means Geoffrey or Ciana will have to go in; probably Ciana. She went to their house this morning at seven-thirty to make sure all of them were fresh and had no complaints and felt loved, but she knows children at school are like people who come to the pharmacy: they time their worst troubles for when everyone else is ready to be complacent. Geoffrey has one-of-many jobs on one-of-many floors at Entergy, which makes him completely flexible as far as Ciana can see, but somehow he figures that if a child is sick Ciana should be the one to go to the school. That's Geoffrey. Ciana is still the girl.

"We've got a problem, Ciana," Geoffrey says.

For Vendetta's benefit, Ciana says, "Who's *we*, white man?" She can feel Vendetta wondering why he's calling. Vendetta's only seen Geoffrey about three times, and she has him completely figured out.

"Not funny," he says, and Ciana gets that sensation in her chest that would make a weaker person in her position steal a klonopin. "Mama fell."

"What?"

"Mama fell down in New York."

Their mother does that sometimes; her heart fibrillates,

and she passes out and scares herself silly, so one of them goes over to her house and dusts her off until they all can go their separate ways and pretend they don't need to set aside differences and huddle about her not living alone anymore. Ciana has been unfazed by it lately because it has happened enough with no consequences; she actually forgot about it before the trip. Surely this call is about a drama starring Corinne. "Corinne's with her," she says. "Mama *ought* to be better off than usual."

Vendetta has come to the back to catch Ciana's eye, as if she needs reminding that their assembly line's deep intelligence rests right now on computers and one licensed human, and Ciana is the licensed human. Ciana signals with her index finger. One minute.

"She broke her damn leg," Geoffrey says, and now Ciana has an image of her poor mother in cold New York, where she doesn't want to be, with Corinne, who is crying piteously. "You've got to go up there," Geoffrey says. "Now."

Ciana can't believe he is stealing her right to panic. "I am so sick of your wife," she says and hangs up.

She dials him right back. "What," he says, seeing Caller ID. "All I mean is that Corinne is an adult," Ciana says. "I don't need to fly up to New York this very minute. Don't think I'm not taking this damn seriously." This time Geoffrey hangs up on Ciana.

When Ciana shoves off from where she's been leaning, all the blood rushes from her head; she's one of those lucky overweight people with shock-level blood pressure. She feels as if she is about to pass out, but she doesn't. She knows she's chalk-white, though, because Vendetta rushes over and says, "Girl, you better set down before you fall down." Ciana never sits when she's behind the counter. For her, there's nowhere *to* sit. Except a couple of high stools, and she's not taking that risk. Ever. She tells Vendetta she's all right. She kind of likes the drama of being so pale. *After* the chance of fainting has passed. "What that man say to you?" Vendetta says.

Ciana tells Vendetta about her mother, but says, "It's what I said to him that scares me. I said practically nothing. And with Geoffrey and Corinne, I've got to say *enough*."

"Seem to me," Vendetta says, "no matter what you say, people like that gonna get it ass-backwards anyway. Maybe saying nothing a good idea."

It doesn't matter what Ciana said. Corinne has practiced turning her words inside out since they were together in first grade at Holy Name of Jesus, and she is damned good at it. Geoffrey's been at it longer, and if possible, he's better. No sooner did Geoffrey tell her as fact that Ciana was not coming up to New York at all than Corinne twisted that to mean, *New York is bad, New Orleans is good; get out of New York, go to New Orleans.* Their mother is in a place up there called Roosevelt Hospital, and that gives Ciana more sight-unseen faith than a place here that everyone calls Baptist even though that hasn't been its name since the corporate takeover. Ciana doesn't understand how a city can routinely rank number one in cholesterol levels or stress levels or violent crime levels and yet all of its citizens have unflinching allegiance. She figures it is because no one ever leaves, and if they all have grown up together, they all make certain assumptions. The only reason Ciana lives here is that she loves her mother blindly.

"She thinks she's going to take her onto an airplane in a wheelchair *with* her leg still broken," Ciana tells Vendetta later that day. A woman with a $3.29 prescription for a diuretic has brought half a week's groceries back to the pharmacy to check out, and Ciana scans them mindlessly while Vendetta clears the other register. Ciana wants to tell this woman that if she didn't buy canned ravioli with 1,180 milligrams of sodium per serving she wouldn't need the diuretic, but she'd have to find the right way. Vendetta would find the right way.

"How a hospital gonna let you take somebody out with a leg still broke?" Vendetta says.

"I think after they listen to Corinne being hapless for about an *hour*, they'll load my mother up with morphine and call a taxi," Ciana says, her voice half wishing for morphine for herself.

The ravioli woman can't help overhearing. "Someone flew a dead woman on a flight I was on once," she says. Vendetta stops what she is doing. Vendetta needs all the details. Ciana already is imagining what they must be. "She just seemed very helpless and quiet."

"It must have been before 9/11," Ciana says, and Vendetta cracks up.

"How'd *you* find out?" Vendetta says, and Ciana knows Jaquilica and Frieda are going to want all the details when this story comes home from work tonight.

"I was the flight attendant," the woman says.

As soon as the woman leaves, Ciana tells Vendetta that she can believe some things, but she can't reconcile flight attendants and Chef Boyardee.

Ciana is not making mistakes because she doesn't make mistakes, but all she can think about is her mother. She wants to talk to her mother. She wants to be sure she hasn't become one of Corinne's parcels. Her mother lit a lot of candles and lost a lot of babies to have Geoffrey, and she lit more candles to lose no more babies to have Ciana, so she and Ciana do a lot of treasuring. Ciana pictures her in a hospital gown and knows that that is all it will take for Corinne to reduce her to freight. No clothes, no rings, no watch—no worth. A person *is* personal effects. Ciana has sensed for quite a while that the day ten-year-old Corinne and she sneaked into her parents' room and tried on her mother's jewelry, something snapped in Corinne. Maybe sunlight reflecting off a diamond, reflecting off a mirror as she twirled faster than hefty Ciana could. Some perfect moment for a girl tired of hearing about suffering martyrs at school. *This* was beatific. Geoffrey was doomed from that day forward. And at the time Corinne didn't even have any concept of the dividends Mr. Jambon's Freeport-McMoRan stock paid.

Ciana's cell phone has a local New Orleans number, so

she dials it and dials it, but she gets her own voice mail every time, and she finally gives up. Her mother learned how to operate the phone while she and Corinne were still at the boarding gate at the airport, but Corinne decided that answering it was quite enough to learn. Since they left they've worked out a deal with Ciana: Ciana can call them any time of day or night and talk to her mother. Her mother worked out that deal herself, and it seemed to make her feel good. Every day, at least twice, Ciana has managed to say to her, "Is she treating you all right?" "Do you want to come home?" She has known her mother could squeeze that little phone up against her ear and say *yes* or *no*, and Ciana would have all the information she would need. She could ask Corinne the open-ended questions. But now is the time when Ciana needs the deal enforced, and Corinne is violating it.

As soon as it is her break time, Ciana phones Geoffrey from the back room. "You can't use cells in a hospital," he says, as if Ciana is some sort of idiot who has no business being involved in this crisis, never mind that last week he was not a cell-phone person. Ciana asks him what number he's using. Corinne's stepping outside and calling from a pay phone. "And Mama?" Ciana says. "She's not stepping outside," Geoffrey says. "Somebody ought to talk to her," Ciana says. "Why?" Geoffrey says.

Ciana bursts into tears, and just when she starts to get loud, Lennon walks into the room. "*Why*? You know what, Geoffrey? I'm not going to answer that question. I'm going to give you about two seconds to tell me how to get Mama on the phone, and then I'm calling the hospital myself and telling them that she's in the custody of a dangerous person and needs some kind of guardian to make sure she's making sensible decisions. The idea of flying down here with a broken leg is criminal."

Lennon walks over and puts a hand on Ciana's shoulder, and she is sure she could cope if he didn't ever leave. But of course he does because he has to.

"It was your idea," Geoffrey says.

"All I said was that I wasn't going up there. And I only said *now*."

"Don't split hairs."

"Give me the hospital number, Geoffrey."

He honestly doesn't have it, and he honestly doesn't see any reason that he should. He reminds Ciana that he broke his arm on a Cub Scout camping trip and came home two days later with it still broken. "Are you saying Mama should toughen up and hobble over to Bloomingdale's before they go to the airport?" Ciana says. "*No!*" he says, as if Ciana thinks he might say yes. "I can't talk to you," Ciana says. As soon as she hangs up she understands what is going on, and she bangs at Vendetta's cell phone with one angry index finger until it gives her what she wants, an emergency room nurse at Roosevelt Hospital. The nurse, however, does not give Ciana what she wants from her. According to the chart, her mother is under no one's influence, not Corinne's, not the doctor's, not the painkiller's. Her mother flat-out insisted she would not have surgery until she was safely within the perimeters of the parish of Orleans. "I've quit saying that now I've seen everything," the nurse says.

"You didn't see what you thought you saw," Ciana says, and since nurses don't have time to be confused, she catches on right away. "I figured your mother wasn't the one wanting to come home," she says.

Ciana knows she will be generous with the Demerol.

Corinne will phone Ciana as soon as she has her mother in a taxi on the way to the airport. No matter what time it is. So now every part of Ciana's intact overworked skeletal system has intermittent lightning cracks of sympathetic pain as she imagines her mother trying to get into a New York cab with Corinne, her luggage, and a makeshift cast as an afterthought. In her mind Ciana moves the parts around like Tetris, trying to make her mother comfortable, but she can't shift Corinne into the front seat of a taxi, and she keeps coming back to a carry-on bag on the floor, her mother's leg stretched diagonally out over it, Corinne hunched in the corner and thoroughly put out. It is not a rectangular arrangement, and it is painful to see.

The call comes just as the shift ends, just as Ciana is thinking that this is the day when she would be well within her rights to ask Lennon if he would mind coming across the street and sitting with her in Burger King over a cup of coffee for a little while, just until she gets a call. Shift change is a conscious time, a responsible time. Not a time when Ciana needs to listen to Corinne breaking up as she moves in and out of the steel and electric infrastructure of New York. Corinne had the cabbie dial the drugstore before he pulled off from the curb, and Ciana is sure he's going to go home and ask his wife what planet area code 504 is on.

"They sent *men* up there, Ciana!" Ciana has no idea what Corinne is carrying on about. "I swear, if I have to send one clean skirt to the cleaners because they folded it wrong, I am going to send them a bill." Ciana asks to speak to her mother, and Corinne goes into a dead zone for a few seconds without knowing it. When she comes out, she is going on that it is hotel policy to send security with the bellman to pack out her room, and why not housekeeping if housekeeping is supposed to know so much about neatness? "Are you talking about the *hotel*?" Ciana says.

"We're paying two hundred fifty dollars a night when you tack on all those taxes they don't tell you about," she says. "Geoffrey and I didn't pay that much for our first apartment—"

"Give me my mother."

"You want to talk on the phone, Mother Jambon?" Corinne says into the white noise of the city coming through an open window. Ciana hears no response, some rustling, no Corinne, no mother.

"Mama?" Ciana says. "Mama?" She gets no answer, but she can tell nothing is happening inside the cab, that all motion is outside, that wherever the phone is, it isn't moving. "*Corinne!*"

Rustling, and then Corinne comes back on the line. "I think it's starting to snow. Wouldn't you know it. Look, Mother Jambon, we're getting a little bit of snow. Come on, just turn your head a little. Oh, Ciana, has she ever seen snow?"

Ciana's shift is over, Lennon has left, her mother is unconscious in the backseat of a taxi, a shard of her femur is probably slicing through her artery; she is probably going to be dead on arrival at LaGuardia.

She closes her eyes tight, so both the pharmacy and the inside of the taxi go away, and only when she feels herself take back control does she open her eyes again. Wordlessly, she motions to Vendetta to close her out for the day; Vendetta knows the routine of every person in the store. And then she says to Corinne, "I don't care if you have to use a hatpin, I want you to get an intelligible sound out of Mama before you get to that airport. I don't expect one out of *you*, but I want one out of *her*."

Corinne is being rough. "Hey, wake up." Letting her know that in some kind of way it's Ciana's fault. Ciana hears the driver say, "Lady, we're going sixty, how about you sit back." "Hear that?" Corinne hollers into the air somewhere away from the phone. Rustling. Unintelligible animal sounds. Corinne in the distance. "Talk to her so she'll leave us alone." Close to the phone, *Mmm?* "Mama?" Ciana says. More rustling. Then Corinne. "You satisfied now? She's zonked out, okay?"

"What's she on, Corinne?"

"They gave her a Demerol shot, and she threw up."

"She should be asleep, *maybe*, not half conscious. What else is she on?"

"Well, like I said, she threw up. So I figure it's out of her system." Ciana looks around the pharmacy for someone to tell this to, sees Vendetta nearby, catches her eye with an expression that says, *Just wait.* Corinne keeps prattling. "So we're out in front of the hotel, and the meter's running, and they don't come right out with our bags, and I've got to go in, and she's getting all restless, so I put the patch on her, and she got a lot better."

Ciana's mother is loaded with Demerol and is wearing a morphine patch that someone probably told Corinne to apply if they got stranded in the Andes. Her mother could die from an overdose.

"I'm sure they gave you pills."

"You can't give a pill without water."

"Take the patch off of her," Ciana tells Corinne.

"They *told* me to put it on her if she got uncomfortable," Corinne says. "She got uncomfortable."

"I'd be uncomfortable, too, if you parked me in front of a hotel in the freezing cold while you went in and got your damn suitcase. *Take the patch off.*"

"What was I supposed to do, wait for them to ship all my stuff? I've got all my personal effects in that suitcase. And your mother's got jewelry."

"Take the patch off."

Corinne protests that Ciana's mother will be frozen and

embarrassed by the time she peels off all the clothes that cover the patch. Ciana reminds her that she did it in front of the hotel in midtown with no problem. At which time her mother had her eyes open. Corinne's sure the cab driver will pull over and make her walk if she doesn't sit still. Ciana doesn't care. Corinne finally gets the patch off, and it's sticking to her finger, and she's sure she's going to pass out herself any second, all gaga with opiate, and then what will she do? Ciana tells her to attach the patch to the instep of her shoe. Just in case they do crash in Peru.

VENDETTA figures no one can complain that both she and Ciana are out sick today because neither has been out sick in as long as she can remember, and they're never late like Maureen. Especially given the fact that a million viruses probably come in on the pieces of paper people hand them every day. Their prescription file ought to be in a lead-lined, airtight vault; she's that sure of how contagious it must be. (Not the file of Schedule II scrips: people who come in for narcotics may be filthy, but God protects children and damn fools.) Vendetta thinks that in the pharmacy they've built up some kind of immunity over time, like parents of little children, but she'd rather think that there's something in the air behind that counter, and they're all protected. They sure don't have their rightful share of mental illness. Given what she knows about her family and Ciana's, anyway.

She's taking off to give Ciana some backup, and this way she can get Lennon to feel free to do the same thing. Ciana needs family; her brother has it, but she doesn't.

Vendetta knows that the second Lennon spells her, Ciana is going to go into a little dream that he's *really* family. She just hopes like crazy that Ciana watches the way she acts with Lennon in front of her brother. From what Vendetta knows of the brother, he's the type to say, *So, Ciana, you're so desperate you had to get a black man.* Not straight out, but in so many words. Vendetta would have to lay him out, right in the hospital. He'd probably say it in front of Lennon, too. Lennon would just roll with it. Though right now Lennon is more bothered about Ciana's mother than even Ciana is. From the little bits of the story he's heard, he's sure that sister-in-law is trying to kill the woman. Ciana says to him, "Oh, Lennon, that's just the way we are down here." Vendetta has to keep herself from laughing, Ciana sounds so white and Southern. And Ciana knows Lennon's from Memphis, too.

Vendetta took Patricia with her and Ciana to the airport last night. They borrowed Frieda's big old four-door Buick so Ciana's mother could ride any way she wanted. Frieda keeps that car because her boy is so hyper that there's no point breaking her heart over anything better. At least that's what she says. Vendetta figured Patricia could squeeze wherever she needed to squeeze. If Ciana had needed to squeeze, it would have been a problem, but Ciana was the driver, and the driver could only sit one place.

Patricia hates riding in that Buick. She goes to school every day in that Buick with Frieda's boy, her cousin Quick, and everybody sees her getting out of that terrible car with that terrible boy. Vendetta knows how she feels, but Frieda works for the City of New Orleans, and Frieda's hours are right, so Patricia has to live with being driven by her auntie. There's nothing wrong with being strange to project children who walk to school from their messy apartments. It helps a child figure out things very fast.

Vendetta felt so good about Patricia last night, right up until they saw Geoffrey Jambon. When Vendetta was growing up, her family was like royalty at Sylvanie F. Williams Elementary, being only one of a handful of families living in houses on South Roman Street; everybody else lived in the Calliope Project. That's probably why she sends Patricia there, because she felt so damn good about herself. Patricia comes home scuffed up, and if Vendetta would admit it, the scuffing isn't just on the outside, but Patricia gets to know how good she has it. Yesterday evening all Vendetta wanted to do was get Patricia cleaned up down to her fingernails because Patricia is always cleaned up down to her fingernails when she leaves the house, and the child looked like she was going *on* an airplane, in Vendetta's opinion. Never mind that Patricia never had been to the airport. Vendetta had been to the airport, but never on a plane.

The first thing Geoffrey Jambon said when he saw

Patricia at the airport was, "I got a babysitter. It's a school night."

"Not everybody get a babysitter every time they feel like it," Vendetta said, all bristly.

"All I meant was, the kids had to do their homework, and I didn't think this was a night I could ask Ciana to sit for me," he said.

"My child go to public school. Public school children don't get no homework," Vendetta said.

"That's a shame," Geoffrey said.

"Ain't it though," Vendetta said.

Ciana's mother came off the plane high as a kite, full of Coca-Cola and some kind of cookies they give people on Delta that she couldn't stop talking about. "Now she can't have surgery for another twelve hours," Ciana said. "She has to fast." "Look who's talking," Corinne said, her eyes wide and wet like she was some kind of martyr who was entitled to say anything she felt like. Vendetta found Patricia a vending machine right away and got her two candy bars so Corinne couldn't think she was shaming everybody out of eating. No chips, though, because Vendetta figured they'd talk about black people and chips. Patricia didn't understand why she could only see parts of airplanes out in the dark. Mrs. Jambon rode up that concourse like a Mardi Gras queen, waving her hand, all googly-eyed, her head swiveling from side to side, and if anyone was shocked by her condition, Vendetta didn't notice. Mrs. Jambon exclaimed as she passed each landmark, *PJs! The Grove! Restrooms! Ciana!* and Patricia caught the excitement and the chocolate and started dancing alongside the wheelchair. When they reached baggage claim, Corinne insisted on taking Mrs. Jambon to the hospital in her car. Geoffrey had been kissing Corinne wetly and patting her bottom, and Vendetta had been sure they wanted to go straight home, but, no, Corinne insisted. Never mind that their vehicle was an SUV, and Mrs. Jambon would have to be lifted bodily and painfully into it. "They don't want you talking to your mama," Vendetta said to Ciana on the way home. "They never do," Ciana said back. "The airport stupid," Patricia said.

Before their shift, Lennon rode Vendetta in his Miata to the Winn-Dixie and paid for a king cake and a huge bunch of stargazer lilies, and she told him about last night. She couldn't figure out for whose benefit she was telling him all this. She has to admit, it was very good, riding around in that open Miata. She isn't interested in Lennon in any way except as Ciana's true love, but she wouldn't mind riding around town in that car a little bit. Lennon doesn't even know that Ciana's sister-in-law ratted Ciana out to Mr. Walker, and he already thinks she's evil, that she broke the old woman's leg. He says Vendetta needs to take a good look at Mrs. Jambon. Vendetta can just picture her black self going into that hospital room and picking up the sheet.

Ciana is sitting on one side of the surgical waiting room, and Corinne is sitting on the other when Vendetta walks in. "Where he at?" Vendetta whispers, pressing the king cake on Ciana.

"He says he might as well be at work while she's in surgery, for all the good it'd do her for him to be here." Ciana whispers, too, as if protecting Corinne from hearing such foolishness. Reflexively, she is opening the king cake as if it is food instead of a big party favor that they ought to be sharing with everyone in the room. "Hold up, hold up," Vendetta says. "They ain't put the baby in. And I got you a gold. Let me put the baby in. And I got to get you a vase."

"Say it louder."

"What."

"You've got to get me a what?"

"I got to get you a vase." Vendetta pronounces it *vaaz*. She sees Ciana looking in Corinne's direction. Corinne looks for friends who try on East Coast pronunciations with a hesitation that lets on that they're new and largely untried. *Vaaz. Ahnt. Um*brella. Corinne shakes out her copy of the "Living" section of the paper. But doesn't look up.

The volunteer at the desk gets the hint, sees no one in the room at the moment except the family related to the stargazer lilies, leaves and comes right back with an industrial-sized jar half filled with water. Ciana arranges the flowers in the jar and says to Vendetta out of earshot of the woman, "You'd think more flowers than people would die in hospitals. Where do all those ugly cut-glass containers go?"

"You know Lennon pay for those flowers?" Vendetta says.

"Want to say that a different way and say it louder?" Ciana whispers. She looks pleased out of her mind.

With the flowers at their feet, Vendetta and Ciana try to

figure out the king cake. Vendetta is willing to forgo the mystery of knowing where the baby is, but she wants to try to fool herself, so she spins the box until she loses all its landmarks, picks up an edge like she's lifting the corner of a mattress to hide her money, slips the baby under and shoves it in. She spins it again, and she's pretty sure she doesn't know where she put it. "It's a shame, yeah, can't get the baby baked in because somebody going to sue the bakery," she says. "That's *low*." "Once I chewed it and swallowed it so I wouldn't have to say I ate the whole piece," Ciana says. "*That* was pain and suffering."

Half the cake is gone in ten minutes. The baby is still unfound. Vendetta is keeping pace with Ciana. "Feel like we at work, you know? Like people watching us, and we better eat fast, because they *waiting*."

Ciana tells her to go offer some to Corinne, and Vendetta carries the flat box over to her like she's selling cigarettes in a 1930s bar. "You want some?" she says in her friendliest possible voice. Corinne looks at the cake, and Vendetta can tell that what she sees is that no one has bothered to find a knife. Corinne works hard at showing that she is hiding her disgust. "I brought an apple," Corinne says.

"A' apple not enough for a day like this," Vendetta says. "Besides, I promise you we ain't touch the part we tear off from."

It's the best king cake Winn-Dixie makes, with pecan praline filling and white icing instead of sugar sprinkles, and Vendetta knows the smell is driving Corinne crazy. She looks around for a microwave oven; fifteen seconds for the cake in there, and Corinne would have her fancy face down *in* it. Corinne takes a confidential tone. "You know, Ciana has a weight problem. If you were any kind of friend to her at all, you wouldn't encourage this kind of behavior."

"Ciana a fine-looking woman," Vendetta says. She keeps her voice down, though she doesn't know why.

"Ciana hasn't been able to get a date in as long as I've known her, and I've known her since we were in elementary school."

"Ciana got mens asking her out all the time," Vendetta says. It's true. Ciana doesn't know what to think of herself, Vendetta knows, but when she's standing up in that pharmacy, she's got a no-shit attitude, and it does something to men. Vendetta would like to explain that effect to Ciana, but first she would have to explain it to herself.

"Men take advantage of her," Corinne says. She sounds almost proud of the fact, like she set it up herself.

"You been there?" Vendetta says, and she flips the box lid over the king cake.

"Yes," Corinne says. "I actually have."

This morning Vendetta promised Patricia that she would pick up her and Quick and take the long way home on the streetcar. She doesn't know why kids are like tourists about the streetcar, but for her dollar and a quarter she sure doesn't mind looking at the avenue instead of all the mess on Claiborne. It's almost two o'clock, and Mrs. Jambon is in her room, alive and sleeping; Ciana ought to be all right without anybody until Lennon can come by after work.

Mercifully nobody is in the other bed, because the room is crowded with her and Ciana and the brother and sister-in-law all sitting around watching each other. The last piece of the king cake is lying on the bedside table with the baby still in it unless Ciana chewed it up and swallowed it, gold and all. The room smells delicately of stargazer lilies. "Jeopardy" is on the TV, and Ciana is making the other two furious because she knows all the answers. "Double Jeopardy" has a category called *Verbatim*, and Alex Trebek is saying it means "words in Latin." The answer comes up. "Daily." "What is quotidian," Ciana says, and her mama stirs a little, like she's proud. "All that medical terminology pays off," she says to Vendetta, as if Vendetta knows the answer, and Vendetta can tell that Geoffrey and Corinne would like nothing better than to throw the two of them out of the room. Ciana doesn't see it, or maybe she *does*. "Hey, Geoffrey, remember when I won the Latin prize?" She turns to Vendetta to bring her into a story the others surely know. "I told Daddy I might be of some use to the Church when I grew up, and he said there might be alternatives. I guess he was looking at this body and figuring having a husband wasn't one." She smiles at Corinne like she's given her a gift. "Anyway, Mama said, 'Well, Ciana, anything you say in Latin will sound like a command, so keep it up,' and when I finished pharmacy school I reminded her of that. Mama?" she says to her mother, and she looks like she's getting ready to cry.

Vendetta watches all three of them take turns trying to get the poor woman to wake up. She might smile a little, or let out a little hum, but to Vendetta she looks like somebody who's just not ready to wake up. Ciana takes one of the stargazer lilies from the jar they've set on the sill and twirls it under her mother's nose. "Lennon sent this," she says to her mother.

Mrs. Jambon opens her eyes, looks at Ciana, and says, "Hi, sweetie."

Ciana says, "I love you, Mama," and Corinne can't contain herself anymore. She edges into position like someone trying to fit into the frame for a photograph. "We had a wonderful trip, didn't we, Mother Jambon?" she says. Mrs. Jambon closes her eyes, and then she starts struggling to breathe.

Geoffrey and Corinne don't move, but Ciana tells Vendetta to ring for the nurse and then goes running out into the hallway. The room fills, and Vendetta doesn't know what to do. "Take the flowers and get out of here," Ciana says, and that is what she does. She'll tell Patricia they're for her, and the whole streetcar will smell lovely.

THIS MORNING Errol Nash got caught stealing baby food, and Lennon has felt lousy ever since. He and Ciana and Vendetta have a tacit agreement that they do not ever turn in anyone they see shoplifting on the baby products aisle. If they see someone doing it, they come out and edge up to the person and ask if maybe ten dollars might help. Errol never has done it before, but they would let even Errol go. Never mind that there hasn't been a baby in Errol's house since his mother brought him home over thirty years ago.

But the sub they sent from Magazine Street to cover for Ciana saw him, and Kasha from Cosmetics who was covering for Vendetta acted like Errol was committing grand theft auto, so within the hour Errol was being frog-marched out of the store by Les with a warning from Mr. Walker that he better never set foot in N.O. Drugs again. "But that plum stuff good, yeah, and ooh, that peach sauce," he was saying, even as the door slammed behind him, and Lennon was feeling a sharp ethical pinch until he realized Errol's mother could still come get his prescriptions filled for him. Still, he was sure that he, Ciana, and Vendetta were the only three people in the world who understood this man, and now Errol's life was going to be ruined. What is bothering Lennon right now is that he isn't sure he can work as a pharmacist if he can't work with those two women. He might be more ruined than Errol.

It takes him a while to find Ciana at Baptist because her mother is not in a room but rather in the ICU. When he walks in, her brother is standing over her, ready to leave, but taking his sweet time about it. He's tall and lean, and Lennon is sure he began bullying Ciana long before she weighed as much as he did and became vulnerable. "You know you might very well have killed her," the brother is saying. "She was doing great until you started that foolishness with the flower."

Ciana turns to Lennon to explain. "I let her smell one of your stargazer lilies, and she went into respiratory distress."

"You admit it?" Geoffrey says.

Lennon says, "She's not admitting that there's a connection. A stargazer lily smells that way so *insects* will pollinate it, not wind. Only plants that depend on wind pollination cause allergic reactions."

"I don't know what you're talking about," Geoffrey says. He says it with such authority that for a second Lennon feels that taking botany was a waste of time. And then Geoffrey gets the look on his face that Lennon has seen a thousand times in this city. It's the look a white man gets when he makes a deliberate choice to ignore everything he knows to be true about Lennon. "Please don't interfere when you don't understand what's going on," he says. Lennon catches Ciana's eye, and her expression says, *Yes, he flunked out of Tulane after one semester.* Ciana once entertained him and Vendetta, telling how her mother gave Geoffrey a choice: throw his inheritance away on tuition or buy a house. Corinne was thrilled because she could marry him and have a house and have a wedding announcement in the *Times-Picayune* that said he attended Tulane University. In New Orleans "attended" is synonymous with "graduated from" or there would be no alumni associations, Ciana said, killing herself laughing. Vendetta didn't need a degree to get the point. Lennon wanted to work with the two of them forever.

"Mama looked like her regular self until you started in on her with that stupid flower," Geoffrey says. "Now she's got tubes coming out every place and her mouth's hanging down like she's mentally defective or something."

"Mama was her regular self before Corinne dragged her up to New York, too," Ciana says, and Lennon feels a hot rush of admiration go through his chest, because she says it in such an unbelievably conciliatory way.

"Yeah, touché," Geoffrey says.

Geoffrey's explanation for leaving now is that there is no safer place for his mother than the intensive care unit of a hospital. Someone's watching her all the time, he tells Ciana and Lennon, "monitored in ways nobody else is being monitored," and she can't fall down or get hit by a car or have a heart attack. "It's like putting a dog in the vet instead of a kennel when you go on a trip." Lennon thinks he is going to develop a case of hiccups right here if he can't laugh, and he knows he can't laugh. He breathes as steadily as he can, tries to pretend he's in church.

"I'll act like I didn't hear that," Ciana says, and Lennon wants to throw his arms around her.

"What'd you do about her dog, by the way?" Geoffrey says.

"Geoffrey!" Ciana says.

"I think you're getting a little hysterical here," Geoffrey says, and now Lennon *has* to take Ciana's arm and hold it. Protectively: that's the way it appears. But her skin is as soft as it looks, and he thinks that touching her this way would be enough to satisfy him for quite a while.

Ciana says she will deal with the dog, and Geoffrey gives her the cell phone without its charger or carrying case, and Lennon keeps holding Ciana's arm, and they might stand in the middle of the waiting room the rest of the night if it weren't ten minutes to ten and visiting time.

"How did your mother break her leg?" Lennon says when Ciana comes back from the ten minutes in the ICU, pale and undistractible. It's not an idle question. She fell,

Ciana says. How? Ciana is sharing a two-seat sofa with Lennon, and he doesn't know why this feels more intimate than standing six inches apart all day, but it does. "I guess she had a heart fibrillation, and she fell," Ciana says. Where? New York. "You don't have any of the specifics, do you?" Lennon says. "You know, it must be that I don't want to picture Mama with Corinne up there. Does that make sense?"

"Sure," Lennon says. "You can ask her about it when she gets better." He hopes he sounds like he means it.

It is Ciana's turn to speak, and she doesn't, and Lennon wracks his brain for something to say, and he feels the way he felt at the eighth grade dance when he had to take a girl, and they sat side by side for three straight hours in complete silence. He is sure he never will forget that evening for as long as he lives. No one else is in the ICU Waiting Room. The television becomes more and more audible, the way the numbers in an elevator become more and more important the longer the ride is. Lennon realizes that the program is "The Biggest Loser," and he can tell from contextual clues exactly what the show is about. Everyone is fat, and everyone is ashamed. He would rather find raw, naked sex on the television while he is sitting next to Ciana; the discomfort level would be lower.

"Well," Ciana says, noticing the TV, "I'm surprised Corinne didn't send me an audition application."

Relieved and grateful, Lennon says, "Those people have something wrong with them."

Ciana plants a big wet kiss on his cheek, but it's too fast to be sensuous. "And you can *see* every square inch of it."

Lennon takes this as an invitation mentally to compare each and every one of the women on TV to what he imagines Ciana looks like in a sports bra and spandex shorts. With Ciana's face and spirit, any one of those women would be someone he'd make love to right now. He stares at the cleavage on the big blonde on the red team, ignoring her face, and *all* of him feels pretty tumescent when Ciana says, "Hey, wake up, this is the ICU."

Because Geoffrey believes so strongly that staying nearby is meaningless, Ciana cannot figure out how she feels about doing so. By midnight she has worked this subject in and out and over with Lennon, and because he is hoping to spend the night here with her and see the morning in this windowless room, he doesn't help at all. Staying or going is not her problem.

Last semester, before he started doing his clerkship full-time, Lennon was taking advanced molecular biology, and at some point he began to worry that he was going to go through life with the perspective of a man squinting through his right eye all the time. His father, after all, was a dentist, and Lennon knew how he was. At least that was his rationalization for reading *Men Are from Mars, Women Are from Venus.* Now he searches his brain desperately from what he learned, and while he's delighted that all of molecular biology is ready and waiting for the NAPLEX, all he thinks he knows about women is that they don't want solutions. And as he recalls from when he read it, Ciana never did fit any of what the book prescribed anyway. Of course, at the time, Ciana was the person *with* the solutions. Right now Lennon's solution would be to call the police and have them take a gentle look at Mrs. Jambon. Mrs. Jambon didn't fall softly. As soon as Mrs. Jambon starts talking, Corinne will be sitting right next to her, interpreting. And if she never starts talking again, he wonders what kind of a conscience Corinne has. "Ciana," he finally says, "everything turns eventually." She looks him straight in the eye. You can't *buy* eyes that blue. He waits for her to think through what he said. She should be able to figure it out, but she seems to expect him to tell her something. Good. He doesn't want her to be a chapter in a pop psychology book. "If you tell yourself you're staying until something turns, you have a plan," he says.

"I like that," she says. She sounds so sad that he thinks she might kiss him.

When Lennon walks up to his front door a little after midnight, because nothing has turned for him, yet, he finds a note taped thoughtlessly to the painted jamb. When he removes it, paint comes off, leaving a small patch of bare wood. The day Lennon moves out his landlord will see that and assume the rest of the deposit is going to be forfeited. In the light of the lamp he keeps right inside the door, Lennon reads the sheet of loose-leaf paper. The handwriting is about 36-point.

So, you do go out late after all. Cool! We checked to see if maybe y-o-u work at the drugstore late, but NO!

See ya, A&A

This is another advantage of being parceled with Ciana and Vendetta. They weren't there, either, to be found and tormented. He can't believe he works in a drugstore and doesn't have even one Tylenol in his house. He could use a couple. At least.

AFTER three days measured out in hours marked at ten minutes of the hour, every hour, twenty-four hours a day, Ciana no longer knew what taking a turn would mean. Her mother's CRP level fluctuated a little bit each morning. And the machine tracking vitals ticked up and down, but Lennon had meant to wait until for-the-worse or for-the-better came, and so far it hadn't. So Ciana decided yesterday to come back to work, and she's paying Jaquilica six-fifty an hour to do nothing more than sit where Ciana was sitting and go in every hour to look at her mother. Vendetta is sure Jaquilica can do that. Jaquilica can even do that with a pint in her pocket, Vendetta says. *Especially* with a pint in her pocket.

Today is slow enough for half-hour breaks, and Ciana

can get *to* Baptist in four minutes. She can get *into* Baptist in ten. That's the way it is in New Orleans; no one is en route anywhere; everyone is already parked when you arrive. Finally she finds a meter and feeds it full because meter maids are the city's only source of revenue. Actually they are called parking enforcement officers, as Vendetta's sister Frieda will be the first to tell you. Ciana thinks this is because Frieda doesn't want to be called Lovely Frieda, but Vendetta says, no, Frieda was born in July of 1976, and that name was as close as their mother could come to freedom and liberty and everything else that was important around then. Ciana points out that no one knew what Frieda was going to do when she grew up, and Vendetta says, I swear, that girl made the rules up, time she was *born*.

Ciana can't wait for the day when she finds out what sparked Jaquilica's name.

Her mother is grimacing when she walks into the ICU, relieving Jaquilica of the ten hourly minutes on her feet. Ciana calls the nurse, who says of her mother's obvious discomfort, "That's a good sign." "Oh?" Ciana says, stroking her mother's head, feeling perspiration and fanning her a bit with her cupped hand until she looks more comfortable. "Brain function," the nurse says. "It means she has some."

"What do you mean by that?" Ciana says. It's a rhetorical question, because Ciana is instantly sick to her stomach, which means the answer is not good.

"She might not," the nurse says, and she walks away as if this is a perfectly normal conversation.

Dr. Hebert happens to be in the hall when Ciana walks

out. He stops to talk to her, and because he sees her lab coat he doesn't talk all the way down, unless it is his way of forcing a lesser professional to ask questions. "What your mother has seems to be particularly intransigent," he says. "She's not making a whole lot of progress." "But she's not deteriorating," Ciana says. He hesitates just long enough to jangle Ciana. "She's holding her own," he says. "We have a pretty strong arsenal of antibiotics, as I'm sure you know."

Ciana asks him if he has some sort of timetable, because it is the kind of question Geoffrey is going to ask when he checks in, and she's going to be able to say that the doctor told her such matters are completely unpredictable. If it's weeks rather than days, she doesn't know why it should matter to Geoffrey, unless thoughtful people are asking him. "Well," Dr. Hebert says, "every day your mother is on a respirator decreases her chances."

"Oh, my God."

She is standing up. In a corridor. With no one around. Except this man she doesn't know. She looks into his eyes, hoping. But she gets nothing back. He acts as if he just has told Ciana her mother has a cold. "I don't feel good," Ciana says. "I'm sorry," he says, as if he has bumped into her, and then he moves on. *Now* Ciana has some specific questions, but she can't run after him. She wouldn't care if the hallway suddenly filled up with dozens of slender, mocking women; public humiliation is not what stops her. What stops her are his answers. He's not the type to be ambiguous just for the sake of letting someone go away feeling better.

She has a choice. If she thinks about it, it is her total

choice. She can call Geoffrey, or she can call the pharmacy, knowing Lennon is supposed to answer. Either way, all the anger is probably going to come out. Either way, she will get to do a lot of crying if she wants. The difference is that with Geoffrey she might also make him feel bad, and with Lennon she might also get to make herself feel good. Actually, with Geoffrey, she has to confess that making him feel bad will make her feel good. She can't help what she feels; she just wants to feel better. She calls Geoffrey. "I'm busy, Ciana," he says when he answers the phone. Her name and cell number have come up on his Caller ID. "Fine," she says. "I'm right outside the hospital." She hangs up the phone.

She gives him a full minute to dial back, and when he doesn't, she admits to herself that she's flat-out grateful that Geoffrey never has learned his lesson. Geoffrey always has lost her and gotten in trouble for it. When Ciana was in kindergarten and he was supposed to walk her home, he got caught up in putting pennies on the streetcar tracks and to be rid of her put her on the next streetcar going downtown; Ciana stood next to the conductor until she wet her pants. Geoffrey had hell to pay for that one. When he and Corinne fixed her up in tenth grade with a blind date who left her in the corner of the DeLaSalle gym, Geoffrey hollered at the boy, "Hey, Ronald McDonald, you forgot about Grimace," and Ciana shambled all the way to the levee behind the zoo in a terrible purple satin sack her mother had found in the old ladies' department at Lane Bryant. "You can't lose *that*," Geoffrey said. Ciana guesses her mother is going to get better.

She is the highest power Ciana believes in, and Geoffrey is going to be in trouble with some higher power soon.

Ciana dials the private line to the pharmacy. "Lennon?" "Ciana!" The pharmacy doesn't have Caller ID. He knows her voice. Forget inductive reasoning. Forget contextual clues. Forget that Ciana recognizes Lennon for the same reason he recognizes her. She asks him if there's a huge backlog. "Honey, you've only been gone twenty minutes." *Honey*. She feels soothed, as if he can hear her sadness, but then she snaps out of it. He calls everybody who might need a pill *honey*. "Sometimes twenty minutes is an eternity," Ciana says lamely. "Not today," he says, and he sounds as if he could be lying for her sake. "You can take all the time you need. Trust us. We can get a lot done while we're locked up. Do what you need to do." Ciana asks him what about Mr. Walker finding her gone. "Mr. Walker can't tell you and me apart," Lennon says.

According to Ciana's date book, her mother is due home from her trip tomorrow.

Her mother's life will start up again, but it is a very small life now. It can go on without her; all Ciana has to do is phone the *Times-Picayune* and check the mail that falls under the slot next to the door. She's sure that ninety-nine percent of that, in sheer volume, can go straight to the trash. Her mother has ordered once from a Coldwater Creek catalog and donated once to the Humane Society, and she gets four catalogs and a half dozen solicitations every day, all of which she opens and reads. "They print it in color," she says. "They go to a lot of trouble." There is nothing Ciana has to do except call the newspaper, and she can almost accept Corinne's having gone on her merry way with no offers to be useful.

Ciana's relieved; she wonders what single call she'd like her own life pared down to. Probably not the *Times-Picayune.*

The dog. Nookie the improbable dog. Nookie, one of the main reasons her mother didn't want to leave town. Though Nookie has had a peculiar ability to survive all his life in spite of what nature and jokesters have given him. He is a miniature dachshund who, the breeder said, was assuredly not the runt of the litter. But he is a peculiar specimen of his breed, and to Ciana's way of thinking the best of the lot. He is smaller than even the usual small ones, and he has none of the manic, blood-vessel-popping character most dachshunds have. He's just *there,* as if a wire shorted, and his expression is one of gratitude; he soldiers on, rarely yipping, and he wins Ciana every time. "Smoke and eyeballs," Ciana tells her mother, "that's his magic."

When Ciana bails him out of the vet's on Freret Street, she is surprised by her reaction to the dog, just as she is every time she sees him. Ciana doesn't believe in souls; she often doesn't believe in *minds.* But she thinks this animal has at least a mind. Nookie settles against Ciana's bosom with none of the aerodynamic problems that make most dachshunds need to be placed straight on the floor. And he looks up at Ciana with one round eye and an expression that says, *Whatever you do is all right.* Thus ends Ciana's plan to drop him unceremoniously at her house for the remaining six hours of her shift. She thinks of other houses. Vendetta's house is empty because Jaquilica is at Baptist. Lennon's house is empty because he is at N.O. And Corinne's house is not worth considering. Ciana tolerates her older niece and nephew living with Corinne, but she aches over the middle one, Madeleine, spending any time at all in that house. An evening there would bruise Nookie's soul.

Nookie fits in the pocket of Ciana's lab coat, and Ciana thinks she is lumpy enough to keep him hidden there as long as no one bumps into her. It's a strange feeling, after all the months of maneuvering to get lined up where she'll brush against Lennon, all of a sudden to have to act as if she has a huge blister that will pop if anyone touches it. She knows she could just come right out and tell everyone back here in the pharmacy that she has a dog in her pocket, but she is the enforcer of standards of purity and precision. Ciana never lets on that she knows her responsibilities because she didn't go into the business for power over people she knows personally and daily. She's in it for power over people who don't know any better.

Nookie is only a small, soft, warm secret against her hip. But he is pleasure. Puppy pleasure. When no one is looking, Ciana peeks down, and he is looking up, all eyes. Ciana would have gone to veterinary school if it had been nothing but well puppies forever. Now she doesn't even have a dog of her own because she works a twelve-hour shift. Besides, a dog's life span is too short. She knows if she got a six-week-old puppy she would start grieving over its decline before it got its first shots. Ciana's already a little sad over Nookie.

The dog's in her right-hand pocket, and Lennon sidles up to Ciana on the left and drops something into her other pocket. In that brief moment she can feel his hand through cloth, brushing against her upper thigh of all places, the pillowy flesh giving way worse than it does anywhere else on her entire body. She wants to protest so he won't touch her *there* again, but because she wants him to touch her anywhere else again, she says nothing, just clenches her thigh in case he does it again. She reaches into the pocket and comes up with a palmful of dog kibble. "Where'd you get this?" she whispers. "Aisle six," he says. "Lots more where that came from." He jerks his head in the direction of the break room. Ciana wonders when he slipped out, got it, paid for it, opened it, hid the bag, slipped back in. *My mother is probably dying, and I am breathlessly happy for a good long moment.* Ciana drops all but one kibble into the pocket with Nookie, and as she works she can feel the dog maneuvering around, ever so politely, finding each little nugget. Ciana has saved one for a keepsake. "You got one seriously busy pocket, girl," Vendetta says later in the day, and Ciana gives up on being any sort of standard bearer. But she knows she can't do this tomorrow. Maybe humans can choose not to drink so they won't have to take breaks for the bathroom during a twelve-hour shift, but dogs can't. A human can make that choice for them, but her mother didn't make a donation to the Humane Society only to have her own dog be treated like a prisoner of war. Ciana doesn't know what she's going to do, but she's positive she'll spend money before she'll ask Corinne for help.

Just before it's time to close out for the night shift, Lennon says to Ciana, "I have a solution to your problem."

"I have a million problems," Ciana says, and she smiles to let him know she doesn't feel sorry for herself. Though she would like to.

He looks straight at her in a way that Ciana thinks says he's going to completely, forever ignore the fact that she's seventy pounds overweight. The night at the hospital, he said that the fat people on television had something wrong with them and Ciana didn't, which to her meant that they were on television, and that was unappealing. She wasn't on television, so she was beautiful. Lennon says, "The only problem I see is that you all of a sudden have a dog, and you work a twelve-hour shift."

Ciana can't help it. Her eyes fill up. She quite simply wants to have him. *Have* him. Absorb him. Own him. Take him home. She nods.

"Can you follow me home?" he is saying. Ciana nods.

She has to go see her mother. She has to spend the night with her mother. Lennon says that's all the more reason to see what he has for her. He has something for her. Ciana is afraid she'll be late to the hospital and be sorry, but he has something for *her*.

9

VENDETTA knows what Lennon is going to give Ciana tonight; he must have asked her a half dozen times if it was all right for him to be coming right out and suggesting Ciana get around people. Really, he is giving her a way to break the rules. And Ciana's job is supposed to be to enforce the rules. Vendetta wanted to tell him that Ciana would be thrilled if he gave her a baggie full of dog shit as long as he said it was a gift from him. But being the person in the middle means keeping her mouth shut and waiting until Ciana and Lennon wise up. Vendetta loves seeing how stupid the two of them are.

The shift is over in ten minutes, and Vendetta doesn't know what to do. She has the pill in her purse, but she'd rather have a cyanide capsule that she will use proudly and bravely. It's one little twenty-milligram tablet, and it would be easy to short somebody's bottle, but she doesn't want to do it. She figures she'll walk out with it, make her decision on the way home, bring it back if she can, replace it without anyone knowing anything.

Frieda says it's all her fault, that taking Jaquilica away for her white friend is messing everything up. "I don't hear you complaining when my white friend give her cash money every night," Vendetta says back.

"Quilica buy a fifth instead of a pint," Frieda says. "All that money doing, making her too high and mighty to help me out. Not that she got the time."

Frieda does not want to take the blame. Frieda was doing her rounds uptown this morning around the Tulane campus, and Frieda was thinking about what life was all about, and it didn't take long for her to think about Tulane students and drugs and how Tulane students sell Ritalin and Adderall and how Quick takes Ritalin and how Quick took his last pill this morning and oh, shit.

At first Vendetta didn't have to cover the receiver when Frieda called from her cell phone, because all the solutions didn't involve Vendetta. "Girl, you know you meet quota. One way or the other, you meet quota. Do it early and get your ass downtown." It was true; half of what Frieda talks about is the tricks she pulls to meet quota, ticketing rich people's cars when they've been in a two-hour zone an hour and a half, knowing they won't contest; ticketing poor people's cars when they're fifteen inches from the curb instead of nineteen because they won't pay. Frieda was messed up in that deal where somebody put epoxy putty in the meters on Magazine Street, and people parked like crazy and kept getting tickets because they couldn't feed the meters. Nobody ever knew it was the parking enforcement girls who did it; rumor was that it was shop-owners from up the street. Frieda could make quota in half a day and fool around with one of the stock boys over at Whole Foods a good portion of the afternoon in parts of that old building where no one ever looked. Vendetta knew that up by Tulane Frieda could meet quota on those dumb students by eleven in the morning. "Shoot," Frieda once said. "You know how up north they send their kids to Harvard and all? They come up with one can't learn, they send *his* ass to Tulane." A Tulane student would see an orange envelope under the windshield wiper and mail it to Daddy. Frieda could get *her* ass down to Charity for a paper prescription and still earn her little paycheck. That was the problem with Ritalin: Schedule II. She had to have it on paper. No doctor could call it in. Not that any doctor at Charity *would*.

"You know damn well nobody walk into Charity, say, 'I would like me a scrip, please,' they hand you a scrip, you walk out in five minutes, no," Frieda said.

"I know damn well that you got City of New Orleans insurance, so you got no business dragging your fool self all the way down to Charity," Vendetta said.

Frieda was waiting for that one. "I like for Mama to hear

you now. Every one of us born in Charity, and they give you *no* gas back then, and you hear Mama complain? No, you did not. You see Mama stop having babies because they act mean to her down at Charity? No, you did not. And you not that far up the line, Vendetta. You could of swum right into a condom."

"Charity is not hoping to hold onto loyal customers," Vendetta said.

"Well, they got me for life," Frieda said. "And today they got Quick, too."

Vendetta has the pill. It's small and generic, round and white. She will take it home with her and try to find a way to bring it back tomorrow. Quick needs one dose in the evening and one dose before school, but Frieda had the good sense not to ask for two. Either she will cut it in half and it won't work either time, or she'll use it midway and keep him up all night, or she'll blow it tonight and suffer in the morning. Or she might save it for morning. Vendetta hopes that's the case, because by then Frieda will see that in just a few minutes she can deposit him on his teacher, and Vendetta can have the pill back. Public school teachers don't have very high expectations.

Everyone is in Vendetta's half of the double when she comes home, except Jaquilica. In her place, for some strange reason, is her son, Everett, who is just watching, as if he's been invited over as a witness, though of course he hasn't. Patricia and Quick are jumping on the beds in Patricia's room. The beds Vendetta bought at Universal Furniture on credit that took three years to pay off. Good Sealy Posturpedic. "Patricia," Vendetta says without raising her voice, and Patricia stops with ankle action worthy of a top-seeded gymnast. Quick lands a belly flop, gets up, looks to his mother for a signal, gets none, keeps jumping. Vendetta walks over and grabs one flailing hyperactive skinny wrist and squeezes until even Quick gets the idea. "You got the pill?" Frieda says.

"No," Vendetta says.

"You see how this boy acting?" Frieda says.

"I see this his normal time for his medicine," Vendetta says. "You not making no special case. I *also* see you got my child all riled up for no reason."

"What I'm suppose to do, put them in separate rooms? How you think that make my Quick feel?"

"Like he could be with Patricia if he don't cut up," Vendetta says.

"Mama!" Patricia says. Patricia feels that she is tortured enough by the boys her own age at school without having to suffer the torments of her cousin's craziness at home. It's bad enough, she's told Vendetta, that everyone in the school is sure she must be a' animal if she's kin to Quick. It doesn't help that she says back, "Well, if you live in the project, *all* you kin to is animals." Vendetta is sure that one day Frieda will call her on her loyalty to Sylvanie F. Williams the same way she's called Frieda on her loyalty to Charity Hospital.

"Half Patricia problems because she show up with

Quick," Vendetta says. Nobody picked at her in kindergarten, first, and second, in fact not until Quick came.

"Quick only go there so Patricia got a ride," Frieda says. She's got Vendetta on that one, and she says, "So give me that damn pill."

"Frieda, I'm a get fired."

That's what this is all about. Ciana does everything perfectly. They never miss a penny or a pill. If somebody gets shorted on their shift, it is either her fault or Lennon's. And Lennon is so much like Ciana in his ways that Vendetta wonders sometimes if it's part of the calling and other times if it's something a little sissified about Lennon. If it's the second, only one person might help, Everett, and he's as useless as teats on a boar hog. Everett never fails to ask about Lennon when he comes over. Everett prefers portly white boys, but for Lennon he might make an exception. Vendetta cringes whenever Everett comes into the store. But so far Everett has done nothing but sashay up to the counter without a prescription just so he can have Lennon ring up his KY. As far as Vendetta can tell, Lennon thinks it's toothpaste.

"They not gonna fire you over one little pill," Frieda says.

"Wrong is wrong," Vendetta says. "Tell you what. You leave that Quick over here with no pill, and we all be happy."

"Except me," Patricia says.

"You sleep over by my house," Frieda says to her.

"Uh, uh," Patricia says, and she starts to cry.

"You sleep in the bed with me," Vendetta says. "He can sleep in your room."

"Uh, uh," Patricia says, still snuffling. "He pee the bed."

Frieda's feelings are hurt, even though it's true. But obviously her feelings aren't hurt enough to have Quick sleeping near her if he's not medicated. "He got pantses. Vendetta, you know they got pantses he sleep in. They sell them right up by the Depends."

At one A.M. Vendetta wakes up because she smells something good. It's been hard to sleep well because Patricia has been sobbing from time to time, and this much she has gotten out of her, that the child is having a nightmare that the entire play yard behind the school is a giant pool of pee, and she has come in from recess, the only one soaked. Vendetta half believes Patricia is going to wet the bed just from expectation.

She sees the light on in the kitchen and tiptoes through Patricia's room until she notices that Quick isn't in the bed, and then she moves fast. There he is, as big as life, standing at her clean gas stove, a hot dog on a fork sizzling over an open flame. The grease is dropping down into the depths of the stove where Vendetta cleans only once a year because she is so careful when she cooks. The hot dog is popping with little flames and has a few charcoal blisters that would make it taste awfully good on a bun at a picnic. "What the hell you doing, boy?"

"I'm hungry," Quick says.

"Give me that fork."

"Uh, uh." Quick goes running through Vendetta's kitchen with the fork in the air, the hot dog flopping like little fat wings. "You can *have* it," Vendetta says. "You got a bun?" Quick says.

When he has eaten the hot dog and two bags of chips, Quick is ready for "Nick at Nite." Vendetta is beginning to feel that special kind of panic that comes when she hasn't had the right kind of sleep. She can doze on the sofa while he watches. Good, "The Cosby Show." Bill Cosby must have the deepest voice of anyone on television. He'll put Quick to sleep. And if he doesn't, at least he'll put Vendetta to sleep.

She has just drifted off when he pushes the volume up to forty-two on the cable box. Vendetta comes awake the way that means she won't sleep again for hours, and Patricia screams from the bedroom. "That's it," she says. She gives Quick the pill.

What kills her isn't that Ciana will fire her. What kills her is that Ciana will hate her.

LENNON lives in a little shotgun in what's called Pigeontown. The intersection of *South* Carrollton and *South* Claiborne, where N.O. Drugs sits on the uptown-lake corner, cuts four sections, and Pigeontown is the uptown-river section. Lennon likes the area because it's possible to walk through there and pretend it's a small southern river town, though he wouldn't do it if he were white. That's the way it feels. Every animal is a stray, even if it has a tag. Every child is a stray, too, especially in summer. The streets are higher than the sidewalks, and they crumble at the edges into clamshell aprons. No curbs. Lennon hopes Ciana can tell he's just a renter because the winter grass hasn't been cut in months in spite of many complaints. A profusion of Japanese magnolia blooms is starting to drop petals over his small patch of a front yard. His is a gingerbread house that would rent for a thousand dollars in any other part of town. Here it rents for what a student can afford. Personally, Lennon thinks it says a lot about him, all good.

Lennon leads Ciana slowly up the front steps, hoping a neighbor might see them and say something to the Hollingsworth twins the next time they drop by. All of his neighbors are over fifty, and their interpretation of Ciana would be a "fine white girl." That would dumbfound those Hollingsworths. Lennon suddenly feels a wash of shame that he wants Ciana defined as something other than what she is. He'd like to think that she really is a fine white girl, but he already knows that's not the term the twins would use. And the damn twins are judging him. *That's* what's the matter. He hurries into the house.

The house is cold because there is no reason to heat it for the twelve hours a day that he's gone. That's the reason it's dark, too. It's a point of pride to Lennon that he never has an Entergy bill over a hundred dollars a month, including those arbitrary fuel adjustment charges. Summer or winter. He checks the meter and does the math and cuts back accordingly. He's not cheap. He's actually not even ecologically sensitive. It's more that he enjoys the mental challenge. "Hold on, hold on," he says to Ciana. He'll make it warm and light, even if he has to use candles and blankets for a couple of hours tomorrow. He lights a gas heater, and Ciana huddles over it, making a warm breast cave for Nookie.

Lennon never has had company here before. It didn't occur to him that he would when he rented it. He has a futon, covered in maroon and green fabric, set up like a sofa, that he got on sale; he would never shop at a garage sale. There is nothing else in the front room of the shotgun except lamps at both doors to make up for no overhead lighting. Shotguns rarely have overhead lighting unless they've been gentrified. Ciana sits at the edge of the futon, very ladylike, looking as if someone is going to bring her tea, and suddenly hot tea seems like a good idea, though of course he'd prefer to bring out *gin* and teacups. Not that he has any. Or drinks any. "Can I get you something?" No, she says, she has to get to the hospital. She seems to be regretful. She pats the dog. Lennon pats the dog. He can't think of anything to say. And then he remembers why she's here. "I'll be right back," he says, weak and thrilled with relief.

The box is not where he thought it was. Lennon considers the third room, the one before the kitchen, his attic. He has fifteen same-sized cardboard boxes, all labeled by general category, along a wall; three file cabinets filled according to whether the material is personal, business, or academic, not easy choices sometimes, along another wall; unhung paintings; his bicycle; a cedar armoire; and shelves of whatever comes up in bulk sale at the store. He was sure he'd go right to the box labeled FAMILY and find it, but that box holds nothing except the flatware and earthenware he ate off of as a child, plus napkin rings, coasters, and a few select items his mother was sure he needed to set up housekeeping.

He's baffled until he deduces that what he's looking for is wearable, so he must have reasoned that it should be in the armoire. And there it is, dangling ridiculously from a wire hanger. Its box is on the armoire floor. Thank goodness. He doesn't have to present it just like this.

"Okay, you won't judge me or fire me or anything, right?" he says.

"You're doing me a favor, Lennon," she says. "I think even if you get me sent to federal prison I'm not going to judge you."

"Good thing," he says, and he opens the package. He can practically *see* the scent of cedar coming out of the poor dilapidated box.

Ciana takes one look at what appears to be a miniature crossing guard uniform, neon orange piped in black, with far too many skinny straps to untangle without good fingernails. "What," she says, and Lennon holds it up so she can see the writing on it. "It's for the dog," he says.

"I'm not taking him *hunting*," Ciana says.

Lennon asks Ciana to give it to him, and he unsnags it with enough patience to make him think that with the right woman he could have become a neurosurgeon. Ciana watches him as if soothed by his motions. He explains why this item has fallen into his hands. "Diana, that's my sister, she carried around this Chihuahua *long* before Paris Hilton and Reese Witherspoon and every other ultra white girl decided a dog was a fashion accessory. I mean, she *loved* that dog. I think something happened to her in nursery school;

she missed out on all that transitional object stuff." Ciana smiles at him, and he thinks it's a conspiratorial smile between two people who don't have children yet, but will be very understanding when they do.

"So when Diana learned at the tender age of nineteen that she couldn't take her dog into restaurants, she was beside herself. My mother reminded her that there was a time when she couldn't have taken *herself* into restaurants, but Diana's not the type to look back. She saw a seeing-eye dog, figured a Chihuahua couldn't pass, found out that Chihuahuas could be trained to sense oncoming seizures, and *voilà!*" Lennon thrusts Nookie up into the air, showing Ciana that the vest says DO NOT PET. WORKING DOG. "It's the only clever thing Diana ever did, so I kept it."

Lennon is shimmering with the excitement of having proffered a perfect gift. "*You* wear a bracelet; nobody asks you any questions. I think you can probably go into the ICU with the dog. They wouldn't want you keeling over in there," he says.

All Ciana says is, "What happened to the Chihuahua?" and every fantasy Lennon has spun around this moment disintegrates into the cold air. "She took it to Paris," he says, and now Ciana looks completely thrilled.

They lapse into complete silence, like a happy young couple with their quiet, swaddled baby. Lennon doesn't want Ciana to leave. Ever. He'd be happy to put in central heating and run it all the time. Though Ciana is a woman who'd love his Entergy game. They could come home at night and jump right into bed and make love by twenty-five watts, not touching each other until their hands were warm. He absentmindedly strokes one of Nookie's tiny cold feet, imagining those feet in the bed with them, and stifles a laugh when he thinks of Nookie as a slightly wriggly hot water bottle. His little vest is that cheap vinyl that doesn't take on body warmth.

He thought Ciana might kiss him when he gave her the vest.

"I have something else for you," he says.

"You're joking," she says, and he thinks maybe he's gone from too cold to too hot. "No," he says, looking her in the eye to make it no big deal. He fishes in his pocket and pulls out the necklace. He's had hundreds of daydreams about her and him, sitting this close, or standing this close away from work, or lying this close, and often he gives her a love token that allows them to fade into each other, Vaseline covering his lens; it's exactly at that point that Ciana tells him he is going too fast, that they haven't even kissed. He presses it into her hand, closes her fist around it.

Ciana holds it closed for a moment, feeling it, trying to figure it out, looking pale with concern that he is, indeed, going too fast. When she does look, and sees that it's a MedicAssist necklace, she still looks alarmed. He's not asking her to marry him, for Chrissakes, and she knows what it is because they carry them behind the counter, where they gather dust because almost no one ever buys one. Ciana dangles it in front of herself, gingerly tries it around her neck without fastening. It doesn't hang as loose as it might, but it's not fitting her like a choker, either. He sees her go pale with relief because it can be fastened, and he gets it now. "I'll get it engraved tomorrow," he says. "I'll go over to Oak Street. If it says you have seizures, you can go anywhere you want with the dog. All you have to do is tell them he can sense an attack coming on, and they *have* to let him in. Even in the pharmacy. Especially even in the hospital."

Ciana leans over and kisses him. Smack on the lips. Just like a little kid, sloppy and hard and too slow, the way she might kiss a girl almost. Lennon's not even embarrassed or excited. He takes the chain and starts to put it on her, but she recoils so he says, "I got a short one so it'll be visible no matter what you wear."

"Oh, Lord," Ciana says, "what if Nookie starts yelping over something? Do I have to keel over and flop around?"

"I think it would be a good idea," Lennon says.

II

HER MOTHER has been moved into the Critical Care Unit, but Ciana doesn't dare ask tonight what this means about her prognosis. All she knows is that it means she can stay all sixty minutes of the hour. Ciana's not foolish enough to brandish Nookie like a trophy when she walks in; he's in the pocket until the curtain is pulled. And then Ciana turns her back to the opening and leans over the bed and pulls him out and brings him closer to her mother's face. It's almost as if Ciana's started to believe Nookie does have extra senses, that he can pick up her mother's brain activity in ways that an EEG would not if it were rolled in there. Nookie practically jackknifes in midair over her mother with excitement, but to his credit he doesn't even whimper. Ciana looks at the panel that monitors vital signs, and the pulse rate rises. Ciana wants to tell the world. She wants to run out into the hallway and announce she's made a great scientific discovery. Someone comes up to the curtain and says, "Knock, knock," and Ciana snatches Nookie back, stuffs him into her pocket, says, "Come in." She's sure she looks like a serial killer.

The nurse checks the catheter line and starts to leave. "When I spoke to her I saw her pulse go up," Ciana tells the nurse, who says that as much stimulation as possible is good. Ciana wants to know whether a little dog beating the air around her mask-covered face actually affects any of the five known senses, but she doesn't ask. "Is being in Critical Care good?" Ciana says. "*I* think so," the nurse says, and Ciana realizes she's asked the wrong question.

Ciana whispers in her mother's ear for a while, to soothe her, to soothe herself, and her mother's heart doesn't seem to hear any of what she says. She tells her that she thinks Lennon is her boyfriend, but the beat doesn't change. She's sure it's because she's whispering. In a monotone. Her mother needs to rest. Ciana needs to rest. Both of them would be too agitated if Ciana made the announcement about him the way she wants to. Her mother wouldn't be able to say a word, but they'd be arguing. She reasons that it doesn't come up to that level if she just whispers the news.

Ciana has been using up what feels like pounds of change at the pay phone, trying to get Geoffrey or Corinne to answer a call from her. She doesn't try from work or home anymore because they absolutely will ignore those numbers, but it seems to her that if Caller ID says "pay phone," it might be worth answering. And she knows Caller ID will read "pay phone" because she's received a call or two from a pay phone in her life, usually from someone who has the sounds of a bar in the background, a bar that has loosened his fingers too much to hit the right numbers but also has loosened his mind enough to give her a most florid apology. But people call collect from jail. And people can't use cell phones in hospitals. That's why she always takes calls from pay phones. Any decent person would. Especially any decent person with a mother in the hospital.

Ciana stays away from the pay phone the entire morning, so Geoffrey and Corinne will think her mother is checking out of the hospital, and then she goes and lets herself into her mother's house. She bursts into tears when she opens the door and wonders if this means she thinks her mother is not coming home. She squeezes her eyes shut, gets rid of the thought, tries to find others. She puts Nookie down on the floor, and the dog skibbles right into the kitchen, straight to his food bowl. The bowl is empty and dishwasher-clean. Ciana pours water into it, and Nookie looks up at her as if he is going to refuse ever to know her again. The house is freezing. Ciana knows why she wants to cry. The house is in what her mother calls dying order. Whenever she has gone on a trip, which has been truly infrequently, she always has insisted on leaving the house in dying order. She's done so ever since Ciana was small, and the family would go to the beach in Mississippi, and dying order was a hard state to achieve when a person was leaving a house with two young children who would make some sort of spill or wrinkle at the last second. Her mother insisted that if she didn't come back, she wanted whoever came in to find everything clean and in its place. Geoffrey always asked why. Ciana always asked *why*. After all, she does not control the mailman, and a very messy heap is cascading around itself under the mail slot. Ciana molds it together into a pile she can lift and carries it back to the kitchen. She starts to do triage on it, but then she realizes she doesn't want to leave trash because that will mess up the dying order, and she doesn't want her mother to walk back in and fuss. Coming *back* to dying order is a bonus of leaving it, but no one's ever dared mention that to her mother. Ciana drops it all into a grocery bag; it'll give her something to do at the hospital.

Nookie sniffs around the house to check out his own dying order, and Ciana settles into the living room and dials Corinne. It's four in the afternoon, homework time; Ciana knows she's there. And sure enough, she answers on the second ring. "Mother Jambon!" she says. "You're home!"

"Hello, Corinne," Ciana says.

"Who's this?"

"This is somebody who had to use a significant amount of subterfuge to get you to answer your phone," Ciana says.

"What are you doing over there?"

Ciana softens up, mindful that Corinne has the delightful option of hanging up the phone. She's not sure why Corinne is avoiding her, but whatever her reason is, it's *extreme.* "Corinne, please tell me why I haven't been able to get in touch with you."

"Hold on," Corinne says, and Ciana can hear her moving away from what sounds like a human hatchery. Something clicks, closing her into quiet. "Okay. You can't get in touch with me because I'm so upset."

"You're telling me nothing here, Corinne."

"I don't know why you think you didn't do anything to your mother, but you're going to have to live with the consequences for the rest of your life," Corinne says, sounding very much like she's been waiting to give this speech for a while now. "I can't believe I went to all that trouble to give her a little fun, a *lot* of fun actually, and then I came back here, and I let you come in the room for, what, five minutes, and before I know it Geoffrey says she looks like she's been beaten half to death. And you did it right in front of both of us. Don't ask me to look at her in that condition. You've pulled some stunts in your day, Ciana, but this one goes too far."

Ciana has no response. She learned a long time ago that there is no point in being rational with irrational people. To Ciana it's purely mathematical, like pressing the +/– key on the calculator. Everything she says flips right over; her sense becomes nonsense because the other person has pressed that key. If she says she never has pulled stunts in her life, Corinne will tell her that her good behavior has been a rotten trick. If she says she happened to be around when her mother's body reached normal temperature after Corinne had taken it to New York and frozen it, Corrine will start some diatribe about how people get the bends when you bring them up from the bottom of the ocean too quickly. "I have no response to that," Ciana says.

Corinne gets quiet for a while. It seems to Ciana that Corinne would have learned by now that Ciana gives her chances for a one-two punch on a regular basis, but she's never caught on. "It's all over town what you did," Corinne says. "If we hadn't put her in the most prestigious hospital in the city, you probably could get away with anything, but I know too many people who volunteer over there. Not to mention all the doctors."

Ciana knows very well that there are *no* prestigious hospitals in New Orleans. Maybe Baptist was prestigious fifty years ago when it was staunchly racist, but she's sure even then people didn't go in there thinking, *Oh, I'm confident I'll get well; no negroes are in any of the other beds.* If a person boasts about having been in a hospital, it's a hospital in Texas or New York. If a person boasts about having been in a New Orleans hospital, it's because he came out *alive.*

"This is Ciana you're talking to," she says. "You do not know any doctors. Unless they're on your health plan."

"I do so."

"Tell me the name of one." Ciana settles back nicely on the sofa. It's not even that cold in the house anymore. She pats the cushion next to herself, and Nookie jumps up, defying all the laws of canine physiology. Nookie and her mother must have practiced this trick a thousand times.

"I don't have to. There's confidentiality," Corinne says,

and Ciana rolls her eyes even though there is no one to see her. "You know as well as I do that when you have your kids at Holy Name you spend a lot of time with a lot of important people."

"I've probably picked up your kids at the yard as many times as you have, and I've yet to see doctors standing out there gossiping about what somebody's sister-in-law supposedly did six units over and three floors up for two seconds yesterday at the hospital."

"Well, I know everything you're doing, and to tell you the truth, you're doing a lousy job."

Ciana's eyes fill up with tears. She knows it's from exhaustion. She sleeps like a cat, waking up whenever her mother gets agitated. She never misses it; Nookie wriggles if she does. Her mother needs to know she's there. She doesn't like to be away, and she tries to have Jaquilica spell her as little as possible. But she has to work, and she's not at the hospital right now. Her mother needs to sense someone's presence. Someone familiar's presence. Ciana believes she's doing a lousy job.

When she hasn't said anything, Corinne says, "I'm sure you're trying your best."

Ciana clenches her teeth. "It'd help if you or Geoffrey would take a turn a few times."

"Look, Geoffrey's got a job. And I didn't see what she looked like, all full of tubes and bloated and all grotesque in the face, but Geoffrey said I'd have nightmares. Do you see any reason why one more person should be exposed to all that? Especially when it's because of something you and that boy at the drugstore did?"

Ciana wants to say that that boy in the drugstore has pointed out that it is scientifically impossible for her mother's respiratory distress to be her fault. She doesn't want to say that that boy in the drugstore thinks Corinne did something terribly wrong in New York. Corinne already has chosen to ignore the first. As for the second, whatever guilty damage she did, it can't be hidden forever. If Ciana mentions that, Corinne might come right out and say that she will have to ask either her mother or the coroner for the truth. Ciana won't let Corinne do that to her. "The *boy* at the drugstore is going to have a doctoral degree in May," Ciana says. She feels good throwing a doctor at Corinne; he's not a make-believe one, standing at the carpool gate.

"Is that what he told you?"

"Yes," Ciana says.

"He's trying to get into your pants," Corinne says. "And you're probably going to let him. I swear, you've never had an ounce of common sense."

"Probably not," Ciana says.

12

VENDETTA always has said there are two kinds of fist-pounders, the ones who are trying to please them, and the ones who aren't. The ones who are trying to please them come right up to the pharmacy, drop the fist down once to within a fraction of an inch of the counter, say, "Gimme my damn Prozac," and wait for them to laugh at the joke like they've never heard it before. She and Lennon and Ciana laugh for them because they know perfectly well that if those customers weren't trying so hard to entertain the entire world they wouldn't be so damn depressed.

The other kind come up and pound their fists on the counter because they've made impossible demands, and they want to make sure nobody in line ahead of them is going to object. This Mr. Earl Roberts is one of them. Ciana just checked the computer, and Vendetta has guessed right: this man never has used this pharmacy, at least not in the past four years. So he can feel totally free to cause a scene. His prescriptions are in the N.O. Drugs system, down on St. Claude, and that makes him a customer, but not a customer in the flesh. He wants his refills, and he wants them in five minutes because his wife is in the car, and the motor is running so she won't be cold. "It's Dilantin and Topamax; you know what *that* means," Mr. Roberts says. Vendetta knows all right. He's an epileptic, and if he took his last dose last night, he's got a chance of blowing wide open right here and now if he doesn't get his medicine. Ciana's got that dog on the floor with that vest. Vendetta hopes nobody asks her to wave it over this fool. Vendetta is not in the mood for Mr. Earl Roberts because she is too nervous about Frieda's stupid pill.

She tells Mr. Earl Roberts that it will take twenty minutes to fill his prescription, and that they're pushing him ahead of other people to do that. "So push me ahead of a few more people; this is an emergency," he says. Vendetta looks at the rest of the people waiting, and she knows one will have explosive diarrhea without paregoric, and another is in the middle of a migraine so bad that the fluorescent lights are going right through her hands covering her eyes. She won't even think about Frieda, who is ready to have a fit because she is going to be late for work, and Quick and Patricia are going to be late for school.

Vendetta tells Mr. Roberts that if he had phoned in the prescription it would have been waiting for him. "No, it wouldn't have," he says. It would have, of course; that's why the phone menu makes people punch in the time they'll pick up, and that's why the computer tells them in the pharmacy what's pending at any given minute. But Vendetta isn't going to waste any time arguing. Seconds count, even for people whose sphincters, cranial arteries, and family loyalties aren't in crisis. "I think you got to bring your wife inside," Vendetta says to Mr. Roberts in a way she hopes lets him know that now he's going to be waiting for a lot longer than twenty minutes. Something in her tone says that she's come to see seizures as what people pretend to have in order to get what they want.

He turns to the others waiting for prescriptions and says, "That's what they do to you here, you know. They get you in for your medicine, which you've *got* to have, then they make you wait so long you go spend money on crap you don't need. Now I'm supposed to drag my poor wife in here. You watch. She's going to find something stupid before we walk out of this store."

Patricia has been watching. "There are a lot of chairs over here," she says to Mr. Roberts, and Vendetta wants to jump the counter, grab the child, run away, and hug her for the rest of their lives.

Quick has his eye on the sphygmomanometers.

Ciana wants to play one of her and Vendetta's games. "What do you bet she looks like?" she says. Vendetta knows

Ciana has the advantage of reading whatever is on the computer screen. "I say big redhead."

"You cheat," Vendetta says.

Lennon looks around, checks the security mirror, gives each of them a puzzled look.

"I didn't say she *right*," Vendetta says. "I just say she *cheat*."

To confound Lennon completely, Mr. Roberts walks in with a big blonde. She is a good four inches taller than he is. Vendetta hears Ciana whisper to Lennon, "He looks sixty, but the computer says he's forty-seven. I figured he's got a lot of money, so she's got a lot of hair." Vendetta wants to say, *What about the fact that they live over by St. Claude?* but the woman already has clacked up to the pick-up counter in shoes that need to be reheeled and is in earshot. Nobody is at the register. "I'd like some service here!" the woman says.

Vendetta is on the phone, and Lennon is out of sight fetching pills, so Ciana says, "We're working on your husband's prescription, would you like us to stop?" Vendetta knows that's a lie because Ciana is dispensing Mepergan, which are huge, ruby-colored capsules, nothing like what the woman's husband needs. Though a Mepergan or two might level him out if they could wait long enough. "*Earl!* I told you don't be coming uptown with this shit. Bad enough we got to go by your mama's in the middle of the damn day, that's still no reason to do business this part of town. Nobody knows you up here. Matter of fact, they make a point not to know you up here." Make a *pernt*.

Earl Roberts comes up to the counter and says, "Baby, they said twenty minutes. Right?"

Ciana says yes, it will be about twenty minutes.

Mrs. Earl Roberts says, "It ought to be about seventeen minutes now. At the most." She looks at Ciana. "I'm timing you, Poppin' Fresh. Seventeen minutes, then I'm asking for the manager. Come on, Earl."

"I think it'll be more like thirty now," Lennon says, and Frieda leaps out of her seat, sure there's a fight she can get into.

"Set yourself *down*," Vendetta hollers at her sister.

Mrs. Roberts turns around, puts her hands on her hips. "Don't you people have anything better to do than play games with customers? Come on, Earl, we'll go to the one on Napoleon." Mr. Roberts gives Vendetta a look that she swears looks almost like one of allegiance. "That'll take an hour," he says. "I could be dead in an hour."

"You're not going to be dead any time soon," his wife says, and then Vendetta thinks she sees a sort of *oops* expression come and go very fast on the woman's face. Mrs. Roberts drags her husband down what Vendetta calls the soft aisle, the one where they sell sanitary napkins and Depends and all the items that help hide the fact that stuff comes out of the bottom of people. She's always said that if she ever had a fight, she'd be sure to have it in that aisle. She hasn't changed her mind since all the minipads have become paper-thin, either.

It's when the Robertses cross into the minimart section

that the commotion starts, and Vendetta thinks this might be her chance to settle up with Frieda. She hears a small crash, then a long series of thuds, and then she gets a view just in time to see a complete display of thirty-two-ounce Gatorade bottles come tumbling down into the aisle. Within five seconds, every single person in the store has converged on that aisle. Except Vendetta, Lennon, and Ciana. Even that damn Frieda. They are under security lock, but evidently Lennon and Ciana aren't going to leave Vendetta in here by herself where she can short Frieda's prescription and even up the Ritalin count.

Mr. Walker hollers toward the pharmacy, "Bring me the dog!"

Ciana goes for the dog before she can stop to think. Lennon jumps the counter, grabs a pack of tongue depressors from the shelf, and runs to the front. And Vendetta is so damn nervous, watching Ciana come to her senses and pat the dog like that was what she meant to do all along, wondering where stupid Frieda is with both those children when there might be eyes rolling back in somebody's head, worrying that as soon as she opens the safe where they keep the CII drugs an alarm will go off; Vendetta is so damn nervous that she does nothing. Absolutely nothing.

They never have filled prescriptions so fast in all their lives. Ciana wanted to make sure all the people who were waiting with the Robertses were out of the store practically *before*

Mrs. Roberts could say "Buddy Homer," and as expected Mrs. Roberts started screaming his name while her husband was still twitching on the floor like a landed fish. Buddy Homer is a lawyer who advertises on television for car accident victims and who trolls to fill up class action suits for fat people who took fen phen and welders who got Parkinson's. He's the nightmare for everyone who doesn't sit still. Vendetta tried to point out that Frieda wasn't going to be a good witness against her own sister, and nobody needed to rush for Frieda, but Frieda must have been able to read lips, because she came up to the counter with a look that said, *I'm a tell*, and Vendetta had to let her walk away from the pharmacy with a full bottle of sixty Ritalin, one of which she shoved into Quick right after he asked if he could pop a wheelie with a shopping cart.

Mr. Walker says to Lennon and Ciana, "You two are going to clean it all up," now that it's too late for Vendetta to take advantage of being alone behind the counter and do something about the Ritalin. So she stands over by Nookie the good little liar dog and watches the Robertses limp out of the store with their unopened prescription bag and another bag carrying the cell phone ruined when Mr. Roberts peed on himself. He's wearing aqua and yellow drawstring pajama bottoms that they sell two-for-ten-dollars; the store will dry-clean his pants, probably for more than he paid for them. Vendetta looks to see if Mr. Walker is angry, because Mrs. Roberts sure blew her story up a lot by the time she left. Vendetta ought to feel sorry for Ciana and

Lennon while they mop, but the truth is that they both look thrilled out of their minds, like somebody has announced over the public-address system that they are boyfriend and girlfriend. Ciana was giggling when the woman said her husband's seizure would cause irreversible brain damage. And that she herself would probably be bedridden for the rest of her life from having a bottle of Gatorade fall on her head. Lennon loved seeing Ciana giggle. Vendetta personally thinks it all got ruined when the woman said they had a freak show in their pharmacy and that downtown they just hired *normal*-looking people. But that's probably because Vendetta is one of the freaks.

Evidently, she's the only one upset. Mr. Walker looks like he thinks this is all kind of funny, but then it probably takes a lot to jangle a person who runs a drugstore at the corner of South Carrollton and South Claiborne. More than Buddy Homer. Way more than a puddle of piss in aisle two.

"That was no grand mal seizure," Mr. Walker says. "A good show, but no grand mal seizure. The pee was a great touch, too."

The phone rings just as Lennon and Ciana are letting themselves back in through the security door. It's Jaquilica, and before Vendetta can think straight, she blurts out, "What you mean, her mama arrested?"

AFTER what seems like a full minute, Vendetta still has not handed Ciana the phone, but she says, "I'm supposed to tell you this not something to be excited about."

Evidently Ciana's mother is not dead.

Ciana does not look as if she wants to hear specifics, so Lennon puts his hand on her shoulder to let her know it's okay just to stand here, and he doesn't even think about it. "What you did?" Vendetta is hollering into the receiver, and then as she listens she makes her expressions readable. She brightens up; Ciana nods questioningly; Vendetta nods vigorously; Ciana starts to cry. Into the phone Vendetta says, "Wait a minute," and then to Ciana and Lennon, who are really standing like a married couple, she says, "You got to understand Quilica. She *very* nervous. Your mama arrest mean your mama go into cardiac arrest, but your mama come out cardiac arrest. Okay?" Ciana nods slowly, then looks around, her hands feeling around as if searching for somewhere to sit. There are a half dozen stools behind the counter, but she never sits on them, Lennon has noticed. He hates to think why. But he can't imagine a gentleman helping a lady in distress to a stool anyway. He can't seem to take his hand off her back, and he leads her to the waiting area. Ciana inhales and exhales slowly, taking in the cool drugstore air the way a marijuana user would take in a lungful of mind-soothing smoke, lips pursed, chest rising high, and Lennon can feel her calming down. He still has his hand on her back.

"You don't want to hear this," he says finally. "But it's time to call your brother."

Her breathing is still calm. "I know."

"That's not an abstraction; that's a fact."

"I know."

Lennon leans around to put his face directly in front of Ciana's, going almost nose-to-nose. He knows his eyes are huge, and he opens them wide to exaggerate his point. He can smell her breath, which is like warm butter. "I bet your mother doesn't have a living will," he says. It's not how he expected this first intimate moment to be, but it is remarkably romantic. He feels as if he smells like warm butter, too. But he backs off, gives her room to take in something besides him.

Ciana shrugs, but it's not with indifference. "My mother's

pretty secretive about her plans for the future that doesn't include her," she says. Lennon smiles at her phrasing. She smiles back, appreciated. "Mama and I have this tacit understanding. At least I think we do, tacit being what it is." Lennon keeps smiling, if that is what it takes. "You know, if we don't talk about it, it'll go away. She went with me once when I renewed my driver's license because it was my birthday and we were going to lunch. When I had to check off whether I was going to be an organ donor, she looked the other way. Know what she said?" Lennon shakes his head, no, still smiling, but now with only the lower half of his face. "She said, 'Surprise me.'"

It is all Lennon can do not to laugh, which of course would be all right with Ciana, but very wrong with the gods and Vendetta. For the first time, he wants desperately for Ciana's mother to get better for *his* sake. "So she's done something," Lennon says.

"I trust she's seen Mr. Theriot," Ciana says. "Her attorney. *He'll* reveal all her surprises when it's the right time. I just hope none of those surprises are general knowledge in the home of Mr. and Mrs. Geoffrey Jambon. Especially if one clause gives Mr. Geoffrey Jambon power of attorney."

"I think she had to sign something when she went into surgery," Lennon says.

"Hmph," Ciana says. "I'm sure she indemnified the hospital and every doctor who might bill her against every possible disaster. What better loophole than not to go to extreme measures? God, I hate extreme measures."

Lennon thinks that anywhere else this would be the most supreme pick-up line ever uttered by a pure intellectual. "What?"

"It was our debate topic in high school. I got up and said that sometimes even common decency is an extreme measure. And then I told my partner, who was *assigned* to me, *Common decency could keep me alive.* We lost the meet."

Lennon wants to remind her that she's forgotten she's supposed to be talking about Geoffrey, but he knows she'd say, *Oh, but I am.*

"Listen," Ciana says. "'Extreme measures' is a topic that makes me very nervous. Bring a Christian Scientist in here, and he'd tell you everything we dispense is an extreme measure. Bring somebody in who lived at the turn of the twentieth century, and he'd tell you the same thing."

"Ciana, this isn't just about 'do not resuscitate,' and you know it," Lennon says. "This is about everything falling on you. You need to talk to your brother about what he's going to do."

Vendetta is leaning over the counter now, listening unabashedly. "You *go*, Lennon," she says. "I been telling this girl for as long as I can remember that she ought to kick that man ass, but do she listen to me? No, she do not."

"Who says I'm listening to Lennon?" Ciana says, and even he can tell she's flirting with him.

Lennon drives Ciana to Geoffrey's house in his car. It's got five-speed manual transmission, and shifting is sexy as hell for the first time. He pushes the tachometer to the limit. The car has no power, and he doesn't get past third, but they are crammed in, and this is better than his hand on her back.

The front door of the house has a large panel of leaded, beveled glass through which Geoffrey can see Ciana before he opens it, but he cracks the door about three inches and peers out at her and Lennon on his porch. "What's going on?" he says.

"You don't answer your phone," Ciana says.

"It's family time. The phone's too intrusive. You leave a message?"

Ciana folds her arms across her chest. Lennon has made the same gesture with Diana. It says, *I've known you long enough to know where you draw lines.*

Geoffrey glares at Ciana, who says nothing, so he calls over his shoulder, "Corinne! Is there a message from Ciana?"

"No!"

It's getting cold out, and Lennon can feel a bit of the heat escaping from the house, so he knows Geoffrey can go on indefinitely, talking to them with no discomfort, family time or no family time. He and Ciana, on the other hand, are going to be miserable pretty soon. At least Nookie is under a blanket in the car, and Nookie is supposed to have a natural way of surviving temperatures below fifty. He's shaped for burrows. "Let me ask you a question," Ciana says. "Do you want to find out your mother died by hearing it from an answering machine message?"

Geoffrey throws the door wide open, and Ciana walks right in. Lennon follows close on her heels, his hand on her back. It's his new right. "That was a hypothetical question," Ciana says softly.

Geoffrey shuts the door hard behind them, a few decibels short of a slam. "That's pretty crappy," he says.

"You came very close to finding out that your mother went into cardiac arrest today by hearing it on your answering machine," Lennon says.

"Who the fuck are you?" Geoffrey says.

Lennon wants to slug him, and Lennon never has slugged anyone, not even his sister or the Hollingsworth twins. "I'm a colleague of your sister who's become a very close friend," he says, more to puzzle Ciana than to enlighten Geoffrey.

Geoffrey ignores him. Lennon thinks Ciana probably is not ignoring him. "What happened to Mama?" Geoffrey says.

Ciana tells him she doesn't know, that she's on her way to the hospital, that she wanted Geoffrey to meet her there, that the doctors are going to want to know what measures they can take, that she needs to know if Geoffrey has any directives from his mother. "Corinne! Get down here!" he hollers. "Why didn't you tell me this shit?" he says to Ciana. Lennon eases into a chair. He doesn't take his coat off, but he isn't walking out of here as fast as anyone would like him to.

"You better make this quick," Corinne says when she plops herself down on the living room sofa. "Bedtime is about the worst time to try to do anything in a house with kids." Lennon can *hear* bragging in her voice.

"I can take a hint," Ciana says. "But this honestly is a matter of life and death."

"Cut the crap," Geoffrey says.

Remarkably, Ciana ignores him, but Lennon feels raggedness in her breathing. "All right, all right," she says. "I'll make this as painless as possible for you two. First question. Has Mama given you any legal powers or papers or anything I need to know about?"

"No," Geoffrey says.

"No?" Lennon can tell Ciana isn't questioning Geoffrey; she's questioning her mother's usual preference for her son. Or, rather, preferential treatment.

"I said no."

"So neither of us knows what she wants done?"

"Don't beat around the bush," Corinne says.

Lennon feels every muscle tighten in Ciana. "That's easy for you to say," Ciana says. "You can't even set foot in the unit without later checking under your bed for old ladies on respirators." Lennon gives her a reassuring pat, lets her know that some things can't be resisted.

"I'll make this simple," Geoffrey says, doing his best imitation of manliness. "Call Theriot tomorrow. Whatever she's said, he's got it."

"I'll bet you anything she doesn't have a living will," Ciana says. "I know I wouldn't have one. I want extreme measures. I want 'please resuscitate' over my bed. I'll never be an organ donor. And Mama and I are just alike. If she doesn't have a living will, it means she doesn't want one. Which means she wants us to keep her alive by all means possible. Especially now. She's got pneumonia, and her heart quivers the way it always does, only in the hospital they notice. You can't let them kill her just because she's there for them to notice what her heart usually does in private."

"If you've got it all figured out, why'd you come over here?" Geoffrey says.

"You are so wrong, Ciana," Corinne says. "Trust me," she says to Lennon for no reason, "Mrs. Jambon has too much dignity for all this stuff. Ciana's out of her mind."

This is the moment Lennon has been waiting for. In his most non-blue-collar-colored-help voice, he says, "Might I ask how the accident happened?"

"You know, Ciana never even bothered to ask," Corinne says. "She thinks New York is just New York. Poor Mrs. Jambon fell down in the Lego department in FAO Schwartz. We were looking for a gift for my son, Lucien, and I don't know if Ciana has told you this, but Mrs. Jambon has these heart spells, and she falls down, and that's what happened. Only this time she broke her leg. The people in the store were so kind. Not at all what you expect in New York. But then these people deal with *children*."

Lennon could swear she hasn't taken one breath. "I see," he says. "That explains a lot."

Corinne looks mightily pleased with herself, as if she has found an ally who will help her cope with her chronically misguided sister-in-law. As Lennon and Ciana are walking to the car, Corinne calls to Ciana, "Did you ever do anything about the dog?"

Ciana nods. "I had it put to sleep."

Corinne looks to Lennon to let him know they're working

together to rehabilitate Ciana. "That was a good decision, Ciana," she says.

In the car, all Ciana can say is, "Lightning is going to strike me. God, I was so mean. Lightning is going to strike me."

Lennon pats her hand while the car is in third. He wants to tell her something that would make her wish she'd pulled far fewer punches, but he thinks better of it. He happens to know very well that FAO Schwartz is in Chapter 11. The New York store has been closed for a couple of months. If Mrs. Jambon's last thoughts before she fell had to do with the interconnectedness of matter, it wasn't because she was looking at a Lego display.

A RESPIRATOR is an extreme measure.

It is ten o'clock in an empty corridor outside the critical care unit, and Dr. Hebert has told Ciana this one simple fact, and she has turned and kissed Lennon smack on the mouth. Quickly like the last time: if she does it this way often enough, it will be easy to do slowly when the time comes. Here they are, her questionable little family, she and Lennon and their baby, Nookie, and Dr. Hebert has surprised himself by making them happy when they shouldn't be, and he stands there and smiles with the kind of puzzlement he's probably had far too often at this time of night in darkened hallways. "That means you'll let her live until she dies," Ciana says. "Well, sure," he says. She asks about the lawyer. Dr. Hebert says not to bother the lawyer. Ciana wants to kiss someone again. Nookie. But Nookie's supposed to be working.

Lennon lingers with the doctor while Ciana goes in to see her mother, and she feels sort of married because that's the way Dr. Hebert acts about her. She hopes she brings that aura to her mother because it is nebulous enough to make her mother feel good. If it were a detailed, Technicolor aura, she wouldn't feel so good. Ciana announces her presence loudly, cheerfully, but there is no reaction. She gets up close, whispers in her mother's ear, "I'm here, and I'm in love with a beautiful black man, and he's right outside talking to your doctor," and her mother doesn't react, but it's still possible that when she wakes up she'll say, "Boy, Ciana, I sure wanted to say something, but you know how your mind wants to do something but your body can't?" Ciana apologizes. She tells her mother she was only saying that to make her wake up.

Ciana's tempted to do her own EEG, which she should have done instead of whispering in her mother's ear. She could pass Nookie over her and try to get a reading. Nookie can't predict if Ciana is going to have a seizure because she's not going to have one, but she thinks Nookie knows whether her mother has brain waves. Ciana's just afraid someone will walk in.

Lennon walks in. He says, "The news isn't very good," and Ciana whispers, "Not in front of her." He beckons her into the hallway, but she has a feeling he's doing it to indulge her. That's an EEG of sorts. "This isn't about you, Mama," she says anyway.

He tells her they may not be getting on top of the pneumonia fast enough. Her CRP levels are dropping a little, which is good because it means they're having some effect on the pneumonia. But all the other systems are going bad from the treatment, and Ciana has to understand it's a balancing act, that they bring one back, and they lose progress with another. Lennon told Dr. Hebert that Ciana is a pharmacist, that she knows there are limits, that the first thing she learned was that society can't put antidepressants/painkillers/blood-thinners/antibiotics into the water supply. Limits. Ciana tells Lennon she understands. She tells herself that for once she's going to ignore science. She's not going to become spiritual; she's going to become simple. Which, in spite of what one might observe in Corinne and Geoffrey, is not the same thing. She'll believe only what she can see, and she'll look only at what a nonscientist would look at. Basically, she'll look at her mother breathing. She realizes that the machine can make her mother breathe for a hundred years, but she doesn't care.

Lennon realizes before Ciana does that if he leaves she is stranded here with no car. "I don't need a car," Ciana says. "I won't have emergencies." There is soap and a washcloth in a tiny bathroom near her mother's bed. Nookie has kibble. Both have nearby bathrooms. Ciana won't even have needs. He will be back tomorrow morning, he says, and Ciana says she will be right here. Smelling of Ivory.

★

It is tomorrow morning, Ciana is right here, but her mother is going to die. She doesn't even ask Dr. Hebert to leave the room for her mother's sake when he tells her. "You told me last night you'd let her live until she dies," she says.

"You know what acidosis is?" he says.

Ciana nods. Greek and Latin aren't that far apart in the way they operate. Her mother's organs are too acidic. She doesn't want to be a scientist right now. She wants to think her mother could drink Liquid Plumber because it has a pH of twelve and be all right.

"Her kidneys are failing, and the rest of her organs are going to follow," he says.

"You can't be a hundred percent positive," she says miserably.

"Do you want to pray for her?" he says. He's looking at Ciana's neck, seeing a medallion with a skewed cross and a squibble that for all he knows from a polite distance is Jesus rather than a snake.

"No, it's not that," she says, and he looks relieved, as if he can deal with irrationality as long as it's reasonable.

"I can give you a day or two," he says. "But keeping her on a respirator makes no sense."

"If this is about insurance," Ciana says, "we'll pay *cash*." She wonders what they charge for a day of life. She would think that a lousy day with strangers and no food ought to be cheap, but hospitals aren't into cosmic issues. She wants to take her mother home. She's starting to cry.

Dr. Hebert asks if there is any family member Ciana

would like him to call. She wonders whether a call from the hospital on Caller ID will go unanswered at Geoffrey's house or office. She supposes Dr. Hebert will leave a message. Doctors probably were the original reason people got Caller ID and Call Waiting. Ciana knows that when she was small her mother literally sat next to the phone until the pediatrician returned a call; if someone else phoned first she treated that person like a telemarketer. At the pharmacy they get doctors to do their bidding hundreds of times a day. Usually by fax. Scissors, paper, stone.

She tells the doctor that she has a brother, and she asks him what would happen if her brother were halfway around the world. "He's not, is he?" Dr. Hebert says, and Ciana says no, but he is religious. He leaves the room with the phone number, and now Ciana is frightened, as if she's in terrible trouble, and when the doctor comes back she'll find out her punishment. She leans over her mother, strokes her hair. Her hair is wet from perspiration. Ciana smells her own fingers. They smell like dirty hair. They don't smell acidic. She leans over and kisses her mother. She just kisses her. "Please help me here, Mama," she says. Her mother's eyes never have been completely closed, and Ciana tries to peer under the lids. Her mother's not seeing. And she hasn't been seeing since she's been on the respirator. But that's because she's drugged. Maybe if they cut back the drugs. They can't cut back the drugs. This is a balancing act. In which someone's made a lot of choices.

The last choice is Ciana's, though. And evidently Geoffrey's, unless he decides to take a pass on this episode, too. And Ciana is going to keep saying no until someone turns off the lights and shuts off the power source. A month ago her mother expected to be alive right now. Maybe she left her house in dying order, but she did that out of pure superstition. She was warding off death. You don't have a two-year-old dog if you expect to be dead soon. You don't go to Sam's Club and buy forty rolls of toilet paper, either. And you definitely don't refill your Fosamax prescription unless you expect to be hobbling around for years, even if you break your leg.

Ciana hears a male voice come in behind her and say hello, far too soon to be Geoffrey, and far, far, far too sweet to be Geoffrey. It's Lennon. She tells him everything, and he says he'll leave, that this is no time for outsiders, but there is no conviction in his tone, and it only takes a pleading look for him to sit by, and so he is sitting in a corner chair with Nookie in his lap when Geoffrey walks in, takes one look at him, and says, "Well, fuck a duck." Corinne, Lennon's new friend, says, "Not now." Ciana watches Corinne looking at her mother, and she can believe Corinne's expression is one of sadness. "Out in the hallway," Geoffrey says without looking at his mother, and Corinne and Ciana follow him.

Dr. Hebert is still on the floor, and he's within earshot if one speaks loudly enough, which Geoffrey makes sure he does. "Look, Ciana, I think Dr. Hebert knows what he's doing. Keeping Mama alive now is completely artificial, and it isn't what God wants. It certainly isn't what Mama wants. What are you being so weird about?"

"Because I'm not a hundred percent sure it's time to take her off the respirator. People make mistakes, you know."

"So they take her off the machine, and she keeps breathing, no harm done," Geoffrey says. "Right, Dr. Hebert?" he hollers down the hall. Dr. Hebert comes over, unfinished papers in his hand.

"Excuse me?" Dr. Hebert says.

"I'm telling my sister here, if we take her off the respirator, and she starts breathing, then we know she's all right, right?"

"If we take your mother off the respirator, she'll expire," Dr. Hebert says.

"I think the Catholic Church would give you a hard time on that," Ciana says to Geoffrey.

"If the Catholic Church wants Jambons to give a hard time to, like in for eternity, I'm not the one they want," he says, giving Ciana a meaningful look. He quit being able to scare her with hellfire before her first communion, but he's never caught on because he's still afraid of it.

"Don't act like you never went to catechism, Ciana," Corinne says. "That respirator is interfering with God's will. Kind of like you did when you went in there with that you-know-what that you were waving under her nose."

Dr. Hebert looks at Ciana funny. "I brought her a dumb flower," Ciana says. "Hush, Corinne."

Geoffrey is a good four inches taller than the doctor, but he pulls himself into full toadying posture anyway. "We'll go along with whatever you think is best, Dr. Hebert. Right,

Corinne?" Corinne nods, and with that they turn and leave. "You forgot to say good-bye," Ciana calls after them. "Bye," Corinne says. "I mean to Mama," Ciana says, but they already are in the elevator bay and can't hear her.

Ciana stands next to the bed, holding Nookie, and what makes her cry the hardest is the cast on her mother's leg. She doesn't know why. She just looks at it, the white plaster that never got dirty, or tattered or autographed, and she is so sorry for her mother that she has to squeeze her eyes closed. Nookie doesn't move. He especially doesn't strain toward Ciana's mother. When Ciana said to Lennon a few minutes ago that she would like an EEG, he said no, she wouldn't, she really wouldn't, that she had to think about how she'll feel in the long run. She knows he's right. If her mother's body is not going to work, it's better that her mind doesn't find out about it. For her sake and Ciana's. Ciana needs to believe she is nothing but a brain stem now. Lennon says he's sure it hurts her to have to go along with Geoffrey, but Geoffrey's right; Dr. Hebert does not shut off life support frivolously. Hebert is a Catholic name. Though then he adds that as Dr. Hebert's hand reaches for the switch, Ciana should demand an autopsy.

Ciana doesn't tell anyone, but when she makes the decision to turn off the respirator she bases it on the date. Today is February twenty-second, two-two-two. She thinks her mother would like that date, the repeating digit. Ciana's birthday is March fourth, and she once complained that it had no particular mnemonic quality, though she didn't use that term. “But Ciana,” her mother said, “that’s the only day of the year that’s a *command*.”

The date is one thing, but the moment is more difficult for her to define, and she desperately wants to define it. And since she can’t exactly take her mother to a warm beach, all she can fix around her is *who* is here. Lennon can’t be here for his own sake.

He has seen dead people, because he had a new church suit every year and his mother put it on him whenever there was a funeral, but he never has seen anyone die. When he finishes school, he will prolong life, and when his customers no longer appear, he will be able to assume they have been cured. Or that they have found their favorite brand of deodorant is cheaper at Rite-Aid. Ciana needs someone with her besides Lennon.

Something about the way Corinne looked at her mother makes Ciana want to give her a try. She answers the phone. “We’re going to do it this afternoon,” Ciana says. “I thought you might want to say good-bye.”

“I did say good-bye,” Corinne says. “I just didn’t say it out loud. Your friend was watching.” She doesn’t sound accusatory, just self-conscious.

“What about the kids?” Ciana only asks this because she expects her mother is going to have everything detached.

“Ciana, if you had kids, you’d know better than to ask something like that. You can’t let a child see somebody looking like a monster that way. Especially somebody they know.” Ciana holds the phone away from her ear. She can tell where Corinne's headed. "The kids are just going to have to remember their grandmother the way she was," Corinne says. "Child psychology is just something you learn from experience, and that's not an area your degree's ever going to do you any good in."

"I might have kids one day," Ciana says.

"Aw, no," Corinne says. "I know where this is going. Don't you already have enough problems?"

"Meaning what?"

"You know very well what I mean. This is no city to have kids that are different."

Ciana pictures a little girl, chubby and light-brown-skinned, not yellow because yellow blacks are neither here nor there. She has tight, good cornrows, big spaced-out front teeth; she is the teacher's favorite, and she doesn't have a problem in the world. The only thing different about her is that she is one damn happy child, and such a child is possible in New Orleans; Ciana is sure she's seen one. This child is in her mind, and for all anyone knows she's in her mother's mind, which now accepts everything. If she's also in Lennon's mind, it has nothing to do with Ciana pushing it there.

She tells Corinne to tell Geoffrey that his mother is coming off the respirator today. Ciana is glad a procedure is involved. She doesn't know what she would say if her mother simply were about to die.

When she tells Dr. Hebert that she wants to *let it happen* at two-twenty-two, he raises no objection. He whispers that this is New Orleans, that he has had some peculiar requests, that he will take hers at face value, that he'll be back a few minutes beforehand. Ciana lays Nookie on her mother's chest, where Nookie rides up and down ever so slightly in perfect mechanical rhythm. She sits beside the bed, holding her mother's hand, and no one comes in for any reason until it's almost time.

Over and over Ciana tells Lennon how her mother died. They're at her kitchen table. She eats half a meatball and sausage pizza, chili peppers straight, and he watches her, his throat closed by what he hears, and Ciana doesn't know why she can eat or talk. She guesses seeing someone die is the best way to go about death. The only experience she's ever had that is remotely comparable was standing in a doorway as a child and pressing the backs of her wrists as hard as she could against the jambs. When she took a step forward, her arms flew up. That is the way she feels now.

"I'm sorry for Geoffrey," she tells Lennon.

"Geoffrey was emptying out your mother's bank box," Lennon says.

Endorphins protect her from that. "How do you know?"

"They thought I was a dumb nigger sitting in the corner, but even a dumb nigger knows what it means when you say, 'Honey, you got the key to the bank box in your purse?'"

"Well, Geoffrey's never going to *know* his mother's really dead," Ciana says. "I *saw* it." Ciana saw her eyes roll back, the monitors go flat, even Dr. Hebert slipping clear liquid into the IV; she's told this to Lennon like a child who's seen a dog hit by a car. Almost singsong. Sometimes questioning. She's left out the very last part, when the flat-line heart monitor suddenly sent across a small squibble, and she cried out, "What's that?" *That* happens all the time, evidently. She was asking out of hope, not curiosity, but no one knew that, maybe not even her mother, so she thinks she left the room looking callow, and she can't tell that part of the story because it's the worst.

"When your mother doesn't ask him for her stuff back, Geoffrey'll know she's dead," Lennon says.

"You know what I mean." Ciana reaches for a piece of pizza from what should be his half. He pays no attention. He hasn't even taken more than a sip or two from the glass of Coke over ice that she poured him.

"He's not going to grieve," Lennon says. "And he's not going to sublimate all his feelings of loss into painful behavior. So don't get your hopes up."

"How do you know all this stuff?" Ciana says, and she gets up and pours herself a glass of gin from a bottle Vendetta gave her two Christmases ago. It's never been opened. Vendetta has great hopes for her.

Lennon shrugs. "I'm in school."

Ciana doesn't like remembering that, even though Lennon is working on his doctorate, so he's not exactly a college sophomore. If he can spout psychology, by now it's because he parroted it back on a test but then saw it up close and personal afterward. Recently, Ciana admits, but in three dimensions. Just because he hasn't seen someone die doesn't mean he's underage. Until this morning, she hadn't seen anyone die. And her older brother, who has three children and a wife, still hasn't seen anyone die. Ciana thinks that's a milestone. Though she's seen enough movies where children stood at the foot of the old homesteader's bed and watched him close his eyes. Of course, those children knew how to wring the neck of a chicken. Ciana's never seen an animal die. She looks at Nookie, who has no memory of a life in another house, and she starts to cry. "It was just me and Nookie and a bunch of strangers, but you know, that's probably good, right?" she says. Lennon nods and reaches for the gin bottle.

He looks around for something to pour into. Ciana expected him to up-end the bottle. She gets up and fetches him a water glass. She's surprised at how wobbly she is; she almost bumps into him when she places the glass in front of him. "You flatter me," Lennon says when he takes the glass, and he pours about a quarter inch of gin into the bottom. She gives him ice to make the glass look fuller, and he is still working on that same gin when the ice has melted completely.

Ciana has had enough gin to make her a very good kind of weepy, the kind in which she has no idea what is making her feel this way, so she smiles while tears stream down her face. She feels sort of beautiful, and she hasn't felt beautiful since she was a child and wrapped her mother's dresses around herself in great dramatic sweeps. She asks Lennon to sleep with her. He's been so wise today. He will know this is a wise thing to do. He won't know how wise it is, how Ciana has funny chains of reason, of conceiving a child right now, if not because she believes in souls, then because she believes in numbers. He'll just think of this as making her feel good. He'll think of the fucking part. He won't think of it as a mercy fuck. Going to bed with a woman the night her mother dies goes way beyond a mercy fuck. She's sure Corinne wouldn't see it that way.

"We don't want to do that," he says.

Ciana is still crying and smiling, so Lennon can't read her. "Forget I said anything, Lennon." She's not going to beg.

"I want to sleep with you. Just sleep with you," he says, and it's far better than good enough. "In my bed?" she asks. "If you want," he says. Ciana tells him it's queen-sized, hoping he doesn't realize that that doesn't leave him a lot of room. *She* is queen-sized.

They fall asleep kissing and kissing, holding each other through their clothes, kissing and kissing. She wakes up in the middle of the night, hears his steady breathing, realizes it's not perfectly mechanical, realizes where she is. She lets her hand travel slowly toward him. It touches his hip, rests on it, presses, moves up slowly, across his belly. He has an erection, and it's because of her. He begins to stir. "No, honey, for your own sake, no, not this night."

It's February twenty-third now, and that is another reason why Ciana knows it's all right not to do it.

15

VENDETTA swears that she never thought about how the day would come when Ciana's mama would die, and Ciana would be off work, and Lennon would leave out of the store, and she could settle up the Ritalin. And that's definitely not the first thing that came to her mind when Ciana called to tell her the news yesterday. But this morning when she got up for work she realized she could pull it off. They were going to send somebody white in to sub for Ciana, because all they have are white people, and Vendetta knows how to play ignorant better than anybody.

She isn't going to tell Frieda. "Look," she tells Patricia, "all you got to do is, you got to make Frieda and Quick both paying attention to you."

"Frieda don't pay attention to nobody," Patricia says.

"You a kick," Vendetta says, and it takes Patricia no time at all to think up a plan. It occurs to Vendetta that maybe Quick's attention problem is something he comes by honestly.

"Where my library book at?" Patricia says as they march into Frieda's kitchen. Patricia has a very square little chest, but no one's looking. Vendetta thinks this is brilliant. Frieda and Quick won't know what to do about a *book*. Patricia is about the only child in Sylvania who checks books out of the school library. The librarian thinks her library is supposed to be a showcase where the teachers can have faculty meetings. Vendetta had to raise a lot of sand with the librarian. And at that it's a secret. The principal has come right out and said she doesn't want her good books lying around that damn project. "I been reading to you about that pig and that spider, remember, Quick?" Patricia says. Quick nods.

"You ain't been in my house reading no book," Frieda says, but she follows Patricia into Quick's room, evidently mesmerized by the possibility that Quick has heard of a book.

Jaquilica is not that interested, but Vendetta doesn't care. If she moves with enough authority, Jaquilica won't notice. Especially now. Jaquilica has lost the only job she's had in years, and she's been drinking heavily. She says she's sad about that poor sweet Mrs. Jambon, but Vendetta knows very well that Mrs. Jambon could have been a cord of wood, and Jaquilica would have had just as much affection for her. Vendetta takes one Ritalin tablet from the bottle on the kitchen table in a move so smooth that Jaquilica might not even have seen it.

"It was in his bed," Patricia announces as she leads her aunt and cousin back into the kitchen.

"That ain't the picture was on the cover," Quick says.

"You weren't paying attention," Patricia says.

Now Vendetta remembers. The kindergarten teacher reads *Charlotte's Web* aloud to the class every year. That's where Quick knows it from. Her Patricia is some kind of genius.

Maureen is subbing for Ciana, and Kasha from Cosmetics is covering for Lennon while he goes to the funeral. Altogether this is none of what Vendetta counted on for today. In fact, it's worse, because she has a sneaking suspicion that Maureen wants to beat out Ciana any way she can. Vendetta has no reason to think that except for the two pictures on the wall. Ugly old Maureen has to do something better than Ciana. And refusing to dispense emergency contraceptives isn't enough. It makes Mr. Walker happy, but Maureen is sure to want more than that. If she asked Vendetta how to win, Vendetta would tell her to get a good haircut for starts, but she's not asking Vendetta.

Vendetta has the pill in her pocket, feeling bad that it's contaminated because pills aren't supposed to be touched by human hands, much less by human pockets that have been through the wash with All and Clorox. The bottles from the manufacturer are in a safe that's close to the front, and unless there's a big commotion like Mr. Earl Roberts's epileptic fit, somebody's going to be a few feet away whenever

Vendetta decides to put the pill back. She can't believe nobody's getting Ritalin today. Though it's not as popular as it used to be. Time was, mamas from St. George's Episcopal School were in here at least one a day for Ritalin; she could tell from the nice little uniforms on their kids. Now those mamas get Concerta and Strattera; St. George's mamas are always on top of things when it comes to keeping their kids good and drugged. "Oh, yes," one of them said when Vendetta asked, "the secretary has two desk drawers full of bottles." Poor Quick. Vendetta opens the safe on three passes as smoothly as she moved through Frieda's kitchen, reaches for the bottle, which has not been opened or unsealed, opens and unseals it, drops the pill in. "What do you think you're doing?" Maureen says. Vendetta has been concentrating so hard that she didn't see Maureen swooping faster than she did. She could have handled Kasha. Kasha works in Cosmetics for a reason.

"You leave the safe open by accident," Vendetta says. "I know you don't want nothing wrong to happen."

"I saw you putting something in there," Maureen says. Maureen takes the bottle from the safe and scurries away with it like a squirrel with a pecan. Ugly bitch. If Vendetta could, she'd call Ciana right now and confess everything. But it's not the kind of thing you can call somebody about at her mama's funeral. And probably not the day after, either. All that makes her feel better is that Maureen is probably thinking she's going to find anthrax in that bottle and get herself on the national news. When she finds nothing but an extra pill that could be the manufacturer's fault, she's going to look mighty stupid. Right.

Vendetta can't concentrate. She is flat-out spoiled by being here every day with Ciana and Lennon, and she knows that's not going to last more than a few more months. Who knows what's coming when Lennon leaves. It's always a student, and usually a suck-up who makes trouble. But the students make trouble with Ciana; Maureen is going to make trouble with corporate, maybe with the police. For all Vendetta knows, this is some kind of federal crime. She can't stand being here. She'd like to go home. What she'd like is to go back ten minutes. What she'd really like is not to be related to Frieda.

Now that it's too late for it to help, a commotion starts up in the front of the store. Not a big commotion, but a small wave of nervousness that means there's a shoplifter or a drunk or somebody with way too few clothes on. Vendetta feels that wave moving in her direction, and she figures it's somebody coming directly at the pharmacy. And sure enough, wiggling their hips through the soft aisle, thinking they're Paris Hilton and Nicole Richie, are those damn twins that are always after Lennon. Vendetta makes sure she gets to the counter before Kasha does. Which is not easy, given that Kasha has an instinct for cosmetics customers. Vendetta wants to tell her that these two don't buy anything in a drugstore. "I can help you?" she says.

"Now, Miss Vendetta, you know who we are," one of them says. "Where's Mr. Israel?"

Vendetta wants to say, *Mr. Israel same age as me*, but the truth is that she and Lennon aren't equal. She just doesn't want to hear it from these hoochies. "He gone to a funeral," she says, and then she wishes she'd said something less specific.

The twins giggle. The other one says, "He doesn't know any live people, much less dead ones."

"Well, he in for a big surprise," Vendetta says, and she starts to walk away.

"Wait," the first twin says. "We can ask you." Vendetta stops. This will be good. As long as Kasha doesn't hear anything interesting. Vendetta's not studying about Maureen. Maureen already has all the news she can handle.

The girl leans over the counter and whispers to Vendetta. Her breath is bad, like she had pepperoni pizza yesterday, but she's too important to care. "Does Lennon ever work nights?" No. "Does Lennon ever let friends back there?" No. "Does Lennon ever, like, you know, *borrow* stuff from back there?"

"All we got back here is pills," Vendetta says. She keeps her voice down, though she doesn't know why.

"I know that," the girl whispers.

"You got to ask him that," Vendetta says, thinking this might be a good way of getting Lennon to get rid of them. "But from what I know, the man very ticky. He don't do nothing messy. He take a pencil home, he bring it back sharpen."

The girls giggle again, and Vendetta looks around the waiting area hoping someone else will notice that they're not very cute. But all that's there is a white man about forty, and he thinks they're plenty cute. "What you laughing at?" Vendetta says.

"You're not going to tell him, are you?" the second twin says. "Because if you do, you're really going to hurt his feelings."

"No," Vendetta says, wondering if she'll wait until tomorrow or tell him as soon as he gets back from the funeral.

"Look, we are, like, the final test. If a guy doesn't want to go to bed with us, well, you *know* there's something wrong with him. I don't think he's had more than two dates in his whole life. Diana—you know who Diana is, right?—Diana has been swearing for years that he's gay. I mean, what kind of man brings pencils back sharpened? We're giving him until the end of the semester, and then I think his family is going to totally *freak*."

"I know for a fact Lennon not gay," Vendetta says.

The twins look at her, struggling with all their redundant brain power to imagine anyone choosing Vendetta as a sex partner, especially as a sex partner when they are available, and they cannot do it. "Sure," one of them says.

Vendetta wants Lennon to get the FBI to put a wire on him and get these girls to ask him to steal drugs. Assuming she'll still be working here when it happens.

16

LENNON'S not sure Ciana gets this way on every birthday, but he would expect any woman in her right mind to be half crazy on a birthday less than two weeks after her mother died. He never has let his own birthday matter. Sentimentality seems to need a lot of explaining in his family. Today Ciana is turning thirty-four on three-four, and she is making a huge deal about making no huge deal about it.

Since the funeral Ciana has quit saying much of anything to anyone, and he wonders if anyone else has noticed. With him and Vendetta, she gets away with an article and a noun whenever she can—the register, the pendings, a break—and she sets in motion many processes by such commands. *March forth*, she says. If he didn't know better, he'd swear she was furious all the time.

With the customers, Ciana hides it; she is sickeningly sweet, and they look at her funny. Lennon has heard Vendetta whisper more than once, "Her mama just die." But Vendetta is a nervous wreck because she thinks Ciana is angry at her over something she refuses to tell Lennon about. "I tell you, I might as well tell Ciana," Vendetta says, and at first he thinks it's because Vendetta sees them as an item, but then he remembers whom he's dealing with. Lennon thinks Ciana is furious at him because he didn't make love to her. He should be glad she's furious because it makes her one of the first women who hasn't walked around after he's shied away and told everybody he's gay. He doesn't get it. How is a man supposed to get good if he's not good already? Lennon does not want to make love to a woman unless he knows how to do it perfectly, but he's never going to know how unless he does it first. He's had too much school and not enough education. And he knows that right now Ciana is walking around thinking she's too fat. He can tell. She's walking around like a fat girl. That's the way she was when he first started working here. A little slumped over, a lot of I-dare-you on her face. It has nothing to do with being an orphan.

He has had to pretend he hasn't noticed a thing, because right now Ciana needs him too much to be rid of him. She shows him bills wordlessly; she leaves her appointment book open on the counter. He went with her to Mr. Theriot's office, and she was too mute, and probably too grateful, to tell him no. Geoffrey walked into the meeting accusing Ciana of undue influence because the poor old lawyer had allowed their silly old mother to do a very short will dividing her assets between the two of them. "Haven't you ever heard of 'from each according to his ability, to each according to his needs'?" Geoffrey said. "I think that's the law in Louisiana. I've got three children, and I earn a lot less than my sister, who's got *nobody*." Mr. Theriot looked at Ciana as if he'd finally lost his own mind. Ciana put her finger to her lips. "So, Geoffrey," she said, loud and clear and polysyllabic, "when did you join the Communist Party?" More words than he deserved. "Can I sue her for that?" he said to Mr. Theriot. "I'm thinking of suing you for everything else," he said to Ciana. "I'll just add that to the list."

It was Geoffrey's big chance to rant. "Get this. We say Holy Name Church. She says Lake Lawn. So where do we wind up? Lake Lawn. Okay, we're not troublemakers. But listen to this. She gets Parlor E, the cheapest, I mean, 'screaming poverty' cheapest room in the place. And of all days. They've got a Dupuy funeral going on. So everybody in town sees us holed up in Parlor E. Like we don't have any money."

Lennon had been there. Any bigger parlor only would have been sadder. When they celebrated mass, there were only seven people. Ciana said, "You looked very rich. Corinne told everybody that Lennon was Mama's groundskeeper. I heard her. And then she took communion."

Ciana spoke in Mr. Theriot's office. To Lennon it didn't matter what she said.

When they walked out, Lennon said to Ciana, "I am highly motivated to find out what that woman did," and Ciana let out an involuntary little sob. He wanted to put his arm around her, but it might have been the wrong thing to do.

Last night he went out to Lakeside Mall and bought a chocolate-chip-cookie birthday cake and on the way home bought a roll of Saran Wrap in which to swathe the entire box to keep it fresh; there might be no way he was going to sneak out today to get one. It turns out he was wrong. It's the thick of Lent, and it's possible that everyone has given up the exact habit that fights antibodies. Gastrointestinal tracts are calm, respiratory tracts are clear; even the over-the-counter products aren't moving today. They aren't dispensing much besides diuretics and statins. The lull is painful. Lennon could swear it's never been this quiet in the pharmacy before. He motions Vendetta into the break room. "You bring it out," he says, unsheathing the cake. He used up the entire roll of Saran Wrap, and it's just as well, because he has no use for the stuff. He crumples it into a satisfyingly small ball.

"A cake coming from you a much better idea," Vendetta says. She lights the candle, and he carries it out, and they present it to her almost at knee level. "We not singing because we not sharing," Vendetta says, casting her eyes around dramatically to be sure Kasha and the rest aren't looking. Ciana laughs like her former self, the one who could sit right in front of Lennon and eat a full third of such a cake like a thin girl with a speedy metabolism and a great love for herself. "You know Lennon the one went to Lakeside for this," Vendetta says. Vendetta has paid retail for the largest card the store has to offer, embossed with a bouquet of white lilies on the front and a rhyme inside that makes Ciana teary-eyed in spite of herself.

"The only thing better than this is that Geoffrey and Corinne are leaving me alone today," Ciana says, and she smiles, and Lennon has a sense that it isn't going to be so quiet for the rest of the afternoon. When he tells Ciana he is taking her out to dinner, she gives him a questioning look, almost as if he is overdoing it, but he doesn't know if he's overdoing it on attention or calories. Japanese, he says, because it's possible to be cold and inattentive and dietetic in a Japanese restaurant. It's also possible to meet every small need and eat tempura. "How'd you know I didn't have plans?" Ciana says.

"Tunnel vision," Lennon says.

"Good answer," Vendetta says.

"Go away," Ciana says to Vendetta.

"Y'all ought to invite me," Vendetta says and limps away with one shoulder drooping.

A letter arrives addressed to Ciana at the pharmacy in the late afternoon, and Lennon sees it before Ciana does. It's a business envelope with a return address of a pathologist whose office is a block from Baptist Hospital. He hands it to her, and she says, "Well, happy birthday to me." She considers it a long while, then hands it back unopened. It's the autopsy report, she says.

"They sent this to you in the mail?" he says.

"I'm a medical professional. I guess they're giving me the same courtesy they'd give a doctor. Which is that I'd have the stomach for anything," she says.

Lennon offers to read it first, and Ciana quickly has the stomach for one of the leftover pieces of cookie cake. The pharmacy's gotten busier this afternoon, so Ciana doesn't have time to watch his face, and despite his efforts his face registers a full range, sometimes many emotions at once. He knew Mrs. Jambon didn't fall down in FAO Schwartz, but he wasn't sure what else he could learn. These results give him a lot more questions to raise. But he's not sure how kind it would be to raise them. And he doesn't have anyone he can ask. Ciana would be the person he would turn to for advice, but this is about her.

"So?" Ciana says after he has put the report back into its envelope and she has put the rest of the cake where she can't see it, either.

"So let me take you to dinner, and you have a drink, and I'll have a drink, and we'll talk about it, all right?"

"Happy birthday to me," Ciana says miserably.

Lennon orders the big tempura platter so Ciana can feel comfortable ordering anything she wants, and he orders straight gin, so she can do that, too. He has enough money for a taxi. He expects he's going to need enough money for a taxi. He's chosen Sake Café instead of Ninja because the lighting is dimmer, and Sake Café is too far to drive drunk, even on New Orleans streets. But dim lighting will help. He hopes the humming in his ears from gin will help, too. He has been composing his speech ever since he read the report, and it sounds brilliant, but it loops around and never comes out the same twice, and he knows he'll freeze up.

"You look more nervous than I am," Ciana says.

Lennon swallows a mouthful of straight gin. It is no elixir. It's like water. He takes another mouthful, and this one does it. He wonders for a second why there are pharmacies. He's found snake oil. He hums. "I think the autopsy was a good idea," he says.

"But you're not sure."

"I don't want to upset you," he says. It seems as if he's going to get advice from Ciana after all. He wishes she would take a sip from her drink.

"It's not going to tell me my mother's dying. It's not going to tell me my mother's dead. And it can't tell me that the stargazer lily gave her pneumonia. She wasn't a computer whose full history could be pulled up so those few molecules flying through the air could be traced from the flower to her lungs. Right?"

"Right." He lifts his glass in a toast, and Ciana drinks to her own innocence.

"You had a lot of suspicions," she says. Yes. "About how she died." Well, sort of. "Okay, about what contributed to her death."

"Listen," he says, and he reaches over and takes her hand, "if you want to play Twenty Questions, I can just give you the report. Please don't do this."

"You know I trust you," Ciana says, and Lennon thinks he knows no such thing. "But tell me one thing. Just one thing, and I could let you keep it. If I saw it, would I be sorry?"

"No, babe, at least not apologetic kind of sorry. But maybe *regretful* kind of sorry for having looked. Sort of like having seen your mother die. You can still picture it, right?" Ciana nods. "Well, that was her last unconscious moment. This is about her last conscious one."

"I don't know, Lennon."

He leans back in his chair. The rolls have arrived, and he takes one so Ciana can start eating. "Listen," he says. "I hate meddling. *Hate* it. I especially hate it when I can piss off somebody I care about. But if you never hear another word I say, hear this. What's in this report might—and I emphasize *might*—make you so furious that you'd have all sorts of problems. But it might not. In which case I'd have upset you for nothing."

"I'd be blissfully ignorant," Ciana says.

"Well, I know I've taken away the bliss," Lennon says. "But you can be trustfully ignorant. Until further notice."

The tempura arrives, platters a foot high, and Lennon starts in on the crawfish rolls to be polite. Not formally polite, but thoughtfully polite. The way he would be if they ate all their meals together. He can imagine that. He feels protective. If they had children, he would feel very protective.

"Here's what I'll do," he says after he has had time to think and eat and even try a little wasabi and get over it. "I'll give a copy to Mr. Theriot—"

"Why?" Ciana sounds panicky.

"He can't show it to anybody if I tell him not to."

"But why?"

"Because something might happen to me," Lennon says. "I mean *happen*. I'm not going anywhere on purpose. And probably not any other way, either."

"Okay," Ciana says. She looks as if she's calmed down, but she reaches for another batter-fried crab leg.

"Then I'm going to do something. I don't know if I'm going to New York, but I'm going to do something."

Ciana is not stupid, and Ciana is not delusional; she knows what Lennon has suspicions about. He expects either glee or cautious neutrality; instead he sees gratitude. "You know, right now I don't think I can handle rage," she says.

"Rage comes from surprises," Lennon says. "You won't have any surprises."

When Ciana invites him back to her house, Lennon tries to beg off. He has his boards to study for, and now he has to fit them around the research he wants to do for her. If he doesn't want to go all the way to New York, he'll have to do it by phone, and he can't make calls at night, so he's going to have to stay up late studying to make up for it. "I have so little time right now," he says.

Tipsy, Ciana says, "You know, when I was a little kid, I thought sex took all night. The mommy and daddy lay together like spirogyra conjugating. I sure was in for a surprise."

Lennon can't tell how experienced Ciana is from such a statement, but it certainly means she's not a virgin. She's not even particularly nervous about sex. That makes him a nervous wreck. A very excited, very willing nervous wreck.

When Ciana turns the lights out in her bedroom, he tells her no, leave them on. He wants to see her naked, and he wants her to see him excited by her. Thrilled, she compromises with the dimmer switch. They lie on top of the bed, concealing nothing, including the fact that Ciana does not own a condom. And the fact that she is quite pleased that he doesn't have one in his wallet, either. "Well, I'm not buying one at the store," he says, kissing her quite perfect pale neck. "Well, *I'm* not buying one at the store," she says back, pressing herself into the kiss. "Now what?" he says, genuinely at a loss. He would almost settle for a hand job; he is that close. "Our first time ought to be personal," Ciana says, reading his mind. He kisses her until he comes. He feels that is personal enough.

If it were up to Ciana, her mother's house would stay exactly the way it was on the day she left it. Ciana would dust it, of course, and pick up the mail until it dwindled to nothing, and she would keep the thermostat at eighty-five in summer and sixty-five in winter. The yard man needs his money, so the yard would keep its seasons. After a year or two, when she finally realizes she has no one to visit in that neighborhood because her mother isn't there, she could let go. Slowly, piecemeal, an armload at a time, no more than she might take if she dropped in and her mother gave her gifts from among her personal effects.

Geoffrey and Corinne want the house on the market before the summer doldrums.

And they win. Mr. Theriot says an asset like a house is forced to sale because it can't be split. She tells him on the phone that he should come up with a Solomonic solution. "Oh, yes," he says, "didn't King Solomon help draft the Louisiana constitution?" "That was Karl Marx," she says.

It doesn't take long for Geoffrey to call: Corinne probably has been waiting her entire life to choose a real estate listing agent. In New Orleans the most important women outside of Carnival royalty are the real estate agents. Corinne wants Anne Rice's agent, but if she can't get her, it won't matter; all that counts is the lawn sign. According to Geoffrey, Corinne has been over at the house working herself sick, trying to clean the place out. Ciana has the picture. No Corinne carting out old newspapers. Just Corinne in a Lilly Pulitzer–colors dress sashaying by the FOR SALE sign, hoping someone will drive past and see her. If she moves anything, it's made of silver. "The valuables have to be divided fairly," Ciana tells Geoffrey. "Well, I don't see you over there helping," he says. "I have a job," she says. "That's exactly what Corinne told me you'd say," he says.

Ciana has told Geoffrey that she has a week's leave at the end of April, when she says she will spend the whole time in the house, stripped down to her underwear, crying her heart out, gently getting rid of whatever no one wants to keep. *Triage* is one of her favorite words. She thinks it's possible in New Orleans to name a little girl Triage. Geoffrey is not interested in such nuanced priorities. Geoffrey wants to haul a dumpster up to the front lawn and shovel anything into it that Corinne can't display in their house. Ciana knows her mother has a file cabinet in which she has a folder for each year of each grandchild's life. Dumpster. Her mother collected hippos. Glass, ceramic, papier-mâché. Definitely dumpster. Her mother has kept most of her clothes since the sixties. Ciana would wear them if they fit because they're classics, not retro at all, and because they're her mother's. But to Corinne they have been worn by a dead person. Dumpster. Not AmVets. Not Tulane Drama Department. Dumpster. Even the forty rolls of toilet paper from Sam's Club. One-ply. Dumpster.

"Selling the house is not an emergency," Ciana says. "If you leave it alone, I'll do it all myself when I take leave in April."

"How're we supposed to get our fair share of stuff?" Geoffrey says.

"For starts you can give me whatever was in the bank box."

"There was nothing in the bank box. Just papers."

"Fine," Ciana says. "But I have lists." She doesn't say that the lists are mental. She's sure that in a court of law she could produce old photos that would prove her mother had a lot of jewelry. And then Corinne would have married Geoffrey for nothing.

"Right," Geoffrey says. Ciana has forgotten that even he knows their mother wasn't the most systematic person in the world.

"Don't be smarmy," she says. "I don't think Corinne

would enjoy showing up in public in a necklace only to have me waving a photo of Mama wearing that same necklace in front of her."

Geoffrey has a suggestion for going through the house and dividing up its contents. It comes from one of Corinne's friends, and Ciana expects something cute because Corinne's friends love cuteness. When he says they have bought packets of colored dots, she congratulates herself, but when he says that each person gets a color, and each family member takes a turn picking an item and marking it, Ciana can't find fault as much as she'd like to. Until he says, "Oh, and you pull cards from a deck to see who goes first, second, and so on." "A coin toss, Geoffrey," she says. "There are *two* of us." She can tell from his silence that he genuinely believed that he was going to have his six-year-old using his sticker to claim the dining room table.

"By the way," Geoffrey says before he hangs up, and Ciana knows a big fusillade is coming. "What the fuck is this autopsy crap about? We got a bill."

"I'll pay it," Ciana says. "I don't know why you got a bill."

Maybe Ciana shouldn't have made the offer so quickly; Geoffrey isn't saying anything, and when he isn't saying anything it means he's working on a terribly erroneous conclusion. "You're covering your ass, aren't you," he says.

"I'll tell you the truth," she says. "I haven't looked at it."

He has no comeback for that one.

★

Ciana buys a packet of colored dots and tries to make Vendetta and Lennon guess what they're for. Lennon is willing to go about ten questions into Twenty Questions; Vendetta takes one look at the packet of neon orange, lime, and yellow circles and says, "Whatever it is, it's too stupid for you." When she tells them that she and Geoffrey are going through her mother's house a week from tomorrow night with those dots, Lennon says she better get an appraiser out there first. "Shit, you better get a camera out there in five minutes," Vendetta says.

Lennon calls Mr. Theriot, Lennon calls the four-hundred-dollar-an-hour appraiser, Lennon locks up the pharmacy, and in five minutes Ciana and Vendetta are in Ciana's car on the way to her mother's house with an N.O. bag full of disposable cameras. "We gonna take pictures of everything," Vendetta is saying. "Everything. Ciana, your mama as nice as they come, but she no different from everybody else. Anything worth something, she put in the living room, right? You got something you like, you show it off. Except maybe one cabinet in the kitchen. Right? Now I'm not counting shit you hide from burglars. But you got to figure that's what your sister-in-law done took while you setting up in the hospital, so nothing you can do about it now."

Corinne's car is parked out front, along with a shiny black E-Class Mercedes. Ciana wants to come back after work. "Uh, uh," Vendetta says, and gives Ciana a little shove to get her out of the car.

In the dining room they find Corinne and a woman who looks as if she's just come from a Junior League meeting studying a full place setting as if they are planning a formal dinner. China, linen, crystal, silver. Arrayed on the table are alternatives for each. Ciana recognizes it all because she's seen it in the cabinet. Her mother never used it often enough for it to be familiar.

Vendetta steps back and folds her arms, saving up details for Frieda and Jaquilica. Ciana says, "This is all a little macabre."

"This is my husband's sister," Corinne says, with a tone that implies shame over Ciana's white coat. Ciana's clearly not a physician; therefore she's a fat girl with a job.

"And you must be Corinne's decorator," Ciana says, extending her hand.

"Heavens, no," the woman says. "I don't work. But you look familiar." She doesn't look at Ciana's nametag. Ciana's still a generic fat girl who works for a living.

Ciana tries desperately to place her. She knows she gets her prescriptions filled at the store. She doesn't want her name; she wants her affliction.

Vendetta steps forward. "Ciana run the pharmacy up on Carrollton. Remember, Ciana?" She leans over and whispers in Ciana's ear. "I don't know who she is, but you can be sure if I whisper, she bound to be embarrass."

They shoot four rolls of thirty-six shots. Including the dining room table.

In the car it all comes to Ciana when she's not thinking

about it. "Celeste Waters," she says. "Remember? The first time I saw that name, I said it sounded like an Indian?"

"Mmm, hmm," Vendetta says. "She come in for Diflucan just a couple days ago. Maybe that why she so grouchy."

Ciana almost feels sorry for the woman. As she recalls, she's on Effexor and Wellbutrin. Now she's also been identified in public with a raging yeast infection. And to top it all off, she's evidently a friend of Corinne's.

Last night Ciana had terrible dreams. She doesn't need a psychiatrist to tell her what they were about. She was a circus performer, and of course through the miracle of metaphor she was startlingly ectomorphic, a high-wire cyclist affected by small puffs of wind or great crashes of sound. This circus operated in three dimensions; it wasn't just at ground level, or even at ground and high-wire level; performers were in the air *everywhere*. So they floated up and around her, and unlike Ciana they were unafraid of gravity. She spent the whole night struggling for balance, and in the morning she had a headache because she was clenching her teeth so hard. She was frankly surprised not to be on the floor. She also was surprised not to be skinny. Or wearing a tutu.

She phones Geoffrey before the pharmacy opens because she needs to swat down a few of those airborne clowns. They're going to play the dot game tomorrow, and while she's armed with a six-page inventory, she knows she's still outflanked. "Who's going to be there?" she says when he answers. "All of us," he says.

Ciana tells him she has been thinking; why doesn't he go over ahead of time, and his family could give him a list, and then he could act on their behalf. She and he could do it alone. She resists saying *go one-on-one*.

"It was your idea to bring them. Don't fucking jerk me around," he says. Ciana tells him okay, but she's bringing someone, too. "Which one?" he says. Which one? "The man or the woman. Don't you have any respectable white friends?"

"Don't *you* have any respectable white friends?" she says back. Ciana has read that when a parent dies the offspring revert to childhood patterns. She thinks that is supposed to mean hierarchies and subterfuges; she doesn't think it's supposed to mean singsong taunts.

On the way over, she explains to Lennon that she's actually terribly fond of her nieces and nephew. "The trouble is, they're such good children, they'll do whatever their mother tells them to do. If she says to put their grandmother's silk scarves in their pockets because it will feel special, they'll do it." The most tractable one is the middle child, Madeleine, who's eight. She looks like Ciana, and she's chubby, and with those two shortcomings she has to work extra hard to please her mother. Actually, with those two shortcomings, she has to work extra hard to please *everyone*. Ciana likes her best. The only thing she wants to change about her is her outlook. She desperately wants the child not to give a damn.

They are already there when Ciana and Lennon arrive, meandering around like shoppers at an estate sale. Ciana waves her inventory list at Corinne with one hand, her sheet of yellow dots with the other. "I don't like to be compulsive and unsentimental," she says. "Don't forget." Corinne is trying to figure out what the printed sheaf of papers is all about, though she is craning her neck in a most uptown fashion. Ciana has no compunction about telling her. "Lennon has a photocopy at his house, and I have one at mine," she says.

"Why are you being such a bitch?" Geoffrey says. "Our mother just died."

Ciana folds her arms and gives him a withering look. It's not easy, given the difference in height, and even the difference in age, but she does it.

"If you want to be fair, we ought to have a copy of that list," Corinne says. "What if we don't get stuff of the same value?"

"Aw, Jesus," Lennon whispers, even though they both hoped he would stay quiet.

Ciana turns to the children because she figures they are the only ones who have a remote chance of understanding her. They're all arrayed around their parents, the way children usually are on television sitcoms to keep them on camera. Ciana thinks they're sticking close because the house gives them the creeps. "Listen, guys. I want to tell you about this list. It's a list of all the things in this house that have to be divided up legally. Your grandmother had a lot of junk, and anybody can take all of it if they want. But the stuff that she'd have put in her will if she'd gone one thing at a time, that's what we've got to split up. But it's got nothing to do with money. It's got to do with keeping track. If it's my turn, and I want the ukulele that's worth a hundred dollars because I remember your grandfather playing it, then that's what I take. Even if I could take the grandfather clock that's worth thirty-five hundred dollars . . ."

"Is that what it's worth?" Corinne says.

"I'm talking hypothetically," Ciana says, "but yes, that's what it's worth." Ciana gives her that much because she's thrilled that she's listening. She knows Corinne's going to go for the clock no matter what, and then she's going to have to figure out what to do about her ten-foot ceilings. "Anyway, this is not about dividing things up so we can see who wins in the end. This is not 'Supermarket Sweep.'"

Caroline, who's twelve and who named her poor unsuspecting grandmother's dog Nookie, says, "If you were smart, you'd take the grandfather clock first and hide the ukulele so you could get it later."

Ciana turns to Geoffrey. "And this," she says, "is why I don't want Fagin and the Artful Dodger loose while you and I are doing this."

In the car going home, Ciana asks Lennon what his favorite moments were. Hers was seeing Lucien come running up the stairs asking for a sticker; he was dazzled by his grandmother's television set. It seems that in half his lifetime of snuggling up next to her, patiently watching "The

Golden Girls" and waiting for a snack, he never had discovered that the 1970s console set housed a hi-fi turntable under a sliding panel in the top. "Oh, sweetie," Corinne said, "this goes to the Goodwill." Triage.

Ciana expects Lennon liked Corinne's tsking about her choice of the Clementine Hunter painting best. "Sort of racist, don't you think?" she said to her friend Lennon. Lennon, who walked around all evening looking at her like a murderer.

"Oh," he says to Ciana, "I think I like best that you walked off with about a hundred thousand dollars' worth of stuff more than they did. And that's just from the list."

"I'll have to even it up," Ciana says.

"I know," he says. "*That's* the good part."

18

THREE DAYS ago they quit betting on which mouse a customer would pick up. It's not funny anymore. On the pharmacy counter Mr. Walker has placed this basket full of toy mice, all in little costumes, that sing when you press their stomachs, four ninety-five. Every single customer thinks it's going to make their day behind the counter to set one of those things off. Vendetta's favorite at first was the girl mouse on her knees singing "Please Release Me"; Ciana's was the Elvis impersonator singing "Are You Lonesome Tonight?" They could *tell* who'd pick which one up. Now they don't give a shit. Vendetta just wishes that she didn't wake up in the middle of the night hearing "Are You Lonesome Tonight?" in her head, sung in that desperate squeaky voice. Her nerves are completely shot.

Vendetta has sworn to herself that she is going to get everything straight with everybody today and calm herself down. She is going to tell Lennon what those twins said and tell Ciana what she herself did, and then maybe when Patricia fusses like she's being killed in the morning because she has to leave the house Vendetta will be able to act like she doesn't feel the same way. She hasn't felt this lousy about showing up someplace every morning since she was the first girl to get titties in her class.

Lennon has been in the corner on his cell phone half the morning. He's not doing anywhere near enough of his work, but Ciana is covering for him, so Vendetta figures he's up to something interesting, and she manages to ease her way past him whenever possible. He's spending a lot of time on hold, which gives her no clues. But she does pass him once when he's saying, "I understand. I will get power of attorney. And then do I hear you correctly that you have complete records?" Vendetta can't wait. This makes no particular sense, but she can't wait.

When he puts away the cell, she waylays him before he can rush back to the computer. "I got something I got to tell you about," she says, beckoning Lennon to come over by the drop-off window, out of earshot of Ciana. "Oh, Ciana can hear anything you have to tell me," he says, and Vendetta thinks she could start to get a little sick of it if these two get too romantic.

"It's about them hoochie twins," she says, giving him a chance to change his mind. Lennon looks like he might waver, but he stays right where he is. It's Vendetta who starts to change her mind. “They come in here a while back looking for you. Why you think they done that?”

“Why?” Ciana says.

“I got to tell this to Lennon,” Vendetta says.

“Why?” Lennon says.

“They saying they spying on you, seeing if you gay. But then they asking questions, I figure out the real reason.”

Ciana stops what she’s doing. Ciana’s not interested in the real reason. “What do you mean, they think he’s gay?”

“Shoot, everybody think Lennon gay. Huh, Lennon.”

Lennon gets an expression on his face that says he believes her and will be ruined by believing her.

“That’s a joke, baby. My sisters want me to marry you,” she says. She looks at Ciana to see if she’s stepped in it again. But Ciana is pleased as she can be with the competition.

By the time Vendetta tells Lennon the real reason the Hollingsworth twins are skulking around the store, he is practically insulted that it is nothing personal. They could be skulking around anybody who could be stealing from the Schedule II supplies. They could be skulking around Vendetta.

The personal phone rings before Vendetta can figure out a way to say, *Oh, long as we talking about me stealing . . .* It’s Mrs. Lawton, the principal at Sylvanie F. Williams School, and she wants to talk to Miss Greene. Vendetta has answered, and she doesn’t bother to correct the woman, that her name is Mrs. Greene, that more parents than the principal suspects do not have bastard children in that school. Mrs. Lawton grew up in the St. Bernard Project herself, and her contempt has no bounds. Vendetta just says, "Yes, this is her," because Vendetta is sure this time Patricia is dead.

"I have your child in my office," Mrs. Lawton says.

Vendetta feels a rush of relief, because Patricia is not dead, and she is not on her way to Charity. Sylvania is about two minutes from Charity, a quick ride over the Claiborne overpass, and if anything were wrong, she wouldn't be in that office. That's another good reason to have a child in that school. "Yes?" Vendetta says.

"Now this is not a child we ordinarily have difficulty with, but we can't get her under control. Would you like to try to speak to her to see what you can do? Before you have to come get her?"

Vendetta knows a threat when she hears one.

Patricia doesn't make one sound that makes any sense over the phone. Except what Vendetta thinks is the word "quick." Or "Quick." With her luck, it's "Quick." Vendetta tells her to slow down. Now she hears the word "peenie." Oh, Lord. As far as she knows, Quick's peenie doesn't do anything except wet the bed. She's going to have to do Twenty Questions with Patricia. And she knows Mrs. Lawton is standing over Patricia, waiting desperately for her to get out of that office so she won't have to be fooling with children. "Shh, shh," Vendetta says. "This about Quick, right?" Uh, huh. "He done something with his peenie?" Lennon walks past and gives her a funny look.

Patricia wails through the phone. "No-o-o-o." Vendetta can't think of any other questions. Patricia starts up making no sense again. Vendetta asks for Mrs. Lawton.

"I can't come get her," she says. "What you do when a parent can't come get a child?" She's lying, since there are always taxis and lost wages and much easier solutions, but it seems to her that somebody at that school ought to be able to talk to Patricia and make her feel better.

"We put the child back into the classroom, and she just has to tough it out," Mrs. Lawton says.

"Your office got a sofa in it," Vendetta says.

"I have business to conduct in my office," Mrs. Lawton says. "I have meetings."

Vendetta went to that school. If someone from the school board came for a meeting, the janitors and teachers made everybody tiptoe. It happened maybe twice a year. If a parent came for a meeting, it was held in the foyer standing up.

"I'm sending her uncle over," Vendetta says. "Or maybe her aunt." She figures she can get away with sending just about anybody but Ciana.

She tries real-live aunts first. Jaquilica does not answer the phone, and to Vendetta that means Jaquilica would be driving under the influence anyway. Frieda picks up her cell on the first ring as if she knows she's got an airtight excuse for whatever Vendetta wants and she can't wait to use it. "Girl, Channel Six doing another investigation. They think they so cool, catching us parking our own cars wrong. I can't move; I'm so sure they got a camera on me." To

Vendetta, she sounds an awful lot like she's keeping her hair combed and her lipstick fresh.

So it's Uncle Lennon. "You sure everybody won't think I look like a child molester?" he says.

"Not at that school," Vendetta says. "You walk in there looking like you got a job, they give you half the third grade."

He brings Patricia into the store looking as if she can't decide whether she has been martyred or has fallen in love. Her eyelashes are clumped together from crying, and her hair is mussed from riding in an open car, and Vendetta is sure that if she makes a nice spot somewhere Patricia would fall right to sleep. But Patricia is not a dog wearing a little vest, so she can't come behind the counter. All she can do is sit in the waiting area with her backpack and pick up viruses off the armrests. Vendetta goes over on aisle eight and gets a container of Lysol wipes, rings it up, then wipes down a chair for Patricia. Two old white women are sitting in two of the other chairs, and they watch Vendetta without hiding their disgust. Vendetta knows very well that in their day those two would have expected Patricia to drink from the colored fountain.

She doesn't make Patricia tell her anything until they get home, and that's a big mistake, because everything can be heard through the walls. Patricia can whisper for about one sentence, for about the time it takes to say, "Mama, I can't go back to that school," and then she starts wailing loud and saying the name "Quick" in every other sentence so that it only takes a minute before Frieda and Jaquilica are in the kitchen, and Quick and Everett come trailing in behind them. Patricia takes one look at Quick and says, "I'm a kick you in *your* dumbass peenie," and she goes straight for him, but she goes for him like a girl, slapping at his face with her open palms. She doesn't have a chance. Poor Patricia. Vendetta is *not* one of the ones who pulls her off.

"Set your skinny behind down," Frieda says.

"Don't be coming in my house telling my child what to do," Vendetta says. "You see her when you pick up Quick? No, you do not. You know why? Because that piece of crap boy of your'n done something to her so bad she wind up in Mrs. Lawton office. And that cow send her home. My child, who never done a thing wrong, *she* get sent home from school. I'm the one ought to whip his ass."

"What you done, Quick?" Frieda says.

"Nothing." He's looking up from under eyelashes so long they actually curl into a complete circle. Even Vendetta likes looking at him.

Patricia finally has found her voice. "Nothing. Nothing. How about you going around telling everybody in the whole school I got a peenie. That's what he done, Mama." She begins sobbing with the awful knowledge that there's no way she can prove she doesn't.

"Aw, that ain't nothing," Everett says. "I been to Sylvania, all the way through. Booker T., too. And people call me a morphodite every day. Look at me now. I'm fine, girl, just fine."

Patricia looks up at her flaming queen cousin who sells coke on Leonidas Street and starts wailing louder.

"Shut up, Everett," Vendetta says.

"Don't be talking to my boy like that," Jaquilica says. "When you got a grown child, then you can criticize my child."

"I'm not criticizing your child, I'm criticizing Frieda child," Vendetta says. "What you gonna do so my child can stay at Sylvania?" she says to Frieda. "*She* the one was there first. Now your damn Quick trying to run her out."

"What he suppose to do, go around telling everybody she ain't got no peenie?" Frieda says.

Patricia lets out a howl of embarrassment.

"Never mind," Vendetta says. This is something Mrs. Lawton should know how to handle. They probably have something about it in the principals' handbook.

"You staying home tomorrow," Vendetta tells Patricia. Patricia smiles and continues to smile, even after Vendetta says, "And you gonna do your studies with Auntie Quilica."

19

LENNON feels that having power of attorney is, in its own way, stronger than marriage. He imagines that one day he could say, *Let's take a step backwards and get married.* He and Ciana have not made love, but he has acted on her behalf in ways that a husband might not have the right to do. If he wanted to, he could destroy her. He has no such wish, but he is stunned that she absolutely knows this.

He doesn't have to go to New York because of the world's willingness to trust fax machines and FedEx and the sound of his educated voice. Between Roosevelt Hospital and the City of New York, he has found every document he needs to corroborate his suspicions. He can't imagine what would have happened if Mrs. Jambon had had an accident in New Orleans. Recordkeeping isn't an exact science in a place where no one can spell or keyboard.

He arrives at the store at the same time Ciana walks in with what looks like a cake box balanced on one hand and Nookie tucked under the other arm. He runs to relieve her of the box before it falls and is surprised at how heavy it is. For someone who once was allowed to eat cake only twice a year, on his birthday and on Diana's, Lennon has been eating a lot of cake lately. "Cake is *boring*," Diana always said. "It's only got one texture." Lennon always has been a single-texture man.

"For me?" he says, joking.

"Yes," she says. "Mostly."

It's not a cake, it's a pie. A Milky Way pie. From Mandina's, made special. No sooner are they in the pharmacy than Ciana is spooning a taste into Lennon's mouth. Not a slice, a spoonful, even though it's a pie. It's Milky Way, caramel custard, and chocolate whipped up into a benediction, and he opens his mouth like a shameless baby bird. He thinks he could keep eating this stuff even when he's not hungry anymore. This is the first time he ever has understood substance abuse fully. "I was going to slip a condom into it, like a baby in a king cake," Ciana whispers, "but I'm kind of fastidious."

"Good thing," Lennon says. His reverent feelings for a future of endless ecstatic mouthfuls of pie are gone.

And he notices she doesn't say how hypothetical this condom is.

"So y'all didn't wait for me?" Vendetta says when she walks in.

"Sorry," Ciana says. "It looked too good."

"That's from me *and* Ciana," Vendetta tells Lennon, and Lennon gives Ciana a funny look. Ciana's smile is cryptic; he probably never will know whether Vendetta was in on the condom idea. "You been doing a lot of shit around here lately," Vendetta says. "We both figure we owe you."

So much for power of attorney being a mystical, scoreless bond. He supposes that if he is standing in for Ciana with no limits, doing her tasks as if she were doing them, in essence *being* Ciana, then if she feels the need to pay him back there is no more perfect gift than a Milky Way pie. It tastes like the food of the gods. He wishes she'd never mentioned the condom. The Vendetta part he understands. Ciana can't come right out with giving him too much. Aside from total control over her affairs. "You might take this all back when I tell you what I'm doing today," he tells Ciana.

"What," she says, and she holds out a full slice of pie to him.

"I'm calling Corinne."

Ciana's pie hand doesn't move, one way or the other. It doesn't even dip a little. Ciana just stands perfectly still, waiting. When Lennon doesn't speak, she says, "I'm having a hard time trying to ignore all this business." "I know," he says, and then the pie hand moves. Absentmindedly, Ciana brings it toward herself and begins eating.

Of all things, the biggest roadblock to talking to Corinne is that she is afraid he is going to rape her. Or worse, that she is going to be seen in public with him.

He has identified himself only by name at first, just to see what she will say. If "Lennon Israel" is familiar to Corinne, she is not letting on. He does not sound black; he does not even sound like he's from Memphis. He has been told this far too many times, as if either fact is a compliment. "Lennon Israel, an associate of your sister-in-law." Silence. "Your sister-in-law, Luciana Jambon." For all he knows, Corinne has a brother or two. A brother might have a wife. Though Corinne doesn't behave like a woman who grew up with brothers. "Yes," Corinne says, still noncommittal. "I met you at your mother-in-law's house the night you went through the inventory."

"Oh," she says finally.

He tells her that he would like to meet with her. What for? she asks. To talk about the death of Mrs. Jambon, he says. That's none of his business, she says. He has Ciana's power of attorney, he tells her. She considers that for a moment, then tells him to call back in five minutes. Lennon has a feeling she's not calling Geoffrey. Not because she's hiding anything from him, but because she figures he has no clue what power of attorney means, either. When he calls back, he hears a click when she picks up. He's called back too fast; she's still on the other line and has to hang up on someone else. "What?" she says.

"This is Lennon Israel."

"Yeah, they said I ought to talk to you. But I ought to ask you first why you want to talk to me and not my husband."

He can't believe it. Even when all she's doing is saying the word "husband," she's bragging.

"Because you're the one who was with Mrs. Jambon when she fell."

It takes Corinne just a little too long to say "So?"

And it takes Lennon just as long to say, "So she didn't fall in FAO Schwartz."

"Listen, mister, I don't think there's any reason to discuss this. My mother-in-law just died, and everybody's upset, and you've clearly got some agenda with poor Ciana, and I think you need to butt out."

"I think you need to talk to me," Lennon says.

"I don't want to talk to you."

Lennon is actually shaking. If he had had the constitution for confronting people in their entireties, he would not have gone into his line of work. "If you want me to show what I've found to Ciana, I can do that instead."

"Is this some kind of blackmail? I'm calling the FBI."

He ought to be laughing, but he wants to cry. He will remember every word from this conversation to tell Ciana. If she doesn't *love* him forever, at least she will love him forever. "All I mean is that when she finds out, she's going to be very upset. If that's blackmail, well, I don't know what to say."

"So talk."

Lennon explains that he has papers he wants to show her, and they need to meet in person. He suggests PJ's coffee shop. Corinne acts as if he has asked her to have sex with him on the streetcar tracks at State Street. "We can't be seen there," she says. He had thought up a list of nice cafés and bistros in her neighborhood where he was willing to treat her to lunch to prove he was a good person, but he sees no point. She can't explain him to her friends. A woman who is someone of significance in uptown New Orleans does not have lunch with her late mother-in-law's groundskeeper. Even if she's having an affair with him. And she wouldn't be having an affair with him if he's black. Lennon suggests that he come by her house. "Oh, no, it has to be a public place," Corinne says.

Ciana will enjoy the implications of that one.

Lennon *tells* Corinne that he will be at the Shoney's on Clearview at noon. If she doesn't show up, he won't mind a few trips to the salad bar.

She's there waiting by the claw machine. They are far from the only interracial couple, but they are the only one not dressed in T-shirts. Actually, they are the only couple of any permutation not dressed in T-shirts. Corinne looks soothed by the conspicuous anonymity. Lennon decides he will take only cold foods from the salad bar, since he figures Corinne expects him to pile his plate high with hot fried meats and cheese-covered vegetables. Corinne comes back with a bowl of thin soup. She's a nervous wreck.

Lennon opens the leather folder he's chosen just for this occasion. He has the originals of all these papers at home because he fears food stains, but the ink is strong and legible. The pick-up location and destination of the ambulance. Notations of contusions and preliminary radiologist's reports. Autopsy report. The inventory of everything Mrs. Jambon wore when she went into Roosevelt Hospital. Including jewelry.

Corinne skims; her eyes glaze; seeing only technicalities,

she tosses it back unread. "Who's to say you didn't make all of this up?"

"Do you see the fax number on the edge?" Lennon says. "How am I going to make this up?"

"People can forge anything these days. You use computers. I've been in drugstores."

Lennon pushes the papers back into the folder and looks around for the waitress. It is hard to pretend to make a dramatic exit in Shoney's. Fortunately, it is easy to fool Corinne. "Okay, wait," she says. "How much do you want?"

"Excuse me?"

"We're getting a lot of money. I assume you know that if Ciana let you know all her business."

"I don't want money."

"Jewelry?"

This is wonderful. Lennon never will have to cut this woman slack for as long as he lives.

"I don't want anything for myself. I just want for Ciana's sake that you know you didn't get away with anything."

"I didn't do anything wrong. I was being damn nice to that woman. Damn nice. Do you hear me?"

Corinne gets up and walks out, punishing him by leaving him to pay full salad bar price for a half-eaten cup of soup. "If you change your mind, you can still call me," she says as she walks away.

Lennon goes back to the salad bar three times, but never for hot food. Just in case Corinne comes back. To entertain himself he studies the dessert flyer on the table. Someone once told him how marketers set up the photographs of food like this, and he studies the symmetry of the whipped cream on the hot fudge cake, the amazing perfection of the way someone has sliced through the filling without smearing it. He wants a big slug of Milky Way pie. He wants to be among the sure people at Mandina's.

CIANA probably has slept because the time has passed quickly, but she feels as if she has stayed awake all night, watching Lennon. Her bedroom is at the back of the house, but it is never completely in the dark because her next-door neighbor has security lights that come on automatically every night at nine o'clock, and her curtains are not opaque enough. She doesn't mind. She knows her yard, too, is flooded with light. And tonight her room has been flooded with filtered light, gold filtered light that makes Lennon look quite beautiful, even when he starts to snore somewhere around midnight. She doesn't mind. He even snores decorously. Rhythmically. If Nookie weren't sitting directly across from her, keeping a vigil on the other side of his head, she would have no perspective at all.

Last night, with all the time in the world, they made love for the first time. Lennon's touch was unlike any other lover's; she did not let herself think about how often he must have done this before, to be so knowing. This body of hers, this body that she never likes bumping up against men; he acted as if it was a treasure. Every little pudge, every broad expanse. "Do this for hours," she said, and he did.

The sun is up by seven, so she starts flouncing around, but just a little, to wake him up. He sits bolt upright. In the light she can see tight little curls of chest hair. She has a lot to learn about men, and probably even more to learn about black men. She might as well just skip over the general information about men. And even the slightly less general information about black men. Lennon's all she wants to know about. "I'm giving myself half an hour," he says laconically, sounding like a man who's woken up in this bed for years. For what? Ciana wants to know. "I have to get down to it," he says. "You notice I don't talk about it. Especially with you."

Ciana doesn't fear the answer, since last night he was quite free with telling her that he'd already had lunch with Corinne and that he had it all under control. Anything else must be minor. "It?" she says.

He whispers the word, and it comes out sounding almost erotic, no small feat for an acronym that seems to come from a military-industrial lexicon. "NAPLEX."

In all the time she's worked with Lennon, it's almost never crossed Ciana's mind that he's been serious about preparing for the exam. She knows he has to take it, and she knows he'd be insane not to be thinking about it, but Ciana believes he knows everything, and he just needs to get a good night's sleep beforehand. Lennon is a natural. When a woman came into the store last week and told him her son had put red wax in his hair for a school play, and she didn't know what to do, he told her to use Tide. Just like that. He knows the world down to the molecular level.

"Aw, sweetie, for you it's just a formality. Show up, and you've got your license."

He shakes his head, and his dreads arc out like streamers. They look as tight as they did when they went to bed. Another question answered. "You know as well as I do that everybody thinks all we're good for is counting pills from bottles," he says. Ciana has to nod in agreement, and she feels her hair is not moving nicely the way Lennon's does. She reaches up slowly and fluffs it into some kind of symmetry. It's naturally streaky blonde and straight and thick; maybe Lennon's learning something new, too. "So what do you want to do with your half hour?" she says.

He looks straight into her eyes for the longest time and finally says, "A half hour's not enough."

Five minutes is long enough, but Ciana is happy not to say so.

She offers to make him eggs, grits, and toast. She hopes he will say no, because the grits are several years old, and the eggs aren't much newer. He laughs. "Ciana, don't pretend you cook," he says, as if she's a runway model who lives in New York with a refrigerator too small to hold anything more than a jar of mustard, rather than in New Orleans with one large enough to hold several leftover pizzas, a case of Coke, and a half dozen Styrofoam containers she hasn't looked into since she brought them home. "Well, I can make toast all right," she says, feeling as if she will just have tea, thank you very much. She's pretty sure there is nothing green on top of the jam. She's lucky she has no appetite. The smell of toast usually makes Ciana want to eat the entire loaf. She can do it, too. She believes anyone can. A loaf of bread is mostly air; it's like cotton candy.

The phone rings before the kettle boils. Ciana looks to Lennon for permission not to answer. He should be the boss all the time. Or half the time. Lennon nods for her to answer, the consummate gentleman. Ciana cradles the receiver on her shoulder and moves around the kitchen like a wife.

"You've got to get over here. Corinne won't get out of bed." No *hello*. No *am I interrupting you?* Ciana doesn't notice because she is too transfixed by this peek into her brother's marriage. She's always labored under the illusion that adults get out of bed without prompting. She's glad Geoffrey can't see her face and that Lennon can. "She's just lying there, staring at the ceiling," Geoffrey says.

"Is she dead?" This is not a hopeful or sardonic question.

"Shut up, Ciana."

"Do you know what a dead person looks like?" It's an honest question, not a jab about his mother.

"She's not dead."

Lennon is holding his slice of toast in mid-air. He hasn't

blinked since Ciana answered the phone. Ciana makes eye contact and holds it while she tells Geoffrey that she is not exactly the one to coax Corinne out of bed, and then she purses her lips and rolls her eyes to communicate to Lennon that Geoffrey is saying that she is an idiot, that he just needs her to come get his children off to school, though of course Lennon cannot pick up on any such particulars. Lennon gestures to her to cover the mouthpiece, then says, "What's he want?" and Ciana says, "For me to get the kids off to school," and Lennon says, "Corinne's sick?" and Ciana says, "No!" She can hear Geoffrey hollering into his phone, "Hey, Ciana, what the fuck?" so she uncovers the mouthpiece.

"Does it ever occur to you that I might have company?" she says.

"No." She knows he's lying.

Lennon puts down his uneaten toast and begins cleaning up behind himself. Ciana gesticulates wildly, wanting so much to serve him, to watch him eat, to have herself and Lennon play house memorably this morning. "Hold on," she says to Geoffrey.

"These kids have school," Geoffrey hollers into the phone.

Lennon leans over Ciana, kisses her, and whispers in her ear, "I'm letting myself out. Don't do Corinne any favors." Ciana shakes her head, no, but Lennon nods his head, yes, and lets himself out the front door. Nookie looks thoroughly bewildered. But he doesn't get up to see Lennon out. The toast he offered him didn't have butter on it.

"Dammit, Geoffrey," Ciana says. She doesn't tell him

he's ruined everything. He would be too happy. "Has it occurred to you that you're a lot more experienced in this business of being a parent?"

"They've got hair!"

"So do you."

"What's that supposed to mean?"

"That means they don't have some strange foreign substance growing out of some strange body part. You know how a comb works. Use it."

Geoffrey's voice gets lower. "I don't want to." In the background, Ciana can hear the kids' voices begin to separate out from distant white noise into cacophony and then into individual screeches. She recognizes Madeleine's voice. "I can't go to school," she says. Ciana tells Geoffrey to put her on the phone. "Who is it?" Madeleine says. "It's me," Ciana tells her. "Ciana, nobody'll help me. All I ask Caroline to do is make me one ponytail. Just one. And you know what she says? She says, 'You are too hopeless.' I'm staying home." Ciana tells her to put her daddy back on the phone.

"Are you listening, Geoffrey?" She waits and hears nothing, so she assumes he's nodding. "You put those kids together the best you can, and you run them past here on the way to school. I'll put on the finishing touches. That's my best offer. They're not in diapers. They managed fine when Corinne was in New York. How do you figure that?"

"*You* came over every morning."

She walked right into that one.

"All they needed was some affection. If you want, I'll give them a kiss, okay?"

"Hey, we kiss our kids." She's sure they do. The same way their parents kissed them. A dry peck at bedtime. A ritual that was some distant cousin to getting the house in dying order.

When Geoffrey pulls up in front of Ciana's house at eight-fifteen, Caroline looks completely put together, probably more so than usual because she seems to have gotten away with blusher. And even though Lucien has that slight popcorn smell of little boys who don't bathe, he looks like he'll be just like the rest before recess. But Madeleine is a tangled mess, and tears are streaming down her round, red face.

"What'd you do to her, Geoffrey?" Ciana says as she tries to reach inside the van to comb her hair.

"Please just do her hair," he says.

Madeleine cries harder, though Ciana is doing a very good job. She's putting a little French braid at the front. Geoffrey has not turned off the motor. Caroline begins rocking back and forth in her seat when Ciana is not even halfway through the braid. Madeleine manages to sob without moving her head. "What's going on, baby?" Ciana says to her.

"I want to throw up," Madeleine says.

"You've never thrown up in your life," Geoffrey says. "Madeleine, you just want to stay home with Mommy, and you can't."

Madeleine catches Ciana's eye and says very emphatically, "No, I don't."

Ciana places her hand on Madeleine's forehead, which feels quite cool, and she tells Geoffrey that she thinks the child is sick and needs to stay home. She hears him take a big inrush of indignant, protesting breath, and then Ciana says, "With me." Madeleine flings her plump, healthy, unnauseated body out of the van straight at her aunt, and they collide so sweetly that Ciana thinks the moment is almost as good as sex. In its own way.

Ciana carries Madeleine to the house before Geoffrey can protest. She's sure they look foolish, like two soap bubbles stuck together, but she doesn't care. Madeleine seems worried, but Ciana calls the school, tells them to give her homework to her *brother*, and Madeleine giggles. "I'm going to get arrested if I go out in public in my uniform," she says. Ciana tells her, "Stick with me, kid; you can go into any bar and order whiskey straight up." Her eyes get wide, and Ciana can see that she has a lot of work to do if this little girl is not going to turn into her.

AmVets is coming to her mother's house in six days, so Ciana has no choice in how she is going to entertain Madeleine. But they're not expecting any particular type of goods, so Ciana can let Madeleine choose in which room to start. She hopes it's not her old bedroom; her history is too mortifying. And she hopes it's not the upstairs bathroom. Ciana knows for a fact that her mother never threw anything away, and she doesn't want Madeleine to be a witness when she learns what form of birth control her parents used.

Madeleine chooses the kitchen. They spend about fifteen

minutes standing speechless and sad in the center of the room with no idea of where to start. "I think if we do big stuff first it'll look better," Madeleine says. So they start in on everything that doesn't have a green or yellow dot, and that consists mostly of items with electric cords. "This is way better than ours," Madeleine says of the microwave or the Cuisinart or the coffeemaker. Ciana suggests it go into the keep pile. No, Madeleine says, it would be far better that a poor person could get it for a dollar. Ciana suggests they put it out on the curb. "That would make them feel terrible," Madeleine says.

By lunchtime the kitchen is in such a state that they tell themselves they are entitled to suspend all known forms of etiquette. They send out for a triple order of buffalo wings, fries, and onion rings and find a patch of floor where they picnic on newsprint. Madeleine has ranch dipping sauce, Ciana has bleu cheese, and they compete to see who can go longer without napkins. The front of Madeleine's uniform is covered, but it is a red, white, and blue plaid made for such times; Ciana's pink T-shirt can go straight into the dumpster pile if she can find some way to go home in her bra. "You're really good, Ciana," Madeleine says. Ciana can hardly understand what she's saying, she is lisping through so much goop. She can tell, though, that Madeleine is incredulous.

All Ciana says is thanks. She's not going to go near the subject of Madeleine's parents and their attitudes toward her or toward her mother or her things; she doesn't even want to know if they vote Republican. She's sure if Corinne can manage to slur out a few words tonight, she will direct them all to debriefing Madeleine. As it is, she's going to hear about lunch and think Ciana's recruiting for Fat Pride, and she can take to her bed for a week over that alone.

The phone rings in the middle of the afternoon, and Madeleine looks at Ciana as if she's seen a ghost. Ciana can tell from her expression that she doesn't want to be the one to answer and say her grandmother's dead.

"Where the hell were you?" Geoffrey says when Ciana picks up on the seventh ring. The phone was under a pile of dishcloths.

"Obviously right here."

"What the hell was I going to do if I couldn't find you?"

Ciana doesn't know what he's talking about. He doesn't need Madeleine. Certainly he isn't worried about her.

"It's almost three o'clock," he says.

Now she understands. She tries to catch Madeleine's eye, but she is in a dream state, in the sort of satiation that would let them both fall right over into sweet afternoon naps. "Let them walk home," Ciana says.

"I can't do that," Geoffrey says.

"You and I walked home when we were their ages, and those weren't the good old days."

"Mama was irresponsible."

It would be so easy to say, *And it is terribly responsible to be lying in bed in a state of advanced spoiled temper*, but Ciana doesn't. It also would be easy to suggest Geoffrey leave work early, but he would create such a logistical drama that she would never hear the end of it.

She tells Geoffrey that she'll pretend she didn't hear what he said about his mother and she hopes God will do the same. And then she says she will pick up Caroline and Lucien and drop them at home, but she's keeping Madeleine with her until he comes to get her. She figures that it is fair all around. Corinne will have to put a pillow over her head for two hours, and Geoffrey will have to walk into this house and see that Ciana is shoveling out the Augean stables the way she wants to. Of course, all he hears is *free ride*, and he's happy.

When Geoffrey comes to pick up Madeleine at six-thirty, he takes one look at the AmVets pile and has a fit. "You can't give away all this stuff," he hollers. He thrusts the George Foreman grill at Madeleine and stuffs his mother's toaster oven under his arm. "No, Daddy, you don't get it," Madeleine says, and she gently sets the grill down on the floor. Geoffrey picks it up, loads it on top of the toaster oven, and bumps Madeleine out the door with his elbow. He doesn't notice that his daughter has her hair in tiny cornrows that make her head look like an overstitched baseball but make her feel terribly glamorous.

"You may have money to throw away, Ciana, but I don't," he says.

"You just inherited a couple million, try to adjust," Ciana says, and then she shuts the door hard behind him.

21

THIS MORNING Ciana said, "You know, spring really does come to New Orleans, but only three kinds of people know it. Pharmacists, pediatricians, and women who have two closets." Vendetta can believe it: the store's been overrun today with people who have no idea what hit them. They all feel lousy, but as far as they can tell, nothing's changed. At the pharmacy they have to tell them that they have seasons here that have nothing to do with how much clothing they wear, or what fabric it is. They're not filling too many extra prescriptions, but the line at the Patient Consultation window is four-deep most of the day. Since the public sees Lennon, Ciana, and Vendetta as interchangeable, against all regulations they rotate, and Vendetta's experience as a mother makes her by far the most qualified. Ciana and Lennon both have begun to parrot her by mid-morning. Vendetta has it in for Robitussin because her mother swore it could cure everything. Now the manufacturer named Wyeth says the same thing. Vendetta will do anything in her power to make sure no one walks out with Robitussin. It thrills her that Wyeth makes Preparation H, the most shoplifted item on the planet.

Somebody who is fussing loudly is working her way up the line, out of turn, and all the cranky snufflers are stepping aside as she gets noisier. "You out your mind?" she says to Vendetta.

"I could help you?" Vendetta says. No one has taught her to say this. She just knows what it will do to a person. She also knows perfectly well who this woman is.

"You talk me into this crap. I can't even pronounce it. I walk out this store. I don't even get halfway to my house, no, and I'm jumping out my skin. Where's the manager at?"

She's waving generic pseudoephedrine, the world's best, cheapest solution to sinus agony, never mind its use in meth labs. It can, however, make a person very agitated. Vendetta may not be a fan of all the big pharmaceutical companies, but she knows enough not to be dangerous. And to be correct.

Vendetta leans forward over the counter. Everyone waiting for her advice watches with ragged, bated breath. "You tell me you got a sinus condition?" she says.

The woman nods.

"How your sinuses doing?" Vendetta says.

The woman takes in a good sniff. It's long and dry. "*They* feeling all right."

"You calm down after a while. Go take you a hot bath. Next time maybe only take you one pill."

"I'm a be all right?" the woman says. Vendetta nods vigorously. "That's all I need to know. I'm not having a stroke or nothing?"

"Mrs. Washington, you know well as I do you got such low blood pressure you halfway in shock most of the time. You ain't got what it take to pump no clot up to your brain."

Vendetta doesn't turn around to see what's going on behind herself, but she has this feeling that Ciana and Lennon are looking at each other like they're her proud parents. She's very happy for both of them, but if they get too sickening, she's going to have to knock some sense into Ciana at least.

"How'd you know Mrs. Washington has low blood pressure?" Ciana says a few minutes later, when the line has slowed down.

"I don't know jack shit about Mrs. Washington blood pressure," she says. "I just figure, woman over fifty, she black, and she never come in here for pressure medicine, she *got* to have low blood pressure. Otherwise, you think I'm a tell her take something blow her head off?"

Ciana seems almost shy when she comes to Vendetta with the note in her hand, but Vendetta still has a good idea what it's all about. The store has dried up during the lunch hour, and Lennon is the one keeping an eye on the Patient Consultation window. It's been a while since Vendetta has been jumpy about being where Ciana can get her alone. Somewhere along the line she figured Maureen couldn't do anything about that Ritalin pill, and she relaxed. But the minute Ciana waves a piece of paper at her, she knows it wasn't true. She should have known better about Maureen. Women like her have nothing better to do than make other women miserable. "Cover for us," Ciana tells Lennon, sounding not at all like a love bird to Vendetta. But Lennon grins like a fool, and Vendetta has a feeling that he gets to play boss some of the time.

As soon as they walk into the break room, Vendetta says, "I'm in trouble. You gonna fire me, so get it over with, all right?"

"You're in trouble," Ciana says. She waits just a second, and then she says, "But not the way you think." Vendetta doesn't say a word. Saying something can't do her any good. "I want to know why you don't trust me," Ciana says. Vendetta still doesn't say anything, but this time it's because she doesn't have a clue about what to say.

"Listen," Ciana says, waving the piece of paper around. Vendetta still can't make out what's on it, but it's handwritten, and it's long. "I don't need to be a rocket scientist to know what this is all about."

"I can see it?" Vendetta says.

Ciana ignores her. "You take an accusation of product tampering, you see it has to do with Ritalin, you know very well that Quick takes Ritalin, you see there's an *overage* in the inventory, and you know exactly what happened. Right?"

Vendetta has seen enough trials and interrogations on television. This isn't the time to confess. So she just looks her best friend right in the eye.

"Damn you, Vendetta," Ciana says. "I'm mad at you because you could have told me your stupid sister ran out and you needed extra. I'd have advanced you a couple of pills. Even though I can't stand Frieda."

"You not gonna fire me?" Vendetta's almost ready to feel relieved. She's also almost ready to get excited that she has permission to quit liking Frieda.

"I am never going to fire you," Ciana says.

Vendetta throws her arms around Ciana's neck. It's the first time they've hugged each other. "I love you," Ciana says. Vendetta pulls back. "Don't be talking like that. People be thinking we a couple of bulldaggers." Ciana looks a little wounded. "Hey, it's all right. I know white people be saying that all the time," Vendetta says.

"And sometimes we mean it," Ciana says.

"So what I'm a do?" Vendetta says after she has processed her embarrassment.

Ciana tells her that she will take care of Maureen "but good." Vendetta hopes that means Ciana will screw up the inventory some kind of way that will make Maureen sorry she ever tried to rat anybody out, but she knows better. Ciana isn't like that. "You, on the other hand," Ciana is saying, "you need to move out of that house."

When the personal phone rings later in the afternoon, only Lennon is not paralyzed by anxiety over what disaster the call might be bringing. Vendetta is sure Jaquilica has turned on the stove without lighting it and let gas fill the house, and Patricia is dead. That is the scene she picks to terrorize her because most other scenes can be outsmarted by Patricia. She hopes the call is for Ciana, even though it means she will have to fight with her brother. The only person who could be dead in a call from her brother is that terrible Corinne, and no one would be too sad over that.

"She says to tell you it's Madeleine," Lennon tells Ciana.

"Did your daddy make you call me?" Ciana says into the phone.

Ciana covers the receiver and whispers, "She says, 'Not exactly.' Good semantics." Then she says into the phone, "Okay, listen. Somebody will be at the gate to get you this afternoon, okay?"

Ciana presses the hang-up button, then releases it and gets ready to dial, but Vendetta steps in and replaces the receiver. "Hold on, baby," she says. "Let's think this one *through*."

Ciana looks happy to put herself in Vendetta's hands, to forget the Frieda foolishness, to remember mostly how Vendetta tended the minds, bodies, and probably even the spirits of half of a very strange zip code most of the day. Vendetta knows everything about the world if her sisters don't confuse her. "Okay," she says, and she pitches her voice up high the way she does at the Patient Consultation window. "F.B. trying to shame you into going to pick up his kids. Right?" Ciana nods. "Now you know those kids got to be picked up, one way or the other, because he not raising them to know what to do, right?" She hopes Ciana doesn't call her on Patricia needing to be driven to school. She doesn't; she just nods. "Well, you could just make him leave work and go get them and get hisself all messed up and pissed at you, but that's no good. And you could go get them and have him thinking he can call you every day, but that's no good, neither." Ciana folds her arms, waits to see where Vendetta's headed. But Vendetta hasn't had this sort of luxury of time with her other patients. She hasn't been able to bad-mouth the whole line of Robitussin products before coming out with her generic recommendation. "So!" she says. "So, come here, Uncle Lennon." Lennon shambles over. He's been listening to all of this, of course, but he's been thinking it wouldn't involve him. "You see where this is going at, Ciana? You send 'Uncle Lennon' over to that school, I guarantee that cow never even think about asking you to fetch her children. And it don't make no never mind to the children. Everybody win."

"Holy Name is not Sylvanie F. Williams," Lennon says. "They don't give kids to just anybody."

"Oh, yes they do," Ciana says. "I'll tell them you're the groundskeeper."

"No," Vendetta says. "You got to tell them he the *uncle*."

★

Lennon's car is just a Mazda Miata, but the kids don't know the difference; they drove off from school with the top down, thinking they were the shiznit, Madeleine told Ciana, and that is all that counts. He brought her back to the store first, then went to drop off the other two at home. N.O. Drugs is playing babysitter to a half-mute wiener dog and a little Catholic white girl whose head looks like a baseball, but Ciana's well within her limits. She's given Madeleine twenty dollars to spend, and she can kill all the time until dinner thinking about that twenty dollars and coming up with nothing. "It's that way with fat kids," she tells Vendetta. "She'll get a bag of Gummy Bears and keep the change. She'll be Mr. Walker's customer until she makes her choice."

Geoffrey comes in at six-thirty with tears in his eyes; he is that angry. "What?" Ciana says. "You fucking well know what," he says. At least it is the dinner hour, when steamy food is clearing sinuses without their help; nobody is back by the pharmacy to hear him. "My wife is terribly ill, and you're not helping."

"Have you taken her to a doctor?" Ciana says.

"Do I look like I have time to take her to a doctor?" Geoffrey says.

"Entergy is not the evil empire," Ciana says. "At least not to its employees. You could take family leave. Or at least an hour off. I know you've taken three-hour lunches. A lot."

"What's a doctor going to do? Nothing hurts."

Vendetta holds her breath for this one.

"A doctor could refer her to a psychiatrist," Ciana says.

Vendetta can't believe it. Ciana has been wanting to say this for as long as she's known her. And now she's saying it flat-out, like she's suggesting Corinne might like a new pair of shoes.

Geoffrey sweeps his hand across the pharmacy. "We don't believe in this foolishness," he says. "You can't just pop a pill and change your personality. Then how do you know who you are?"

Ciana takes one small step backward, like she's not about to get into it with Geoffrey on this subject. So Vendetta steps forward and says in her patient-consultation voice, "Some personality ways aren't worth keeping."

Geoffrey looks at Ciana and says, "Neither is fat," and he stalks out.

LENNON can't believe that, of all people, he is sharing a secret with Corinne Jambon. He despises the woman, he would be perfectly happy if she spent the rest of her life in a darkened room pretending to be ill, turning pale and consumptive, but he has no way to call her a malingerer. At least not without giving specifics, and he can't see how that would be a good strategy. Ciana would blame Corinne for her mother's death and, wracked by regret and bigger grief, she would go after her brother. A man like her brother would not take it like a good sport.

So this afternoon when he delivered Caroline and Lucien, he walked them to the door, rang the bell, and waited for their mother to come open up and ask him in to hear her admit all wrongdoing. He stood on the front steps with the two children for so long he thought maybe she might not answer, and he even had time to look back a few times to be sure Madeleine hadn't opened her door and stepped out into the street and occasional traffic. But Madeleine had found the radio control and was bouncing around, making the car bounce, too, so he figured he'd give Corinne five minutes, and then she opened the door slowly. Not out of caution, but drama.

"What the hell is this?" she said, already knowing.

"We rode in a sports car," Lucien said.

Corinne put her hand on the top of his head and moved him into the house like a grocery checker moving a head of lettuce down the conveyor belt. "You, too," she said to Caroline, then called to Madeleine to get her ass in this house immediately. Madeleine didn't move; the music was too loud.

"Ciana's deal is that she'll pick up your kids if she keeps Madeleine," Lennon said.

Corinne tried to look him in the eye, but she couldn't quite focus. She wasn't drunk, and she couldn't have been drugged because it would have been in the computer. More drama. "She can keep her forever, far as I'm concerned," Corinne said, pretending to be in general pain. Lennon turned to go. "Hey, aren't you proud of what you've done to me?" she said.

"Beg pardon?"

"Don't pull that ignorant act on me," she said. "I know you're educated. You've literally made me physically ill."

Lennon felt a sense of urgency to get away. Not that he had to get back to work. Not that his motor was running. But that Corinne was in a bathrobe that was being kept closed by a tie at the waist that couldn't be trusted. "I really need to be going," he said.

"I haven't told Geoffrey about what happened in New York," she said. "It'd make him too sad. Imagine how Ciana would feel."

"I know," Lennon said. "I respect your decision."

Corinne smiled. She actually believed him. "By the way," she said, "Tell Ciana Geoffrey is going to kill her for telling Holy Name you're their uncle. *I'll* let it slide."

"Maybe I will be one day," he said. All the way back to the car he was furious at himself. It was a great line, but Corinne shouldn't have been the first one to hear it.

His mother has left a message on his voice mail at home, and Lennon has a hinky feeling about it. Even mechanized and scratched, her voice is portentous. Not in a death announcement way. And not in a simple authoritarian way, one in which he can confess and move on. He knows he is going to call her back, and she is going to say something straightforward and superficial and benign, and he is going to be correct when he worries, possibly for weeks, about what she actually means.

"I saw Mrs. Hollingsworth this morning," she says when he calls, and he smiles triumphantly to himself, knowing he was right, and knowing this is his last moment of feeling good for a while.

Lennon doesn't say anything.

"Those poor girls are having a rough time," his mother says.

Mrs. Hollingsworth only has two girls. "What girls?" Lennon says.

"Don't be petulant with me, son."

"You can't possibly be talking about the twins," Lennon says. Andrea and Antonia are the only twins he knows, but from watching them he always has assumed that twins are automatically comfortable wherever they go, as long as they go together. They constitute a crowd. The world has to adjust around them. The Hollingsworths certainly have lived this way. And from the little he has seen them in New Orleans, no one ever has been able to mistake them for newcomers, not even for freshmen. Life is not rough for Andrea and Antonia; life is rough *around* Andrea and Antonia.

"I'm just telling you what their mother said. And I gather that you haven't been particularly avuncular toward them."

He knows the images the mothers have, of him and the twins dressed in church clothes, going out to dinner, his treat, his invitation, his making small talk about their course work. He knows, too, that the twins are cagey enough to have complained that Lennon didn't deliver on this precise scenario. He's just wondering how they garnished their complaint. "And what did Mrs. Hollingsworth say exactly?"

"These really are very young girls, you know," his

mother says. "And that is a very menacing city. It would have been gracious of you to have made an effort to be certain they were safe. You know, orient them to the parts of town they should avoid, that sort of thing."

To the best of his recollection, Antonia and Andrea were sneaking out to Beale Street in Memphis long before either one qualified for a driver's license. He can't tell that to his mother, at least not this early in the game. "I've seen them," he says. "They seem to be able to navigate quite well."

His mother gets that huffy tone that enrages him. "Their mother says you are terribly rude to them. She and I had a long talk. I'm very concerned about you."

This is about women. With his mother it is always about women. She never has had any grounds to pick at him about academic performance because, to her knowledge, he always has surpassed all family standards and most of his own. She never has had reason to fuss about behavior because, to her knowledge, no teacher or traffic policeman ever has caught Lennon misbehaving. It hasn't even been about religion, because he never has told her that he calls Bellevue Baptist "Six Flags over Jesus" and thinks going there is a form of mental illness. His mother has only one subject she likes to probe, because it's the only subject she thinks he has secrets about. Women. Or, rather, sex. He's pretty sure she's let her imagination run far afield, encompassing not only women, but also virginity and homosexuality. Even if no one actually sent the Hollingsworth twins to New Orleans to test him on his mother's whole gamut, they've proven s*omething* to her.

"I'd like to bring a friend home with me for Easter," he says suddenly.

"Oh?" his mother says. He would love to see her expression.

"Would that be all right?" he says.

"Sure," his mother says, and she lets him get off the phone without volunteering any more information. He can't wait for her next phone call.

He's surprised that he doesn't have a phone number for either of the Hollingsworth twins. He has to use the university switchboard, and he gets Andrea because she appears first alphabetically, but Antonia answers because they're rooming together. The Hollingsworth twins are a redundant waste of protoplasm, as far as Lennon can tell. "We had a feeling we'd be hearing from you," she says.

"Well, here I am."

"So, you want to go out tonight?"

"Is that what it would take to find out what you've been telling your mother?"

"Pretty much."

Lennon has to admit that he's always wondered what it must be like inside a place with the unlikely name of Snake 'n' Jake's. It's a smoky bar, and the music is loud and meaningless, and Lennon knows if he sits on the sofas near the door he will be sick tomorrow, but Andrea and Antonia behave as if this is the reason they have come to town. Their eyes shine, and they sway in place just a bit, and Lennon despairs of having a conversation. "You can buy for us," Antonia says. Lennon hesitates, because no answer is the right answer. "First I want to know what kinds of things you go telling your mother," he says. "Shh, shh," Antonia says, as if he is an old man who is going to embarrass the hell out of her in front of her friends. "Nobody's paying attention to you," Lennon says. "Hush!" Andrea says. As if to prove Lennon wrong, three boys walk by and say hello. And they say, "Hello, Andrea or Antonia or whatever," and grin knowingly.

He gets two beers, but doesn't give them to the girls. He can drink them himself if he has to. "If I give these to you, how do I know you're not going home telling on me?" he says.

"We can't exactly go telling anybody that we drink, can we?" Andrea says, and Lennon hands over the beers.

As he watches the twins put away the beers with the casual finesse of party girls, he notices that far too many people in this place know them. It might be that they are conspicuous and memorable because they are beautiful and identical, but he doesn't think so; he thinks it's because they are familiar. When he was a college freshman, there was not one single place he could have walked into with such a high level of recognition, and that included his lab classes. "I feel so sorry for you both, not having had my help getting adjusted here," he says.

Antonia sidles up close and gives him a sloppy, beer-fueled kiss in front of his ear. He recoils. To Lennon the Hollingsworth twins always will be a pair of big-eyed ten-year-old twigs on Rollerblades screeching in the neighborhood dusk. If they are capable of sensuous behavior, he doesn't want to know about it. "Cut it out," he says.

Antonia pulls back fast, perfectly happy not to have to waste her affections on dried-up old Lennon, now that he's proved how easily he can resist an irresistible girl.

"Here's the deal," she says. Both girls fold their arms. "You get us Xanax and Vicodin, we give you five dollars a pill. Zero profit for us," Antonia says.

"Maybe some Soma if you feel like it," Andrea says.

"You mean steal," Lennon says. He is grateful to have to scream over the noise. Voices and bodies go out of control so easily in a place like this. He senses he might let his voice *and* body go.

The girls look at each other as if they've just had a brilliant idea simultaneously. They're not just a waste of protoplasm; they're a doubling of bad energy. "You wouldn't have to steal if you could fake stuff in the computer," Andrea says.

"Why would I do anything like that?" Lennon says.

"Because otherwise you're going to have to live off a *salary* the rest of your pitiful life," Andrea says.

He's not going to come back at them with a line about seventeen cents an hour in the federal penitentiary because then they will think that his only concern is getting caught. Somewhere along the line he learned not to argue with people who lacked consciences because they were almost as difficult as people who believed in Jesus Christ. In both cases, it was better just to say no.

"I won't do it," he says.

"We thought you might say that," Antonia says, and she wiggles a bit from side to side as if she's not worried at all.

"You know your family thinks you're gay, don't you?" Andrea says. She is trying to sound menacing, and Lennon would find her entertaining if she weren't a young girl playing with fire.

"I don't actually know that, no," Lennon says.

"Diana told us to check you out," Andrea says. "She doesn't give a shit if you're gay, but she thinks you're a complete loser if you're not going to come out of the closet."

"What business is this of any of theirs?" Lennon says, *feeling* gay as he speaks.

Antonia has been waiting to hiss at him. "Well, like, your mother thinks you'll go to hell if you're gay, that's all."

With the mention of his mother, Lennon comes to his senses. "I'm bringing my girlfriend home for Easter," he says, turning to leave them to get killed walking through the university section by themselves.

"Mmm, hmm," Antonia says. "Even your mother is not that dumb."

23

Last night Lennon called her from outside a bar, and afterward Ciana could not sleep because it seemed to her that now she could be secure. Being secure made her nervous and insecure, and she turned the conversation over and over in her head until she was quite confident that it made no sense. He was outside a place called Snake 'n' Jake's, and all the ambient sounds were true, a car door slamming once or twice, the door to the bar itself opening and letting out the unearthly thrumming of people thinking they were unbearably happy, even a few shouted conversations Doppplering past. "I don't think there's any way you'd find out unless someone tries to cause trouble, but I think someone will probably try to cause trouble," he said. "So I'm calling to tell you I was here." "Why?" she said, figuring that would elicit the most answers to the most questions.

He told her the Hollingsworth twins wanted something from him, and he wouldn't give it to them, and they were going to make him sorry, and that was why he met them there, because he was trying not to set them off. "No specifics?" she said. "Too upsetting," he said, and she left it at that. For the duration of their conversation. For the rest of the night, she considered the only possible specifics, which were sexual, and while his call essentially told her flat out that she was secure, she was wild-eyed with worry until dawn, when she finally realized that she could not live with being reassured.

She needs the voice of Vendetta. She wishes it didn't have to come from the actual person of Vendetta because it's a gift from her. But Ciana thinks that's the way life is for Vendetta, dispensing wisdom everywhere and getting a huge kick out of it. She's sure if she tries hard enough she can find some value for Vendetta in being with her. Lennon says that the three of them being interchangeable means the world to Vendetta and that's all she needs, but she's too inscrutable for Ciana to know. Ciana thinks lunch is a good idea. She can always tell if Vendetta appreciates what she eats.

All she says when Vendetta answers is, "Are you free today?" Ciana's her only white voice, at least the only one that doesn't ask for her by name.

"Oh, girl, what you need?"

"Nothing."

"I hear you. Neither me." She covers the receiver so her voice doesn't leak out. "What I really need, a child not so miserable all the time."

Ciana looks at the clock. It's eight-thirty. Vendetta shouldn't have a child in the house. She asks if Patricia's home. Ciana had to laugh when Vendetta first told her the child's name. She said she wanted a child with a name nobody could make her sorry over. Ciana didn't bother to tell her about the poor Patricia at Holy Name who accumulated rolls of fat and three nicknames when she got breasts.

"Yeah, she home. I'd say Quilica homeschooling her, but you know that's a story. What I'm a do? Quick tell all the children she got a peenie. The child can't go to school, everybody call her a morphodite. I'm suppose to prove different?"

"You have the federal government on your side," Ciana says.

"Aw, baby, ain't nobody got the federal government on their side. You watch the news?"

"Oh, they're too busy taking away your civil liberties. I don't think they've gotten down deep enough to your civil rights yet," Ciana says.

"Hmph, you ain't try to send no child to school next to the Calliope project. They got civil nothing over there."

Ciana never has understood why Vendetta insists on sending her child to that school. She knows Vendetta's mother thought it was a pretty swanky school to send Vendetta to because it had air conditioning, unlike the tumbledown wooden buildings that had stood there when she was a girl. Never mind that the same teachers with the same fistfuls of rulers and work sheets had moved from the old building right into the new, and some are still there. Vendetta thinks it's swanky enough to lie about her address. And she might have a point. Her neighborhood school is Lafayette, which is dying a little bit every day, being carried out with the sweeping compound.

Suddenly it seems like a good idea for Ciana to take Vendetta *and* Patricia to lunch. "What you mean, 'to lunch'?" Vendetta says. "You mean like I got to put clothes on her and comb her hair and everything? Tell you the truth, her staying home kind of a break. Some of these mamas, they send they children to school looking like they just crawl out the bed. Which matter of fact be true. But this girl not going nowhere except if she look like she ready for church." Ciana thinks about her mother's dying order.

"Aw, shit, Vendetta," Ciana says. "Tell you what. I'll come over there and get her ready. Let's take her out. I mean really out. Like the Windsor Court or something."

"You don't know nothing about combing no hair."

"I did Madeleine's hair."

"And that poor girl look like a baseball."

"Because she's white."

"Tell you what. Madeleine tell me, the other evening, the best time she ever have in her whole life, she eat all them buffalo wing on the floor by your mama house. I bet Patricia think that be pretty different, too. Long as it a onetime thing."

Ciana knows she is going to be slathered in dipping sauce and grease any time now, so she doesn't mind distracting herself with the books while she waits. Of all the physical labor in her mother's house, this should be the lightest, but it isn't. Her family had a startling number of books for people who never seemed to read. The work is going to be repetitive motion; she will feel it tomorrow.

The wall is all bookshelves, floor to ceiling, and they have filled up over her lifetime, so they've evolved into a backdrop that she's ceased to pay attention to. Now that she has to look at the particulars, she's grief-stricken. More than any other possessions, these books chronicle the part of her mother's life when Ciana knew her. She feels that each one should be looked at because each one has a reason for being there. If she can't figure out the reason, she can discard it.

Shelving is in order of acquisition, so her copy of *Horton Hatches the Egg* sits right next to her mother's copy of *The New Orleans Garden.* This is the point on Ciana's timeline that marks when her mother went wild over caladiums, narrowed down to when Ciana was a simple reader. All colors, all sizes; they came home with dozens of paper sacks full of knobby caladium bulbs and watched them take too much time to emerge into a showplace big enough for Ciana. She was satisfied with the emerging. Two books, good value. Actually three if she counts the book on the other side of the garden book. Ciana stuck *Candide* there after she read it in twelfth grade, trying to be deep. But that's a reflection on her, not on her mother, unless she counts the fact that her mother saw her do it and didn't roll her eyes.

Ciana has done one shelf out of thirty-two when Vendetta and Patricia arrive. Poor Patricia has had her hair all greased and rebraided, and she's not wearing clothes Ciana would wallow in ranch dressing in. Ciana leans over to kiss her and says loudly, "I'm calling Child Protective Services on your mama." Patricia grins; she is a very sharp girl.

Patricia is as creeped out by a dead person's house as Ciana's nieces and nephew are, even though she never knew the dead woman personally, so she can't be sent upstairs to rummage. Ciana thinks Patricia should go through her mother's clothes until she finds something she would like to dress up in for lunch. Patricia thinks she should lean against her own mother. Vendetta thinks the television would be a nice compromise. Ciana doesn't. She thinks a pile of formal dresses that have been worn once each, decades ago, should come downstairs, and Patricia can try them on. In front of the television if she wants. All Vendetta can think about is organza and barbeque sauce. Even though she has declared that her child can eat a wet mule and not spill a drop. All Ciana can think about is organza and barbeque sauce, and she thinks it's wonderful.

Until it's a reasonable time to eat, Vendetta watches Ciana fail miserably to make headway with the books. Ciana doesn't particularly want to take them home, but she feels she owes them a place where they can rest together as they've been all along, catalogued only by her family's frame of reference. Finally Vendetta says, "Tell you what. See how they got the title on the side?" Ciana nods. "Remember I told you, the only thing you ever need a throwaway camera? Take you a picture. One shelf, one picture. You get all your books on one roll of film. Then give the whole lot of them to the library. You want to visit, that's what the library for." This makes sense to Ciana. "Let me ask you," Vendetta says. "Your mama reading anything when she die?" Ciana nods. There was one book on her bedside table. Closed, but with a bookmark. Dying order. "Okay, you keep that book. Easy, huh?"

"Oh, God, no," Ciana says. That is the one book she absolutely cannot have in her house. Her mother was reading *The Art of Happiness* by the Dalai Lama. She was stuck on a chapter about compassion. Ciana can see where compassion might be linked to happiness, but that's not the route she wanted her mother to be taking at the very end. Anyone but her mother.

She only has been gone twenty minutes. She's gone to Walgreens instead of N.O. to get the roll of film developed because she didn't want to get ensnared in conversation. She left Vendetta and Patricia at their picnic site in the foyer playing Monopoly, Patricia still in the dress her mother wore to the Comus Ball in 1965. Patricia had managed not to spill one drop of food on it.

When she comes back, the house has four more people in it, and the only ones who are not crying are Geoffrey and Caroline. Vendetta isn't *spilling* tears, and her tears don't make her vulnerable, but she's crying all right.

"What the hell are you doing in here?" Ciana says to Geoffrey.

"I could ask you the same thing," Geoffrey says.

This is the time when Vendetta would be saying something arch and wonderful about Ciana having found family slaves under the floorboards, but Vendetta is in a mute rage the likes of which Ciana never has seen. And Vendetta has been called a lot of terrible names at the pharmacy. Especially by white people.

"You left them here by themselves," Geoffrey says.

"Well, so far all that's missing is Mama's jewelry and silver," Ciana says. She hears Vendetta sigh with vindication.

Geoffrey has no comeback because he has to dump his children on Ciana so he can take Corinne to the doctor. Ciana pulls him by the coat sleeve toward the front door, not kindly, because she can't shift that quickly. "I thought you two didn't believe in medical solutions," she whispers.

"I don't know what you're talking about," he says in a normal tone of voice.

"You know very well that you've stood right in front of my pharmacy and as good as called me a snake oil peddler."

"Yeah, for drugs."

Madeleine runs up with Ciana's purple satin prom dress, which on her will have draping shoulders and a train and much drama. "Can I?" she says. "May I?" Geoffrey says back. Ciana tells her she'll be gorgeous.

"Corinne is in horrible pain. I'm taking her because she can't move," Geoffrey says.

"You're not taking her to a shrink?"

"No!"

"Have you poked her where it hurts?"

"I don't have to stand here and listen to this."

Ciana hopes Vendetta is listening. That last line would make up for a lot.

"Listen, Geoffrey, I told you the other day, you're about to be a wealthy man. Not a ridiculously rich man, but a lot better off than these guys you try to run around with whose grandparents had too many children with no brains who all spent their inheritances and have nothing left but a French last name. If you need a full-time housekeeper, hire one. If you need a full-time housekeeper who drives, you can hire one and buy her a car. You do not need to keep bothering me. So you've got to ask yourself, why do you keep doing it?"

"If you resent my kids because you don't have any of your own, that's your problem," Geoffrey says. "Just don't take it out on me. And please don't take it out on them." With that he is out the door.

★

The girls have flounced around in ball gowns. Lucien has not, but only because the girls have locked him out of their dressing room. Instead he has earned ten dollars in Ciana and Vendetta's bucket brigade, unloading the top eight bookshelves. Half the time Ciana has been close to tears because she loves these children so much, and she wishes desperately that she didn't. Vendetta has been fanatical about time. She has been sure that Geoffrey will take exactly an hour and a half, the time it takes to pick up Corinne, wait for her during a psychiatrist's appointment, and drive her back home. When an hour has passed, she plucks Patricia out of her purple fantasy and has her running for the streetcar. She has no desire ever to lay eyes on F.B. again.

Geoffrey actually takes two hours, but Ciana hopes this just means the psychiatrist took extra time. She'd hate to think he chose some other kind of doctor. Geoffrey is such a literalist that she'd expect him to take her to a rheumatologist because she said she hurt all over. Corinne needs to talk.

Geoffrey is alone. Ciana has looked over his shoulder at the front door, and the van at the curb is dark and empty. She takes that to mean that he has time to come in and sit down. The children are at the dining room table doing their homework. Ciana tells him they had a snack an hour ago; they'll be hungry for dinner. He is not going to have a thing to complain about, because she's not an aunt who kills their appetites and spirits.

"You look like hell," she says to him and motions for him

to have a seat in the living room. He doesn't chafe at being treated like a guest in his childhood home. He seems to think Ciana sounds sympathetic. "Thanks," he says.

He cranes his neck to see whether the children can hear him if he speaks. He's flattering himself if he thinks they're interested, but Ciana doesn't tell him that. They haven't come right out and said to Ciana that they've had quite enough of their father for one day, thank you very much, but she and Vendetta overheard Caroline saying to Patricia, "My dad is, like, a different generation, so he is totally clueless about how people are supposed to act." There the three girls stood, pinching and tucking those old dresses into haute couture and trying to do runway moves with no breasts or guile to hold anything up, and they were, in effect, announcing that Ciana and Vendetta were anachronisms. Vendetta looked at Ciana and said, "Uh, *uh*." "What." "Maybe *he* born old and stupid, but you and me, we still got a clue."

"I'm glad you finally understand the agony I'm going through," Geoffrey says, settling into the sofa in a spot that might very well have a memory of him.

"Did I say that?" Ciana says.

Geoffrey sighs. Ciana has heard that sigh all her life, and she doesn't know how he figured out its impact when he was not yet in kindergarten. It is so eloquent, expressing contempt, exasperation, and a history of infinite patience that no one could possibly question. "Listen," he says, "you know I'm as liberal as the next guy, but even I have had enough."

"What?"

"This business of hanging around with black people," Geoffrey says. "It's understandable. If you can't make friends with socially acceptable people, you hang out with whoever will have you. And black people are always glad to have white friends."

"Oh, you mean like nerds in school gravitate toward other nerds?"

Geoffrey nods eagerly.

"Like Corinne and I were friends at Holy Name?"

Geoffrey does not look at all caught out. He looks impatient. "Being thin was a problem when Corinne was little. Now it's not. Being fat is something else."

"Get out of here," Ciana says.

"Look, all I want to tell you is to stay away from that person. He might have gone to school, but he is no good. He threatened my wife."

"You don't seem to mind his driving your children home from school."

Geoffrey doesn't hesitate. "They're not the ones he's after. Why do you think Corinne's so sick she can't eat or sleep? She's terrified. I don't know what he told her, but until you get rid of him Corinne's never going to get better. She's physically ill."

Ciana can believe him. Psychosomatic illness probably accounts for half of the business she does, if she thinks about it. And she thinks about it a lot.

"Goddammit, Geoffrey, if Corinne's sick she's no

fifteenth-century *saint* in some swoon. Lennon knows how Mama died. I don't, but only because Lennon knows I'd make somebody a lot sicker than Corinne claims to be."

"He's bullshitting you."

"I don't think so. I think Lennon told Corinne he knows something *she* did, and he scared the shit out of her."

"See how stupid you are?" Geoffrey is practically shouting. "He's after Mama's estate."

Ciana wishes she had a tape recorder. "Is that why you have all the jewelry?"

"Get rid of him," Geoffrey says. "We're worried about you."

VENDETTA knows in her heart that Patricia probably learns a lot more from watching Bob Barker on "The Price Is Right" than she ever learned sitting up in Mrs. Cole's classroom doing work sheets. She probably even learns more listening to Jaquilica reminisce over her arithmetic textbook. "This look like *algebra*," Jaquilica is saying over a problem in which Patricia has to supply the number which, when subtracted from fifteen, will leave nine. Vendetta is tempted to keep the child out of school this year, and possibly forever, except that she knows she will have to deal with people at the school board that make Mrs. Lawton look like a model of leadership. When Patricia has been out of school for six days with no call from the school asking about her absence, Vendetta gets herself as angry as possible and picks up the phone and dials.

It's hard to hold on to the anger when poor Mrs. Trotter answers the phone. Of course poor Mrs. Trotter would answer the phone. She is the secretary who does all the work at the school, and she alternately knows everything and nothing. Mrs. Trotter must weigh less than a hundred pounds, and Vendetta is sure it's because Mrs. Lawton never gives her time to eat, so it's hard to holler at the woman, even if she's the only message center for the bitch who deserves the hollering. "This Patricia Greene mother; has anyone notice she been absent?" Vendetta says.

Mrs. Trotter is silent. Just as Vendetta expected: Patricia is too well behaved to be a front-office regular.

"Never mind," Vendetta says. "She been out six days on account of she been sexually harass. I guess it too much to expect, somebody take care of a *good* child problem. You think Mrs. Lawton might want to call me before I call the school board?"

Vendetta has forgotten that little Mrs. Trotter routinely deals with mamas in all stages of withdrawal and children up all night staring at crime scenes. Nothing scares Mrs. Trotter except annoying Mrs. Lawton.

"Mrs. Lawton doesn't deal with problems. The counselor comes on Thursdays. You want an appointment?"

"Oh, Lord, it's gonna be a white girl nineteen years old don't know shit," Vendetta says.

Mrs. Trotter actually laughs a little. That means Vendetta's right.

Frieda is off on Thursdays, and it's a good thing, because she is driving Vendetta to the school, and she is going to stay there with her. *Right* with her, as the mother of the perpetrator. “If Patricia stay home, that mean you better not be dragging my Quick into this,” Frieda said when Vendetta told her what they were doing. That seemed like a fair enough plan. Patricia is never setting foot in that school again, and as for Quick, there is no room in which Vendetta desires his presence, not even the school principal’s.

Vendetta can’t help feeling a little sentimental, walking in the front door of the school with her sister, almost like they are children. It’s different from walking in with a child. The school was designed to seem large, with floor-to-ceiling numerals in the stairwells. It feels that way today with her sister; Vendetta thinks places from childhood are supposed to strike you as a lot smaller than they seemed when you were little. She’s as scared by it as she ever was. “Ooo, this place look tiny when I come in here with you,” Frieda says.

The counselor is sitting at a clean empty desk in a clean empty office. She is white and looks nineteen. Vendetta has to jostle Frieda to be able to walk in first. They have been sent in with nothing more than Mrs. Trotter saying, “Go on in”; Vendetta already can see where this is going. “I’m Patricia Greene mother,” she says. “I’m the auntie,” Frieda says. “She Quick Saunders mama, and he the one start this whole thing,” Vendetta says. The woman tells them both to take a seat. She doesn’t introduce herself.

“What seems to be the problem?” she says.

“The problem is, my child ought to be in school, and she not, and nobody doing nothing about it,” Vendetta says.

"She keeping her home," Frieda says.

"Hush up," Vendetta says.

"What's the matter with, um . . ." the woman says.

"My child name Patricia Greene," Vendetta says. "Don't you think it might be a good idea, you got a file on her or something?" The woman gets up to go to the outer office to ask Mrs. Trotter for a file, and Frieda says, "She useless as teats on a boar hog." "You, too," Vendetta says. The woman comes back, looks through Patricia's file, says, "Nothing seems to be wrong here."

"Not even that she absent?" Vendetta says.

"Not until next grading period," the woman says.

"Look, all the children calling my child a name, they calling her a morphodite on account of her cousin say she got a peenie, now what I want you to tell me is, how you make those children stop?" Vendetta says, and then she sees the expression on the woman's face and she adds, "No, she ain't got no peenie."

"I think you have to transfer her out of the school," the woman says. "And that might be a great opportunity for her." She looks at the file. "If you can get her out of this project environment eight hours a day, you'd broaden her horizons."

"What you talking about? That child don't live in no project," Frieda says.

Vendetta hopes what has just come over her sister is pride and not pure-dee meanness.

"You don't live on Erato Street?" the woman says to

Vendetta, referring to their brother's address that is on Patricia's census card. Another brother's address on Galvez is on Quick's.

Frieda still has not caught herself. "Shoot, no, she live on Burdette Street. Her and Patricia got the whole half a double."

The woman stands up. "Sounds like you've got your problem solved."

Vendetta doesn't utter a sound until they are in the car. "I'm a kill you."

"What," Frieda says.

"What my fucking ass. For starts, you should be on your bony knees thanking me. They putting *my* child, the one never done a thing wrong, in Lafayette, because *you* walk in there and good as holler that I'm lying about her address. And who lying-ass child, with his lying-ass address, still going to Sylvania? Your'n. Know why? Because I sat right there and ain't say a word."

"Thank you," Frieda says.

"Aw, shut up," Vendetta says. "Take me to the library."

It is almost worth having the whole day go wrong just to see Frieda in the public library. She has nothing to do. She acts like every item in the place has Arabic writing on it and would be no good to look at, so she just strolls around trying not to look stupid. It's hard for Vendetta to concentrate on the computer, especially when there's so much information she needs to write down, and she can only find those little slips they give you to write down book numbers on. She wishes she had the nerve to buy a computer for herself and Patricia, but she knows it would have viruses and gay pornography and a drowned keyboard in a week from everybody else in the house. Before Frieda can become the first conspicuous loiterer in the Nix Branch Library, Vendetta manages to get a fistful of notes on how to be a homeschooling parent in Louisiana. She doesn't think she can stomach it. Nothing she's read says it in so many words, but she thinks she is going to have to become very bored, sincere, and Christian. She doesn't want that for herself or Patricia.

"You know, we could get good money for the house," Vendetta says in the car.

"I hear what you trying to say," Frieda says. "Why you don't just move out?"

"Because I want my share."

"You probably thinking your share half the whole place, right?"

That's exactly what Vendetta is thinking. She has been reading the Real Estate section of the paper for as long as she can remember because it is the most interesting part aside from the obituaries. A person can know more gossip in New Orleans reading those two sections than even by having a thousand friends. Somebody once told her that she should read the bankruptcies listings, but the print is way too small. The Real Estate listings for the seventh district lately have been showing that houses like hers can get over two hundred thousand. Vendetta figures she gets at least half since she pays the taxes and insurance and fixes everything that breaks. With her half and a little mortgage, she can get a little condo out by the lake. She's seen them in the second district.

"Mama ain't leave no will," Frieda says. "That house belong to all of us. The boys, too. Your part maybe the size of your kitchen. You want to sell that, you walk away with jack shit. Matter of fact, I been wondering how long it gonna be before the boys get tired of letting us live in there rent free. You better keep your mouth shut."

Vendetta walks into her kitchen with the realization that she will probably never, as long as she lives, be able to walk around naked in her own home. She will stay in this half of the house forever, with people who pick at her and damage her, and unless Patricia grows up and becomes very rich, she will die here. An old woman with no privacy, who will mess herself and babble, and her sisters and their terrible sons will stand around and look at her. She walks into the kitchen with no hope, and Everett is waiting for her. "That man you work with, he sure is nasty," he says. He pushes a fistful of torn pieces of newspaper at her.

It all looks like nothing to Vendetta, like the parts of the paper she would use if she had to put something on the floor to protect it. Classifieds. "What this is?"

"He running ads all over the place. *Gambit*. *Ambush*. *Times-Picayune*. And you know what he looking for? A white boy. That's why he ain't talk to me. He looking for a white boy." Everett shoves a page in front of her, and she reads a circled ad. She can't deny it's Lennon. Good-looking, brown-skinned, dreadlocks, uptown pharmacy intern, mid-twenties, Memphis native. With a post office box on McAlister Drive. And a zip code of 70118. Looking to meet white counterpart. "Lennon don't live on no McAlister Drive," she says. "Nobody live in a post box," Everett says.

Vendetta has lived in New Orleans all her life, and she's never heard of McAlister Drive. Maybe this is some gay thing. But Everett never has heard of it, either. Frieda should know it if anyone does. It's Frieda's job to know the streets. "Frieda!" Vendetta calls, for once grateful that her sister is close by.

Frieda knows very well where McAlister Drive is. She works that area all the time. That's the street that runs through the Tulane campus. "Oh, yeah, all the kids got mailboxes there. They run you *down* at lunchtime."

This is the first time Frieda has been useful in as long as Vendetta can remember. Vendetta might owe her for this one, but she'll never say so.

25

IF ASKED, Lennon would say that the single factor that has driven his every decision in life has been deviancy. Or deviation. He's never been sure of the difference. All he's known is that variance from the norm always has given him such a high level of discomfort that he will do anything to avoid it. He knows if he told Ciana this she would say that she has too many standard deviations away from average for him to like her, and he would have to explain to her why she is a perfect specimen of symmetry and therefore beautiful—so he never has told her. Instead he quietly lives every day fighting disorder and pathogens and fever. In the past twenty-four hours, though, everything has spun out of control in the way people are behaving. He's pretty sure it's the general lawlessness of

New Orleans, but he thought it never was going to affect him personally. Last night Vendetta called him and told him somebody at Tulane was running classified ads saying he was gay, and he knew that meant two girls from Memphis had been in town less than one school year and were getting him in a world of trouble. He has managed to sleep in two-hour cycles of mystification, and when he wakes up Ciana is calling to say that Corinne just has made the feeblest suicide attempt in pharmaceutical history.

"She took a whole bottle of Advil," Ciana says. "But get this. She does it right before Geoffrey brushes his teeth, so he sees the empty bottle with the box and the cotton, and even he's capable of figuring out that sixty pills have disappeared in a matter of minutes. Though for all he knows, fifty-nine went down the toilet."

"Sounds like she finally got medication into herself that'll help her," Lennon says.

Ciana says that yes, Corinne is at the mighty Baptist, pumped full of charcoal and not needing a pathologist to check for blood levels, but being kept for observation. Ciana takes this to mean that the ER doctors think she should be under the supervision of professionals, not Geoffrey.

"I'll go with you to see her," Lennon says.

"I was going to see her?" Ciana says.

Lennon looks at his watch. She has called him with plenty of time to visit before they have to be at work. If not on a conscious level, Ciana definitely has intended for them to do this on a subliminal one.

The thing he likes about hospitals is that they make people sitting ducks. Only patients under death threats have guards at the door; the rest just sit up there in their beds like merchandise on the seasonal specials aisle, with rapid turnover. He and Ciana can go see Corinne without invitation or authorization. As he goes through the lower corridor of the hospital, he passes the gift shop and sees Ciana inside; she is holding up two stems of stargazer lilies. When he walks up to her, she says, "The issue surely isn't the price." Even though they are ten dollars a stem. She twirls one, and the scent fills the tiny shop. She takes two, and a vase.

"You know," Ciana says, "this is probably the first time in my whole scientific life that I'm going on instinct. I can't give you one good reason why seeing Corinne is a good idea. For all I know, Geoffrey's up there, though I doubt it. I bet that even if Corinne died last night, he'd have gone to work this morning because he thinks that's what he's supposed to do."

"I know exactly why you're here," Lennon says. "Corinne is under the influence."

Ciana knocks at the partially open door. No one responds, so they walk in. The bed closer to the door is empty, and a curtain screens Corinne's bed. Ciana has the flowers arranged nicely in the vase with greens and a huge pink satin ribbon, and when she gets up to the curtain she reaches around it with the hand holding the vase so all Corinne can see if she's looking are the lilies. They wait a few seconds, and then they hear Corinne's voice, slow and sleepy. "Holy. Shit."

Lennon follows Ciana as she steps into view and says in a Hannibal Lecter voice, "Hello, Corinne."

Corinne is stoned blind. Whatever they have given her, they'd better give her another dose fairly soon, or she's going to be cranky and not as tractable as Lennon wants her to be. But right now her eyes are half closed, and she has a dreamy little smile on her face. Ciana whispers in Lennon's ear, "I bet I could go up and tickle her and she'd kick off the sheets like she's thrilled out of her mind, and she'd act like I'm her best friend."

"So this is what it takes," Corinne says with a drawl. She sees both Lennon and the deadly stargazer lilies, but she doesn't care.

"Sure," Ciana says, having no idea what Corinne is talking about.

"Geoffrey says you don't care if I live or die," Corinne says. She shifts around and moans a little. Then she looks at Lennon. "And he thinks you want to kill me. Pretty good, huh." She lowers her voice to a confidential whisper. "But Geoffrey doesn't trust black people."

Lennon doesn't know exactly what sedative is working these miracles on Corinne's personality, but he hopes the veracity part sticks for about ten minutes. "So, what have you told him about me?" he says jovially.

Corinne rolls dramatically slowly in the bed. "Now you know I'm not telling you that in front of Ciana," she says. He could swear she almost sounds flirtatious. "I wouldn't want to make her *sad*."

"Don't worry, I know it all already," Ciana says. "I just want to know why."

Lennon would love to give Ciana a great big squeeze right now. She is an improvisational genius.

"You told Ciana her mother fell on the rocks in Central Park and not in FAO Schwartz?" Corinne says.

All the blood drains from Lennon's head, and if Corinne had her eyes open she would find out what it means for a black person to look pale. He tries not to look at Ciana to see if she, too, feels like keeling over. All he knew was Central Park. *Ground level* in Central Park. The rocks in Central Park must be two stories high. At least they seemed that way to him when he climbed them as a child.

"The rocks in Central Park?" Ciana says.

Corinne closes her eyes.

Lennon gestures with his hands, high, wide.

"I want to know *why*," Ciana says, a tremor in her voice, and Corinne's eyes fly open, her expression one of puzzlement, because all her mind holds is the *why*.

"What?" Corinne says, with great eagerness to cooperate.

"*What* was my mother doing climbing the rocks in Central Park?" Ciana says.

"You don't know your mother very well, do you," Corinne says. "She *needed* to climb those rocks."

"Tell me," Lennon says softly, pushing a thoroughly riled Ciana to the side a little, for the sake of them all.

Corinne actually gets up on one elbow and speaks loudly to the completely sympathetic-looking Lennon.

"Three days in New York with that woman. Just what I expected. Not a generous bone in her body." She flops back, worn out. But now she speaks to the ceiling, slurring like a drunk. "Like it's always been. Never about me. Always about Ciana. All the way up there, Ciana, Ciana. The woman had a credit card with no limit. I'd be *wonderful* to shop for. Got a knockoff Burberry scarf for seven dollars. On the sidewalk. Shit."

Lennon suddenly realizes he is not playing around with a simple family drama, or with a large family drama. If he is following Corinne's train of greed, she is confessing to manslaughter triggered by a fit of spoiled temper, and this is deviation he hates to be a part of. "Ciana, this is worse than I imagined," he says.

"She didn't push her," Ciana whispers, trying to convince herself more than him.

"Hmm?" Corinne says. Her eyes are closed, but she is smiling to show she is alert.

"You feel better now?" Lennon says to Corinne. Ciana is across the bed from him, mouthing something that he cannot interpret. He furrows his brow, asking for a repetition. "Don't say anything," Ciana says, this time almost aloud.

"I don't like the looks of this," Geoffrey says, having walked in behind him.

Geoffrey edges Lennon aside, not roughly, not even brusquely, but meaningfully, and he shakes Corinne's shoulder. "You okay, Corinne? Wake up. Wake *up*." Corinne opens one eye with enormous effort, sees Geoffrey, and with what looks like terrific wisdom to Lennon, slams that eye shut. "What'd you do to her?" Geoffrey says, eyeing the flowers.

"We made her feel better," Ciana says. Only Lennon catches her tone.

"You two work in a *drugstore,*" Geoffrey says. "If somebody writes something on a piece of paper, you know how many pills to put in a bottle. The only thing you know how to do is kill somebody." He picks up the vase with the lilies in it and starts to carry it out to the nurses' station.

"I bought that in the gift shop," Ciana says. "They don't sell poison in the gift shop."

Geoffrey doesn't leave, but he doesn't put the vase back down, either.

"Corinne talked to us," Ciana says. "You might think about the therapeutic benefits of her talking."

Lennon tries to shake his head, no, in a way that Ciana can see him and Geoffrey can't, but he has a feeling even Corinne is aware of his movement. He has been watching Corinne's body language, no small trick when she's playing dead. When she was truly giving in to the drugs, her breathing was slow and steady, and her expression had the innocence of the unconscious, but now she's listening: he can see a slight raggedness in her breathing, a small frown, a flare of nostrils that are straining to keep her ears open. She, too, is hoping desperately that Geoffrey will not become a listener.

"We go to church," Geoffrey says. "We don't need therapy."

Lennon moves just slightly to block the monitor that

shows Corinne's vital signs. He knows his own just slipped into the range of readiness to pop.

Geoffrey follows them into the hallway, still clutching the vase full of lilies. "I'm going to need you with us for Easter," he says to Ciana.

"If you said you wanted me, I'd feel better," Ciana says. It sounds like a *no* to Lennon.

"Okay, I want you with us for Easter."

Lennon steps forward, thinking without thinking. "Ciana hasn't given me a definitive answer yet, but I've invited her up to Memphis to meet my family," he says. As soon as the words are out, he congratulates himself on how quickly he built in a loophole for Ciana. At the same time he feels lousy. This was supposed to be a terribly romantic invitation, a milestone that maybe would become anecdotal because he would do it cleverly. This doesn't seem like the right kind of clever.

Lennon could swear Geoffrey's expression says, *Black people do not have families.* "I'm glad I mentioned it before you made plans," Geoffrey says to Ciana.

In the car, Ciana asks Lennon why he doesn't want Geoffrey to know about the rocks in Central Park. That is how they are going to refer to her mother's death from now on, the rocks in Central Park. Because of the rocks in Central Park, Corinne deserves no spoils. No silver or jewelry or her half of half of the estate. "She doesn't deserve to lie in the bed,"

Ciana says. "She should be lifting books off high shelves and wiping out corners of closets that haven't been seen since the 1950s. She needs punishment greater than anything meted out by the Catholic Church." The car is filling up with rage.

"Would you want to know what happened?" he says.

Ciana thinks about it. "Of course I should want to know what happened. But it would *feel* better not knowing and pretending it was an accident. As compared to some purposeful act. I mean, imagine how my mother would have felt, knowing even for one second. I don't like to think about her feelings being hurt like that. *That's* almost what makes me the angriest at Corinne. The idea of hurting Mama's feelings."

"And if you were Geoffrey?" Lennon says.

Lennon can sense Ciana going through all the permutations and combinations of knowing how her mother died; he sees washes of anger and sadness. "Oh," she says. And then, "But you know, Geoffrey might not think Corinne's the villain no matter what."

"But if he does?" Lennon says.

"At the very least, he'll leave her."

"And then?"

"All I care about are the children."

26

When N.O. had to have each customer sign a HIPAA release last year, a woman named Jane came into the pharmacy and said, "Well, of course I'll sign. But as for confidentiality, you know so much about me that if I had any worries I'd have to kill you." She's one of Ciana's favorite customers. Ciana's watched her graduate from just Prozac all the way up to a cocktail of Cymbalta, Topamax, and Seroquel, and Jane would be the first to confess that she no longer exists. Thanks to psychopharmacology, she has no shame and therefore no secrets. Ciana wants everyone to be like her. Today Jane is in the waiting area. Ciana has noticed that she's content just to sit there, physically healthy and not bored and perfectly shameless, and if she could, Ciana would go out and ask her the secret of shamelessness. Jane would probably say, “I think it’s the Topamax,” and Ciana would tell her to give herself more credit. Though Ciana might consider Topamax if she ever got past that *medice cura te ipsum* business she prides herself on. If physicians can’t heal themselves, it only follows that pharmacists can’t medicate themselves, either.

Except that Ciana definitely is going to go to Memphis, and she needs shamelessness *right now*. When she didn’t tell Lennon yes right away, he said, “I know your reluctance has nothing to do with Geoffrey,” and she said, “Maybe,” and he said, “Bullshit. My parents will think you’re beautiful,” and she laughed. But she knows without asking that Lennon’s mother doesn’t have an extra ounce of fat on her. She knows, too, that if his mother is old enough to be his mother, she is probably a product of something other than the bourgeoisie, and that means she once mingled with black people who knew everything there was to know about fat. She will know what *kind* of a fat person Ciana is; Ciana is sure black people have a taxonomy of fat the way Eskimos have a taxonomy of snow. Now that half of America is said to be obese and not just poor blacks in the South, the nuances will work their way into the mainstream, but for now Ciana is the type of fat person who pretends no one can tell she has pudding sacks for thighs and a belly that hangs down so she has to sling it into her panties. She has fat parts she tries to hide from people. Ciana can be judged. Not aesthetically. Morally.

For an ungodly person, Ciana is going into Easter feeling like a girl with a lot of confessing to do. Even if it's only confessing what she's hiding under her clothes, and that's no sin; only the pride part is. She always has felt that the best way to become an atheist is to have a Catholic education, and in that respect her mother succeeded with her, at least on the deity idea, all three parts of it. Of course, her mother saw only that she succeeded with Geoffrey, who's been a true Catholic siring his own little true Catholics until he and his true Catholic wife came to some true Catholic understanding about birth control. Ciana and Geoffrey see Easter very differently. He sees it as the most important holiday of the year, marking the resurrection of his Lord. Ciana sees it as the time when the seasonal specials aisle is loaded with jelly beans. She can't very well argue that point with him when he's so recently orphaned and has a wife in the hospital. Even though he probably wants her to stay home in great measure so she can hand out candy.

Before she had so many other options, Ciana planned to spend Easter cleaning out her mother's bathrooms. She figured each one counted as a room, and she would have a sense of accomplishment, ticking them off her list. Bathrooms would be easy because there would be so little to dither over; not much is worth having secondhand. And everything is diminutive. Medications and cosmetics have short shelf lives; no one buys them in bulk. And everyone's fickle about bathroom products; who would commit to a caseload of deodorant when a new and improved version might come out in six months? She intended to go into each bathroom with two small garbage bags and remove everything. She might have kept a bottle of Charlie perfume if she'd found it because that was what her mother smelled like, but she could have put it in her purse, and that would have been easy. She figured that pushed back on the shelves were going to be explanations of how her parents groomed themselves, but she would look at each item as a relic of drugstore history, straight razors and douche bags and Vaseline.

It doesn't seem to Ciana that deciding to go to Memphis instead of sorting through her mother's bathroom memories or filling in for her mother's murderer is an unreasonable choice for Easter. But when she calls Geoffrey at his office to tell him her decision, he acts as if she is refusing to perform some sacrament.

"This is our first holiday without Mama," he says.

She tells him that she knows, that she originally planned to spend it going through their mother's bathrooms, stripping her of her last vestiges of privacy. He ignores this statement, and Ciana would like to think it's because he can't allow himself to consider his mother's privacy. "I could spend some other time with the kids," Ciana says.

"I want you to take Mama's place *on* Easter," he says solemnly, as if he is bestowing a great honor on Ciana.

"Geoffrey, a grandmother is not like a guinea pig that you can go replace quick before they come home from school and find out it's dead."

"Oh, I don't mean that crap. I just mean how she liked

getting them their Easter clothes and coming with us to church and everything."

Ciana happens to know that her mother chafed at taking the children to The Esplanade every year to buy their Easter clothes. She would have done anything for those children, and she would have done even more for their spiritual lives, but she thought it should have been her own idea. Somewhere along the line, before Lucien was born, the annual trek had become her responsibility, with specific accessories, specific stores, specific designers, and her mother had said to her, "This is not what a grandmother does." Ciana wonders what pronouncement her mother made on the top of the rocks in Central Park.

"I buy them candy," Ciana says. "I'll still buy them candy. If there's a God, he probably sees mysterious perfection in the jelly bean. He does not see it in Ralph Lauren."

"You're a bad influence anyway," Geoffrey says, and he hangs up.

Ciana learns far more about Lennon's parents by pestering him about a house gift than she could by any other means. Her usual way of being the guest is to play the New Orleans card, to arrive with all the clichés, usually food. Pralines are the easiest, though she's noticed over the years that they are an unerring failure: people are curious, yes, but they take one bite and cannot in good conscience imagine taking another. Eating pralines is like drinking condensed milk. It's too wrong. Ciana has debarked from planes lugging boxes of live, scrabbling crawfish, a dramatic and thoroughly annoying gesture for any host, who must immediately scare up a large pot and who can only hope garbage pick-up is the next morning. Lennon vetoes food. Period. His parents buy everything at Wild Oats. And they think everything ethnic is plain rude. Coming from Ciana, he doesn't need to add, it would not be helpful.

A plant? For eight hours in a Miata? "I wish we still lived in ashtray times," Ciana says. A picture frame with a photo of Lennon? "Ask yourself if you think they want their friends to know about these," Lennon says, fingering his dreads. Ciana settles on an unopened bottle of Chivas Regal she found that her father saved for years. Lennon says his parents will make it last for a long time, as if that explains why it is a fine gift. "Aren't they Baptists?" she says. In public, he says. She dusts it in full daylight.

The whiskey bottle is sitting next to the motel TV where Ciana has her purse and room key so she won't forget it when Lennon comes to pick her up. They have driven all day, and for the two of them the effects work in opposite ways. Their heads hum, and the lines that define them are fuzzy, and while Lennon is protected, Ciana is not. He wants to evade comment from his family by being vague. Ciana wants to be sharp, with long, intricate, coherent sentences; she wants to look bright, with primary colors and clearly delineated perimeters, like a good lipstick line and a bold pattern in her dress. She doesn't feel such possibilities at dusk in Memphis after they have set out in the morning in New Orleans.

Lennon's parents cannot be fooled by Nookie's disguise because they already have seen his vest on a Chihuahua that they barely tolerated. So Nookie is going to have to stay in the room alone with the television set on HBO. Ciana figures he's best off with voices that aren't interrupted by laugh tracks. She can't imagine what a laugh track does to a dog's central nervous system, but she imagines it's not pretty. She doesn't want Nookie broken of his muteness. Particularly in a motel where she hasn't mentioned his presence. Still, it's better than leaving him home with Vendetta, who's housesitting. Vendetta is there to escape her family, but there's no telling how successful she'll be. That nephew Quick would leave Nookie a paraplegic, and he wouldn't do it on purpose, either.

When Lennon walks in, they're both in front of the mirror, and they both look good, and he smells terrific, and there's a bed behind them, its headboard visible in the mirror for whatever that's worth, and Ciana thinks at least they can kiss for a long, long time. She tiptoes up to kiss him, and he kisses her back, but then she makes the mistake of opening one eye and seeing them in the mirror, and even though she closes it fast, she still sees them and the incongruity of them, and she backs away and says, "All right." "Time to go," he whispers. From now on, the only person in the relationship Ciana is looking at is Lennon.

Of all places the Israels live in an area called Germantown, and Ciana asks if that means anything. Israel sounds so ungodly, and right now it sounds too Jewish. Lennon says that living in Germantown means they have more of a sense of humor than Ciana has been suspecting. And? "And when you walk through their door they're not going to keel over in shock." She wonders if he's told them anything other than the fact that she's white. She has a few other characteristics that are probably also hereditary and not altogether pleasant.

His parents' house is two-story brick, neocolonial, a huge structure on a huge lot, and almost identical to every other house on its street to Ciana's urban eye. It looks lovesick, sort of like her purple prom dress. She doesn't want to feel sorry for his house.

She tells herself it's worth well over three-quarters of a million dollars, but she only feels sadder.

A little bronze plaque, mounted next to the doorbell, reads HOUSE OF ISRAEL. Lennon sees her noticing it. "I told you they have more of a sense of humor than you think."

He rings the bell. "You don't have a key?" Ciana says. Just to the back door, he tells her. He has his hands clasped behind him, and he's bouncing a little on the balls of his feet; he's taking this moment very seriously. And it's not just his parents he's worried about. Somehow Ciana is not calmed by this notion.

A young black woman in a maid's uniform answers the door. Ciana hasn't seen anyone in a maid's uniform since she was a child, except for the occasional companion to some very old woman who insists on coming into the pharmacy for her Coumadin. Those women's uniforms usually have seen better days and are worn only to please a mistress with cataracts. But this poor woman has to use spray starch and an iron. Ciana sees no humor so far. "Your mother says to wait in the library," the woman says to Lennon. If she could, Ciana would pray for there to be no fireplace, and no roaring fire.

But of course there is. The fire isn't roaring, because a gas log is as controlled as it needs to be in this house, but it's cranked up to high. Ciana feels like a character in a penny dreadful. Wood paneling, moss green velvet drapes, lithographs of hunt scenes, a full wall of double-wide books. But the dust jackets aren't new. Herman Wouk. James Michener. Leon Uris. "They've all been read," Lennon says. Ciana scans further. She doesn't find James Baldwin or Richard Wright. But she doesn't find Margaret Mitchell, either. "Sit," Lennon says finally.

Ciana probes for the umpteenth time about Lennon's parents. She can recall that his father is a dentist, and it's easy to attach to that the fact that his mother doesn't have to do anything. But she forgets what she does instead of nothing. She writes novels, but she's not a novelist. No wonder Ciana can't wrap her mind around that. "My mother's not the one to ask for an explanation," Lennon says.

The door opens, and his mother sweeps in. She really does; though she is model-thin, her sleeves and skirt cut her a broad swath through the double doorway, and neither Ciana nor Lennon possibly can rise gracefully. "Victoria Israel," she says, extending her hand to Ciana. Ciana almost thrusts the

Chivas Regal bottle into her outstretched hand, but she does a nifty quick switch and gives her a cool well-lotioned palm. "Luciana Jambon," she says. "But everyone calls me Ciana." Evidently everyone calls Mrs. Israel "Mrs. Israel."

Ciana has a feeling Lennon's mother regrets the choice of the library for the dimness of the lighting. Ciana is in the paddock, and Mrs. Israel must decide whether to bid at the auction. The conformation is easy to see through the sheath dress, but not the molars, the hair texture, the skin pigment. Ciana can't think about what she is saying, she is trying so hard to show off her good eugenic qualities. No silver in the back of her mouth because she's paid for three crowns; no crowding because she had braces. Swingy hair because she went outside N.O. Drugs for Paul Mitchell products. Skin she's not sure about because skin has different qualities, the shade on the palette and the age it reveals; white cracks. Ciana grins and tosses and gleams and hopes Mrs. Israel thinks being fat is an environmental condition, and it takes a while to realize that Mrs. Israel, too, is grinning and tossing and gleaming. Ciana catches a quick glimpse of Lennon. He looks as pleased as any man would when two women are fighting for his love. She thinks her expression says to him that she and his mother are going to love him together. "I'd like to see one of your novels," Ciana says.

"What's that supposed to mean?" Mrs. Israel says.

Ciana thinks she is going to wet her pants.

She looks at Lennon, who seems to be straining with all he's got to make her remember something that she never knew to begin with. "I'm sorry," Ciana finally says when Lennon has not come to her rescue, "I'm a dull scientist. I don't know what to say to an artist."

Mrs. Israel actually smiles. And this time she is not showing off her anthropological superiority and marital status that resulted in good dentition. She is smiling as if she has not had an ally since she moved into her house. "My husband's a dentist, you know," she says, and she sounds as if she is in an Al-Anon meeting admitting something far worse, though being married to a dentist sounds about as bad as it can get, unless having showy teeth matters. "I don't know how to tell him the difference between writing and having written."

"You don't know how to tell *me* the difference, either," Lennon says.

Ciana gets it right away. She writes novels. She doesn't publish them. Or maybe the publishing industry doesn't publish them because they're god-awful. It doesn't matter. She gets out of bed.

When Dr. Israel comes in, and he's two inches shorter than his wife and fat as a tick, Ciana is not surprised.

She overhears Mrs. Israel say to him when she thinks Ciana and Lennon aren't paying attention, "I think those Hollingsworth girls might be full of c-r-a-p."

"I really like you," Ciana whispers to Mrs. Israel when they are called in to dinner. Even though it's going to be served by the maid.

VENDETTA can't imagine anywhere feeling more Christian than N.O. Drugstore on Easter Sunday. Very soft Simon and Garfunkel music is playing, and Patricia is in her Easter dress in the waiting area with the biggest basket the store carries sitting on the chair next to her. Patricia has not broken through the purple cellophane to take even one candy, but she's not deprived. All morning people have been treating the basket like a Christmas tree, placing little paid-for presents on the chair next to it, Gold Brick eggs and plastic SpongeBob SquarePants containers of candy. Mid-morning Mr. Walker gave Patricia a coloring book and a box of sixty-four crayons, and Patricia started on page one like it was her job. Vendetta doesn't tell her that Mr. Walker is not the boss because Patricia looks very happy being a worker. And that is a lot better than feeling like the baby Jesus, which is what she said she felt like when the candy first started rolling in. Vendetta wasn't in the mood to explain that the baby Jesus had done a lot of growing up by the time Easter came along, so she let it slide. Come to think of it, Easter colors are better baby Jesus colors, and Christmas colors would work fine for this part of Jesus's life, at least for Good Friday. Vendetta is thinking too hard, but then business is naturally going to be slow on a day like today, and thinking hard fills in.

Patricia has a peanut butter sandwich and an apple in a paper sack for her lunch. So does Vendetta. That is a sorry excuse for an Easter dinner, but Vendetta will make it up to both of them this evening some kind of way. It won't be easy, because she is trying to leave no traces of herself in Ciana's house, but she is going to give Patricia some kind of pig meat, even if it's only a hot dog.

Vendetta is about to go out and set up a little lunch picnic for Patricia when Les, the security guard, strolls into the store. The place is so empty that Vendetta can see him on the security mirror almost as soon as he comes in the front door. He heads straight for the pharmacy. "Anybody cutting up today ought to be shame of himself," Les says to explain his absence from the parking lot. Everyone within three aisles just looks at him. Everyone consists of about five people, including Patricia and Vendetta, but it's enough to make Les self-conscious. "I been thinking," he says in Patricia's direction. "Any beautiful young lady feel like coming with me to Burger King?"

"No, thank you," Patricia says, but she says it with the expression of a girl who has only a peanut butter sandwich.

"I'm a treat you," Les says.

Vendetta thinks she's never going to be able to laugh at Les again. This is really a good Easter at N.O. Drugs. And to think it was founded by two old Jews, at least that was the story she read in the paper one time. "Aw, no, I'll give her five dollars, thank you, Les," Vendetta says.

Patricia is very intent on coloring an entire bunny pink, including the insides of his ears. She does not look up. "No thank you very much."

Les folds his arms and looks smarter than he ever has before. "Tell you what," he says. "You say what you want. I'll bring it back. How about that?"

That works. Patricia can look at Les just fine, and Patricia can order more than five dollars' worth of food, and when Les has left the building Patricia can explain. "He *big*, Mama," she says. "I don't know how to talk to no mens."

Each time they have walked into Ciana's house, Vendetta has said, "Act like you a burglar." They don't tiptoe, but they try not to leave fingerprints. Vendetta has brought her own sheets to replace Ciana's sheets, and her own towels and pots. She can get plates and glasses clean enough. She wants Ciana to come back and say, "Are you sure you stayed here?"

Each time Vendetta tells Patricia to act like a burglar in

Ciana's house, Patricia has said, "I act like a burglar in my *own* house, Mama."

Today has become the day to call Robert. It is Easter, and Patricia has as good as come out and said she is ruined about men. Vendetta puts on her Easter dress because making this call is going to be as holy as going to church. She worked today so she could stay away from her family, which meant not going to church. She puts on makeup and pantyhose and heels, and she tells Patricia to settle in by the TV; dinner will be ready after a while. And then she goes into Ciana's bedroom, checks herself in the mirror, and phones.

He is home; he answers right away. "Hey," she says. He has no idea who it is. "You don't recognize me?" she says.

"I think I know the voice, but the Caller ID say L. Jambon."

"It's me," she says.

"Something the matter?" he says.

Vendetta hesitates. "Kind of. But not really." Robert is completely quiet, but she can read his quietness. She gets on his nerves very easily since she threw him out. "I mean, Patricia got a little problem. Now you know she always got a little problem because everybody always got a little problem, but evidently this one the kind maybe I need to talk to you about or why I would be calling?"

"Chill, Vendetta, I ain't hanging up on you."

Vendetta takes a deep breath, but she does it with the phone away from her mouth so he can't hear her. "Okay, look. This morning, this very nice man, a man I trust, mind you, say he take her to Burger King, and she act like he going to take her in the woods and kill her."

"Sound to me like you got cable," Robert says.

Vendetta has to smile. She has to admit that Robert has a lot of good points. "Sound to me like the child scare of men. On account of she don't know none."

"It just so happen," he says, "I been standing in the Shell station on Claiborne and know what I seen? Now tell me I'm wrong, on account of I ain't seen the child in a while, but I swear that been Patricia, big as life, riding up in some cheap little sport car with what look to me very much like a man."

"You crazy?" Vendetta says. "I don't know no men."

"Well, he coming in the direction of where you work at, and he got a big head full of dreads. Acting like he your husband, driving your child around and everything. I swear, if I'd've been paying at the pump, I'd've been right after him."

"For what?"

"Never mind," Robert says.

Vendetta feels a wave of sadness come over her, and she feels herself starting to perspire, wrecking up her Easter dress. She'd like to take it off, but there's no way to do it now. "Tell you the truth, that *was* Patricia, come to think of it. But that just Lennon. He ain't studying about me; he getting his doctoral degree and he got a white girlfriend. He don't scare Patricia none."

"Probably because he don't scare you none."

Vendetta tries to figure out if Les scares her. She's never noticed until today that he's actually a man. "Don't start psychoanalyzing me," she says. "Start thinking about Patricia before she need a psychiatrist."

"What you want? You want money?" Robert says.

"Hush up," Vendetta says, and she hopes he can't hear her thinking that, yes, on top of everything else, it would solve a lot of problems if she had just enough money for rent.

"What I'm a do, call the child up and say, 'Oh, honey, your mama tell me go away, I'm a bad influence, now she think I'm a good influence'?"

Vendetta did say that. She thought Robert was a bad influence because Robert fought with her sisters all the time. Robert didn't say anything in his defense; Frieda and Jaquilica, on the other hand, presented argument after argument in favor of his eviction. Deep voice, scary. Occasional beer, lowlife. Mid-range salary, useless. Influence over Vendetta, eventual ruination. By the time Robert moved out, Vendetta was convinced that she was well rid of him.

"I could tell her I made a mistake," Vendetta says.

"You doing this without thinking."

"You right," Vendetta says. "But I think Patricia got to get to know you."

Vendetta has given up on looking holy and fresh for Easter, but she has not given up on a good-looking Easter dinner for Patricia. The Sav-A-Center was still open when they left the store, and she has frozen roasted pork dinners for both of them. They looked good on the package. In her own house she would have fixed up a rack of pork ribs, but the grease would go into Ciana's air. She let Patricia have the half-off cake shaped like a bunny head. They are never going to eat even a whole ear of that thing.

This is the first Easter Vendetta can remember when she is not eating in the middle of the day after going to church with everybody in her house. Easter dinner is always good with Frieda and Jaquilica because they are full of the Lord and they serve everybody right, and Vendetta goes through the whole time full of the sweet spirit of the holiday. She wants to be smart this year, and that is why she's at Ciana's house. Vendetta has to get away from Frieda and Jaquilica. Well, really, if she thinks about it, she has to get away from Frieda. Jaquilica is just extra. Trouble, but just extra.

They are eating in the kitchen, and all the lights in the rest of Ciana's house are off. Patricia has talked Vendetta into eating without knives and forks, and Vendetta has to admit that it is even better when it is just the two of them, without Ciana and her mama's spooky house. If she and Patricia lived alone together, really alone, they would use knives and forks, but eating meals would be so calm like this, not thinking any minute Jaquilica would slam in and sit herself down and complain about something she saw on television. Or Frieda would walk in and look at their plates and ask if Quick could have some of that. Patricia looks like a little angel sitting up here, poking a fine strip of pork into her mouth and leaving her lips all happy and shiny. Maybe Patricia doesn't need a daddy. No, she could go to

Robert's house every now and then and be all happy and shiny, too.

The doorbell rings, and it scares Vendetta so bad that she doesn't hide it at all from Patricia. Her eyes won't blink. "Nobody can see us from the front," Vendetta whispers. "Be quiet, and they'll go away."

The doorbell rings again, and then someone pounds on the door. Slowly, like she's woken up and is having a hard time getting out of bed, Vendetta motions to Patricia to squeeze into the corner of the kitchen, and she reaches for the phone, then steps in front of Patricia to hide her. They hold their breath. The pounding begins again, and a male voice comes through the mail slot. "I know you're in there!" Vendetta dials 911.

In five minutes a man's voice hollers, "Police, open up!" Vendetta doesn't move, because it might be a trick. From behind her a choked little voice says, "Mama, I see blue lights."

It's the police, but they have not come because Vendetta called. They've come because the person who was pounding at the door called. The person at the door is Geoffrey. Geoffrey ignores the police. "Who the hell are you?" he says to Vendetta.

"He know perfectly well who I am," Vendetta says to the officer standing next to Geoffrey. There are two officers, and unfortunately this one is the white one.

"Where's my sister?" Geoffrey says, but he's not looking directly at Vendetta.

"She done told you she going to Memphis," Vendetta says straight at Geoffrey. "I say right now she *in* Memphis."

Geoffrey talks to the white officer. "You have to understand. I drove past just to check the house, and I saw my sister's car. And I saw the light on. No one answered, so I put two and two together and thought she might have tried to kill herself."

This is one of those times when Vendetta knows she has to keep her mouth shut.

"Do you know this woman or not?" the black officer says.

"I know who she is," Geoffrey says.

"Good thing," Vendetta says.

After they leave, all Vendetta can think is that maybe Lennon is going to fall crazy in love with Ciana right now and ask her to move in with him, and her house is going to be empty and need someone to live in it. Though Lennon probably lives someplace smaller. Hell, she'd take that. Hell, she'd take a chicken coop. She bets Patricia would, too.

28

It was hard for Lennon to explain to Ciana that he could abhor Six Flags over Jesus and still be a good Baptist boy. He tried to tell her yesterday, remembering the epiphany he had as a child, driving through Palm Springs, California, and seeing the windmills, which looked to him a lot like the crosses over Bellevue Baptist. His mother had to admit that, unlike the windmills, the crosses caught nothing, not even air, and Lennon had his first lesson in showmanship; it wasn't a favorable one. Ciana thought that he should be like her; having debunked everything Holy Name offered, she extrapolated it to all of Christendom. Lennon supposed that for him, church just had nothing to do with religion.

"My parents don't want to *know* white people; they want

to *be* white people," he said. "Bellevue Baptist has only a smattering of African-American members, and my parents smatter every week." Lennon was getting a kick out of this level of candor, and Ciana didn't stop him. "You know, if you're black, and you sit in a room full of white people, you don't see yourself, you only see everybody else, so you figure you're white. That's why they go. That's probably why they vote Republican, too."

"What's that mean about me?" Ciana said. "I haven't been the majority in a room while I've been here except when I've been alone with you."

"Shush," Lennon said. Ciana had filled up the motel room and all his senses, and he would have told any other woman just that, but Ciana would have taken it the wrong way. They had had to make love in what they hoped was the amount of time his parents might think traffic would add to the round-trip from their house. He had not felt this sexually explosive since he was fourteen. He had been back in that house for almost three days, walking through those rooms, aroused every second it seemed, sure that those same two people were looking at him and wondering what it was they thought they were seeing. His parents had been watching far too closely, and he was not sure why. But in a few minutes Jesus and the Israels were coming face-to-face, and as the sun rose over Fort God, maybe he would have a good old epiphany of the lowercase kind.

The parking lot of Bellevue Baptist was larger than those of most shopping malls, and because they were far from the first to arrive, Lennon and Ciana had a long walk to reach the assembled congregation. They took turns carrying Nookie, whose neon orange vest was not a proper pastel shade for the occasion, but it served its purpose of meaning business. Not that the three of them needed extra reasons for strangers to give them a wide berth. Christianity wasn't on parade this morning, at least not before the sun came up.

Ciana saw his parents before Lennon did, but it was no surprise. "I recognize the dress," she said. Ciana spent all of yesterday following his mother around Memphis, learning how much time it can take to fill a suburban life. They had taken seven hours to find plants to fill a shady bed, a dress for church, and food for brunch. Ciana would have done none of those things, but she had come back amazed by her heightened awareness. "I was looking at everyone's flower beds when we drove down the street!" she said to anyone who would listen.

With the Israels were another couple and two girls who could have been identified even if their backs had been turned. Ciana's step faltered. "Look beautiful," Lennon said, and he kept up his stride. He was fairly sure he saw the twins wilt simultaneously. Just slightly, but enough. They mirrored each other, tipping toward center. Antonia immediately gave Andrea a nudge, and they straightened up, ready to deal with whatever had taken them by surprise. Lennon assumed it was Ciana's presence.

His mother, on the other hand, looked like someone who until a moment ago had despaired of being proven right in a court of law, and had just seen her attorney's assistant come rushing in through the back door waving a crucial piece of evidence. "Kids!" she said. She rushed up and kissed the air around Ciana's face as if she had done so before.

"And this is Dr. Luciana Jambon," she said to the Hollingsworths, taking Ciana's Nookie-free hand and leaving Lennon to stand behind her.

In the silence that followed, Lennon heard Mr. Hollingsworth ask his mother how the lovely Diana was doing. And in the most audible polite voice she could muster his mother said, "Oh, Diana says Paris should be lovely in about a month." Lennon knew that his parents sent a hefty allowance precisely so his mother could utter that sentence maybe twice a year.

"So how's it going, Lennon?" Andrea said.

"Fine." He was sure she wanted hyperbole or rage out of him, and she wasn't going to get it.

"You two work together, right?"

"Yes."

Everyone was looking at him and Andrea, and all Lennon could say was, "What," before the Hollingsworths walked off to be what their mother called flies in the buttermilk. He often had thought that if Mrs. Hollingsworth had not been in the neighborhood, he never would have had any sense at all.

"At least they didn't come up to your mother and say I'm covering for your boyfriend," Ciana whispered.

"Andrea was gearing up," Lennon whispered back.

Since the last time he was here, Lennon had been to a couple of funerals around his house in New Orleans, and he had realized that what this church lacked was percussion. Those hot little churches back in Carrollton thundered inside enough to make his heart pop with the holy spirit, and while this service was loud and fervent, it filled him with nothing more than cynicism. He couldn't abide pious white men who rolled up and down their lines like they were on some kind of sine curve on the monitor. Pious black men weren't a whole lot better, but at least they wiped their brows when they were really sweating. The crowd was buying. Their voices were rising. Lennon's mother was in a thrall, and he wished he could see whether the twins were pretending to be in one, too. The pastor yelled out, "He is risen!" and the congregation yelled out, "He is risen indeed!"

Lennon could feel Ciana begin to tremble all over. The woman on the other side of her looked at Nookie closely, then tried to catch Lennon's eye. He looked at Nookie, who wasn't doing anything, and pointed at the dog, the barometer of Ciana's brain waves. He mouthed, "She's okay." He handed Ciana a handkerchief, and her entire guffaw exploded noisily into it. "Indeed!" he whispered into her ear, and now she was allowed to laugh out loud.

He never understood why, when everyone was surely hungry and ought to have felt full of goodness and high visibility, no one was heading for the parking lot. Hundreds were in line to speak to the pastor, in no hurry, wanting to be seen. The maid probably was waiting at the house, wondering how to time the cooking. His parents had some level of consciousness in the sixties, and they should have had some residue of it now. That would have meant letting the maid be with her family on Easter. But that was not how Republicans behaved. And he was afraid Republicans didn't pay time and a half, either. He never learned these women's names and faces. It would be too condescending when they all quit within six months.

The four of them moved in a pack, like an announcement; his mother's eyes scanned the crowd hoping someone would look in their direction so she could smile and nod, *Yes, this is what it looks like.* They were an easy target, and the twins tugged their parents into the line behind the Israels with the same exponential strength that always had gotten them what they'd wanted. A lot of body English, and before Lennon could do anything, they were a party of eight, moving up to the pastor, listening to Dr. Israel carry on about the wondrous, wondrous service this morning, and Lennon counting on his fingers how many of the eight of them might agree. He couldn't figure if his father was in the number. Lennon looked at no one but Ciana because it was a good idea to look at Ciana. But not lovingly.

The twins did not use their New Orleans slither style for church, but managed nevertheless to present themselves first to the pastor, like happy, ready virgins, each taking a cheek, which was attached to a waiting pink ear. What they said to him, only he and the air behind him knew, but he was certainly ready for Ciana. "I'm so pleased to meet you," he said when Mrs. Israel presented Dr. Jambon, Lennon's *friend* from New Orleans. "You are a very patient young woman."

The Hollingsworths were well on their way to the parking lot, but it didn't matter to Lennon. "Did those girls just tell you I was gay?" Lennon said.

"Oh, son," the pastor said, looking over his shoulder at the long, eager line behind him. "We have been praying for you for such a long time."

His mother did not want a scene in the parking lot. His mother did not want a scene in the car. His mother did not want a scene at the table in front of the help. The maid whose name and face Lennon refused to learn was passing around the table with a silver platter from which they could choose to take a serving of Eggs Benedict or Eggs Sardou. The food looked simply outrageous to him. Queer. Queer-making. He wouldn't take a thing from the tray. "I can't stand another minute of this," he said.

"Son, don't you think this is a matter you want to keep quiet?" his father said.

"You think I'm gay," Lennon said, as audibly as he could, because he knew that for some strange reason his parents feared the poor little housekeeper in the kitchen more than they feared the woman at the table with whom he was sleeping.

"We have never asked you about your personal life," his mother said.

Lennon felt a need to behave at the table more than he

felt a need to try to overturn three hundred pounds and two centuries of cherry wood laden with china, crystal, and silver. He realized he was that repressed. "I want to *tell* you about my personal life," he said, and he gave Ciana a quick look to let her know that current events didn't figure in this at all.

His father sat up a little straighter and put down his loaded fork; he clearly was a man who hadn't had good sex in years, possibly in his entire life. His mother said, "No."

"This is history, Mother," Lennon said.

"Still no," his mother said.

"Listen to this, Ciana," he said. "You grow up in a house where your mother actually brags that you can eat out of the toilets. You wear collared shirts and she buttons the top button. You want to tell me what people are going to think? You want to tell me what I was going to think?"

Ciana kept on eating, but he noticed she was taking the smallest possible bits of egg on her fork that could be speared without falling off. She was reaching her mouth by rote; her eyes were on his.

"Stop this, Lennon," his mother said.

"Kids in school aren't polite, Mother," he said. "Kids will call you a sissy and feel damn good about it."

"Please don't talk like that at the table," his mother said.

"*Res ipsa loquitur*," Lennon said.

"The way you acted had nothing to do with the way I raised you," his mother said, missing the point.

"I am not fucking gay."

"He's not," Ciana said.

"Oh, Luciana, you've known him, what, less than a year, and we've known him his whole life," his mother said. "Maybe someone like you has been what it takes."

"You mean that she's white?" Lennon said.

"Son, you never went on dates in high school," his father said.

"It didn't help having a sister going around telling everybody I was gay," Lennon said.

"Now why would she do a thing like that?" his mother said.

"Because she was just like every other high school kid I've ever known. She was a complete asshole," Lennon said.

"I told you he hates women," his mother said to his father.

Lennon and Ciana are deep into Mississippi when night falls, and he aches from her talkativeness. It's as if she took an inventory of his parents' house, at least the few parts, the public parts, where she was allowed to set foot, in case she found it necessary to fill time with idle chatter. If he didn't know better, he would take her for a Corinne, a woman imagining an upgrade on the furnishings of her current home. But Ciana doesn't like most of it, and she has long philosophical reasons why. They are his parents, so she's general about leather sofas and sure death from the overuse of Lysol, but she makes her point. Which is that she'll talk about anything except suspicions about his sexuality. She doesn't bother to wait for him to answer half the time.

"You're always going to have doubts now, aren't you," he says somewhere past Tylertown.

"No," she says, but he thinks she hesitates just a little.

"You hesitated."

"Because I was talking about whether I would heat a whole house if I only lived in a tenth of it when you interrupted me."

"Sorry," Lennon says.

"I wasn't listening to me, either."

"Look," he says. "I'm not going to bring this up again. I just want to tell you one thing. Just remember this. This morning you were standing under a bunch of insanely huge crosses with me and six other people, and those six other people probably believed everything that pastor said. Think about that."

29

EVERY TRIP Ciana ever has taken ends exactly the same way. She descends at the Carrollton exit, and where she has been is relegated to memory, to perspective stored deep. Carrollton Avenue is that way, dilapidated and out of place in America, and it makes her find it hard to believe she has just been somewhere else. If she has come from an international flight arriving at the airport, if she has come from Baton Rouge; it always has been the same. Ciana figures this is probably why no one ever moves away from New Orleans; natives find everywhere else impossible to believe. This stretch of Carrollton works like Versed, inducing retrograde amnesia. Tonight she has forgotten whatever has happened to her in the past three days. As long as she doesn't try to think.

It is not until Lennon has pulled up in front of her house and taken her suitcase out of the trunk that she has to realize that they are home from a trip, and they are a day early. Lennon walked out during Easter dinner, leaving so many beautifully cooked eggs for garbage, not worth reheating even by the poor woman who cooked them. Ciana kissed and kissed at his parents, grateful because she could do it across rooms and not have to mean it. Lennon had to let her do it. She wasn't sure for whose sake, but he had to let her do it.

She is about to ask him to come in when she realizes she can't. "Vendetta's in there," she says. He asks if she wants to stay at his house. Her answer ought to be yes, for the sake of all that she now remembers from their trip. "I want to be home," she says. "I hope you understand. That's all it is. Now that I'm here, I want to be *home*." He nods and smiles, and Ciana thinks that what matters really is a certain understanding. More than anything else, it is that certain understanding.

Patricia yelps when she finds Ciana on the sofa in the morning. Her voice is high and sweet, much less startling than an alarm clock, and Ciana is not so much rattled out of sleep as amused out of it. "Hey, you, isn't it a school day?" Ciana says. Patricia's hair isn't combed, and she's in pink cotton pajamas that show the complete flatness of her chest, and Ciana wants to be her mother. "Mama! Ciana here!" Patricia calls toward the bedroom. It takes over a minute for a bedraggled Vendetta to shuffle into the living room trying to push her hair out of her eyes while pulling the folds of an XXL white T-shirt together in front of her. "This don't look good at all," she says to Ciana. "Go run watch TV," she tells Patricia.

"Lennon's back, too," Ciana says.

"Never mind," Vendetta says to Patricia.

Ciana doesn't need to ask any questions to know that Patricia is not in school, home or otherwise, and Patricia is going to grow up with some funny lacunae in her brain if she doesn't get back to books soon. Ciana was absent with chicken pox the week her class learned what a vector was, and to this day she still doesn't know. "Get this child dressed," Ciana says.

Vendetta looks miffed. "I just got woked up," she says. "And you not suppose to be here. First thing I got to do, I got to clean up your house." Ciana tells her never mind the house, just get Patricia ready; she has a plan. "How you know I ain't already got plans?" Vendetta says.

"Because you don't," Ciana says, and when Patricia giggles, she knows she's right.

Patricia has play clothes, and Patricia has an Easter dress, and Vendetta chafes when Ciana says neither is quite right for what she has in mind. Vendetta did have a plan for today, which was to stay away from her own house. "I'll *buy* her a new outfit," Ciana says, and that is all it takes for Vendetta to fold. She will go back to her house. "Just my luck, this probably Frieda day off," she says. "Maybe they won't cut up in front of company. But I doubt it."

No one is in Vendetta's side of the house when they arrive. No one comes over the entire time they are there cleaning up Patricia, and Vendetta looks almost disappointed. Then she discovers her kitchen in shambles. "That's just what I been afraid of," she says. Ciana is sure she can see a smile on Vendetta's face. She opens the refrigerator. "I bet they been eating all my food up," she says. She lifts out the half-gallon milk container and holds it up to the light as if checking for forensic clues. It looks close to full as far as Ciana can tell. Vendetta puts it back without comment. "Shit," Vendetta says. "You don't have to live here," Ciana says. "You want to keep sleeping on your own sofa?" Vendetta says, and before Vendetta can find Patricia's comb and brush, Ciana has found a locksmith who can be over in fifteen minutes. He gives Vendetta two sets of keys, and Ciana appropriates one.

When Ciana makes a turn off Claiborne Avenue, Vendetta says, "Hold on, pull over." "What." "This Calhoun Street." "Yes." "You think I don't know what on Calhoun Street?" Ciana pulls over in someone's driveway. This neighborhood is close to Tulane's campus, and there are no legitimate parking places. "You not putting my child in no mental hospital."

"Oh, Christ, Vendetta," Ciana says. "I am not an idiot."

DePaul Hospital is at the other end of Calhoun Street, and aside from parts of Loyola University and the side entrance to a synagogue it is really the only nonresidential building on the entire riverside stretch of the street. Except for Holy Name of Jesus School. And that is where they are going. Ciana is relieved that Vendetta is having a fit over a mental hospital. A Catholic school will look like so much more salubrious a place for a child. She thinks.

Vendetta still waffles. She's not a Catholic. Neither is half the school. It's April. So what's Patricia getting on her school record at home? Vendetta knows before they get out of the car that she has to talk about money, so Ciana chooses to do it for her. "Don't say a word to me about tuition," Ciana tells her. "Do you hear me?" Vendetta nods her head. "What that is?" Patricia says. "It mean your Auntie Ciana ridiculous," Vendetta says. "And you better thank Jesus." Ciana says to herself, *Don't thank that Jesus in whose holy name schools charge a semester's tuition for eight weeks of class.*

The three of them squirm through almost an hour of questions they don't want to answer in front of one another, then take a Mr. Toad's Wild Ride into the housing project and through all the satellite hospital clinics, the ones that make a person feel like she doesn't go to Charity, collecting documents. "These are all welfare places," Ciana says. "You deserve better." "You try starting out with no money," Vendetta says.

By ten-thirty Patricia is sitting up in a classroom with more white faces the same size as hers than she ever has seen in her entire life, plus enough other shades and Madeleine's down the hall to make her comfortable. Vendetta is at peace with the notion that her child will have to have a tutor every afternoon for the rest of the school year, not because she is stupid, which is what Vendetta thinks tutors are for, but because no one has taught her. She even is at peace that the tutor is not free. Unlike Geoffrey, Vendetta can be told what small fraction of Ciana's complete portfolio an expense is and she can have perspective. Ciana tells her that the amount of the tutor's fee renews itself as dividends accrue, and she feels almost as if she and Ciana are conspiring against some power so big the two of them never will fully understand it.

Patricia can wear one of the emergency uniforms they keep in the office today, but Ciana and Vendetta have to outfit her for tomorrow. Vendetta thinks this is too bad, because children are like New Orleans plants and grow wild in summer; whatever they buy today still will have stiff pleats in eight weeks, and Patricia will have no use for it by August. Ciana doesn't care. She tells Vendetta she'll pay. She wants to go to the uniform store. She wants to buy uniforms that aren't a size with an X after the numeral. "Oh, shut up," Vendetta says pleasantly.

While Vendetta does the terribly boring business of checking items off the list, Ciana wanders around the store, and other schools have uniforms that make her want to weep. It's the prekindergarten versions that get to her, the manly little pants, the serious little jumpers. They are so small, at least compared to the eighth-grade versions, that she doesn't understand how parents can take such destructible babies and dress them up this way, put them down on their little feet, and send them in through school gates to cope. Ciana is holding up a size 2T polo shirt when Vendetta finds her and says, "Oh, Lord, Ciana, oh, Lord."

What.

"You holding that thing up and you thinking it cute."

Well, sure.

Vendetta takes it from Ciana gently, suspends it from the shoulders so it hangs two feet off the floor, as if holding it up in front of an imaginary child. "What you suppose to be thinking, this thing gonna have juice stains all 'round the neck, better get dark blue. And then you thinking, oh shit, this child going to school, he still peeing his pants, what the teacher gonna say? Better buy extra socks. That's not what you thinking, no. You thinking, this my little sweetie, he gonna stay home with me one more year, no rush." Vendetta takes the tiny shirt, crumples it up gently, and kisses all over it.

"You got me," Ciana says.

Vendetta loosens up the shirt, smoothes it out reverently, puts it back on the rack. "I put your baby shirt back, okay, Ciana? I bet it look good on Lennon Junior."

"My baby's going to be a girl," Ciana says, "and her name's going to be Triage."

Vendetta looks stricken. And then she looks at Ciana's round middle. Which is no more or less round than usual.

"Not *yet*," Ciana says.

"Don't make me no never mind," Vendetta says. "Triage odd. That's good. Odd good. You could call her Tree."

30

BLACK WOMEN are waiting for black children, black women are waiting for white children, white women are waiting for white children; all that is missing are white women waiting for black children. Vendetta doesn't count the Mexicans and Chinese because she's not sure how they fit in New Orleans anyway. All she knows is that picking up Patricia from this school is all kinds of strange. Just for starts, they don't open the doors and set them free like at Sylvania.

"What are you doing here?" someone says coming up at her. Vendetta doesn't turn to look because it's a white voice and nobody knows her here. Though that should be a perfect reason for turning to look.

Corinne presents herself in front of Vendetta. She studies

Vendetta's face like a white woman who hasn't spent enough time around black people to tell them apart very well. Especially black people she's seen most often in uniform. "Aren't you the one . . . ?"

"Oh, *Corinne*, good to see you," Vendetta says in a Corinne voice, hoping she will be heard by someone Corinne wants for a friend.

"Never mind," Corinne says and starts to walk away.

"No, you asking me what I'm doing here."

Corinne stops, knowing better. Vendetta sees her take a glance at the clock on the far wall. It says they have one minute until the bell. It will be forever until the bell for Corinne if Vendetta can help it. "You remember my Patricia? Oh, I can't remember if you met Patricia. I know Madeleine play with her. Caroline, too. Anyway, she coming here now. Oh, that's right. *Geoffrey* the one met Patricia."

"That goddamn Ciana," Corinne says.

"Excuse me?"

Corinne lowers her voice. "That fat pig put you up to this, didn't she."

"I don't need to talk to you, no," Vendetta says.

The bell rings, and children begin to swarm, but it is as if someone has stomped an anthill on the other side of the room, the effect is that small on Corinne.

Corinne grabs her arm, and Vendetta can swear she can feel through her shirt that Corinne hates touching her. "Listen. You tell her this. For as long as I can remember, everything has been hers. *This* is one thing that's mine. And if she thinks she's getting even by ruining this one thing, she's done something worse than I could've ever done."

Madeleine comes screeching up to Corinne. "Mama! Patricia's in our school!" She notices Vendetta and is too excited to make the connection. "Did you know Patricia's here?"

"This is what I'm talking about," Corinne says.

Patricia comes out in a crowd of children about her own size. A white girl is holding her hand, explaining this final step in her regular day. Vendetta knows this is the twenty-first century, and she has seen MTV and a million movies, but she can't believe *this*. What she especially can't believe is that Patricia looks like it's the most natural thing in the world.

Madeleine runs over and grabs Patricia around the neck so hard that almost everything pops out on Patricia's face. "You've got to come over after school," Madeleine says.

Vendetta wishes like crazy that Ciana were here right now. She checks Corinne out of the corner of her eye. Sure enough, Corinne looks pretty sick at heart; that's good enough. "You have homework," Corinne says to Madeleine. Madeleine's little balloon arms fall to her sides, but only far enough to go akimbo in defiance. "Homework takes twenty minutes," she says.

"I got homework," Patricia says. She sounds as if the teacher has given her a gift. Maybe, Vendetta thinks, the secret to having a hardworking child is to send her to public school and make her so hungry for learning that she'll do anything.

"You see," Corinne says. "Your little friend needs to keep up on her first day."

Caroline has come up. "Her name's Patricia," she says.

"You know what?" Patricia says to Corinne. "Not liking black people is very old-fashion. You *not* cool."

Vendetta lets herself be led away by the most heartbreaking girl in the world.

It is lonely in the locked house. Patricia has babbled herself silly; Vendetta has no idea how she could have learned so many names and life stories when they're attached to little people in uniforms. Tomorrow Patricia might sort them out by color. Tomorrow the girl who was assigned to tour her around today might not be her best friend. Ciana has warned her of this, that her recollection is that children cross the lines when they aren't thinking, but usually they move in their ancient packs, and Patricia probably will be pulled into a pack of little black girls who will chase after little black boys. At least that was the way it was when she and Corinne went to the school, sometime between *Brown v. Board of Education* and now, but closer to now, and the most popular girl had been lithe and athletic and brown-skinned, and Corinne had despised her for everything, but she had tagged it onto color. Ciana purely had been confused that boys would like the girl for having the same skills *they* had. Merry was her name, Ciana said, and Corinne had spent most lunch periods watching Merry make the smoothest runs with a ball, boys *and* girls tumbling in her wake, Corinne hissing that she was so stupid she couldn't even spell her own name. Ciana hated Corinne on those days, wanting desperately to be a girl who dared be visible in the open spaces of the playground. Maybe Patricia will confuse little fat white girls and make skinny little white girls furious because she gets to be popular, but that doesn't make Vendetta all that happy. At least at Sylvania the girls weren't mean. Just the boys.

The mean boys. She forgot about the mean boys. She forgot about the mean teachers. She forgot about how Patricia is happy out of her mind. She must be losing her own mind. If Jaquilica were sitting in her kitchen right now, Vendetta would be telling her about Corinne, and she'd be getting ready to tell her how smart Patricia was today, and then Frieda would walk in, and she'd start yelling at her for putting that child in a white people's school, and then Vendetta wouldn't be losing her mind. Or maybe she wouldn't be having the mind she has right now. The one she got back this morning.

She phones Ciana. She needs to phone Ciana anyway because Corinne said something Ciana needs to hear, she really did. And Ciana might very well have the right to get a call after school every day until Patricia finishes the eighth grade. "Boy, have I got something to tell you," Ciana says when she picks up the phone.

"Must be damn good," Vendetta says. "Or damn bad."

"It can wait," Ciana says. "I completely forgot about school."

"It was good. It was real good. So now you can tell me."

What Ciana says doesn't make a whole lot of sense to Vendetta. It seems like she bumped into Jane. That makes sense. Vendetta knows who Jane is, Ciana's favorite customer, the lady who walks around glued together by a few milligrams each of about ten different drugs; Ciana can't tell if Jane's psychiatrist is a genius or Jane is the most magical person in all of 70118 and 70125 combined. It turns out that Jane is a lawyer. Evidently that doesn't bother Ciana in the least. Vendetta has no idea how that subject came up to begin with, but Ciana right away felt completely free to ask for legal advice, which Jane didn't mind giving, standing right there in the grocery because after all Ciana knows all her secrets and likes her anyway. Ciana gave her a hypothetical—a *what if*, which is what she could have called it to begin with—and Jane knew the answer right there in the grocery. What if a slew of brothers and sisters owned one house and one of them wanted to sell the house? Vendetta stops her again to explain a word. She thinks she knows what "slew" means, but she wants to be sure that it's about her and her sisters and brothers and not about Ciana and her F.B. Ciana is talking about Vendetta. Jane says there's something called partition by licitation. She says it right there on the canned goods aisle. Vendetta pictures the two of them on the canned goods aisle, which is an aisle where she feels very comfortable. A lot of what she ate as a child came from that aisle, none of it DelMonte. Partition by licitation sounds mean. And it is mean. With it you can force your brothers and sisters or anybody really to an act of sale. Frieda and Jaquilica can be sitting up in their half of the house as big as life, needing to get by on no rent, and Vendetta can hand them a paper that says they have to put this house on the market and walk away with their little piece of the money, and they have no choice.

"Why I want to do that?" Vendetta says, even though she wanted to do exactly that a few days ago.

"I don't know," Ciana says. She sounds all embarrassed. Vendetta can't decide if maybe Ciana *ought* to feel a little embarrassed. She's done one good thing, a very good thing, with the school, but now she's all overexcited, like she's going to spend all her time fixing all of Vendetta's problems instead of her own. Vendetta has seen people do that before, and it has gotten sickening. Usually those people have called themselves social workers. Ciana is too good to turn into one of them. Ciana needs to work on being a little selfish. "I just thought you wanted to get away from your sisters," Ciana says, and she sounds kind of weak.

"I did," she says. "I do." Vendetta is completely confused. She wishes Patricia would come into the room and make something happen.

"You know, it's just information," Ciana says, not sounding so embarrassed anymore. "I'm not telling you to *do* anything. I'm just telling you to *know* something."

Vendetta feels like saying, *Don't* tell *me to do nothing.* But even she can see that today has made her a little crazy. Telling somebody to know something isn't bad, as long as it's just a fact. A Louisiana law is a fact. Ciana's not telling her to *believe* anything.

She thinks about it. She thinks about selling the house, moving out, taking her little share and making a down payment on a little house and paying a little note. Her brothers each would have a chunk of change. And Frieda. Frieda's never paid rent; maybe she could pay rent. But what stops her is Jaquilica. She would drink it up in a month's time. And that would be the end of Jaquilica. Vendetta has to stop thinking about it.

"You don't see what I'm telling you," Ciana says, reading her mind. "If you know something, you don't have to use it."

"I like that," Vendetta says. She hangs up the phone, forgetting to tell Ciana again that that Holy Name is very good. But it's on purpose that she'll wait until she sees her in person to tell Ciana what a racist bitch Corinne is and to give her that nasty message. They will laugh their asses off.

31

LENNON should be studying for NAPLEX, but he's spent a good part of this evening working on a clinical definition of *sissy*, and he's come up with one that would be worthy of the *DSM-IVR*. His text of reference is fairly unassailable. The Bible. A sissy is someone who doesn't seek revenge. All the sissies can be found after a very simple point of delineation: where the Old Testament ends and the New Testament begins. He doesn't know why Philip Roth always writes about Jews as nonphysical men. He does know why the world is turned on its side because the Israelis mean business. He likes the message of the Old Testament. He knows the president likes the Old Testament, too, and somebody ought to remind him to be a little more sissified. But it's Lennon's misfortune that his mother used only the New one to instruct him. "Don't *chase* that boy through the mud." "But he hit me." "Those sneakers are only a month old." Well, maybe she wasn't all that interested in eschewing revenge. Maybe she had a touch of Methodist in her, godliness through cleanliness, and that was decidedly New Testament, too. And definitely sissy. Just for fun he looks up the word *vendetta* in the dictionary.

Lennon's not sure what to do with this information, though studying is a good place to start. He has to get his license; failure is the ultimate vulnerability. Particularly now, because yesterday a job offer came through, and while it doesn't hold revenge for him, it might do so for Ciana. He can have Maureen's position at N.O. Drugs. There's an opening at the St. Claude Avenue store, and corporate is willing to transfer Maureen there or send Lennon; it's his choice. He refuses to let himself think about the possibility that this is about race, that so far N.O. has no black pharmacists and they would probably like his face on display uptown. Surely it's because Maureen has something in her file. Lennon only has seen the woman two or three times, aside from her off-putting photograph on the wall next to the check-out counter. He's not sure he wants her job precisely because he's rarely seen her. She has all the days that Ciana doesn't have. On the other hand, he imagines that the St. Claude store is wall-to-wall Earl Robertses, scam artists who pee in their pants.

When he put in applications he only tried chains in two

cities, New Orleans and Memphis, and he has five other offers, all in those two cities. He feels ruined in those two cities; even the woman he sleeps with, the woman who never has had reason to question his sexuality, now seems to question his sexuality. Ciana has a lot of nerve, letting herself be swayed, even the tiniest bit, by fools like his mother and the Hollingsworth twins. Lennon is angry with every woman he can think of. He can't tell this to anyone, because anyone would have the right to turn around to him and say, *See?* But he's not a woman-hater. Women have made him impotent, just not the way they think they have. He can't defend himself. He thinks of Vendetta's poor little girl who can't go out onto the school yard and holler that she doesn't have a peenie. He just remembered. He's not angry at Vendetta.

Vendetta is uncharacteristically happy to hear from him, even though he never has asked to see her outside of work before. When he arrives at her house he finds out why: she has locked out her sisters, and this is her first night trying to be alone with a child and a television set in her own house. She's not sure what to make of her own company. Her first words are a paean to "Court TV." Her second words are to tell Patricia to hush, that Uncle Lennon doesn't want to hear about school; he's spent his whole life in school. "And I haven't learned a blessed thing," he says to Patricia.

"What you need to know?" Patricia says, filled to the brim with a day of Catholic education.

"What you need to know?" Vendetta says, and Patricia is out of the room before Lennon can think of an answer.

Lennon starts to tell her the whole story, the parts she

knows, the parts she might or might not have heard, and before he can get too far Vendetta pulls him to the left side of the house. It's the side with windows, the drafty side, the more menacing side, but Vendetta whispers that the walls have ears. "They probably already heard a man voice," she says. "Though what they gonna do about it, I don't know."

Under a window that looks almost directly into Vendetta's neighbor's empty bedroom, Lennon brings Vendetta up to date. He can tell from her expression that Ciana has come back from Memphis and not uttered one word about why they left early. "Why you telling me all this?" Vendetta says when he finishes.

"Because you're the only person I'm not angry at, and I've got to decide on a job."

"Why you mad at Ciana?"

"Why didn't Ciana come back and tell you what happened?"

"*Evidently* it ain't no big deal to Ciana."

That certainly would be what Lennon wants to think. "Or else it's such a big deal that she won't mention it," he says.

"You don't know womens very well," Vendetta says. "Now you going out with her, it's all right to tell you, every time you turn around, it be, 'Vendetta, what you think that mean?' 'Lennon smile just now. You think he like me?' We talk you to death behind your back."

"Really?" Lennon says.

"For true," Vendetta says. "Some things you better pray not on that test. You a seriously ignorant man."

Lennon studies Vendetta closely, though not so closely

that she can tell, and Vendetta can tell everything. He loves her as much as he can love anyone, but her sexuality never has crossed his mind. Vendetta is a little pocked and disheveled by time and circumstance, and Lennon is so fastidious that it is almost impossible for him to look past an accumulation of such flaws. Yet Patricia resembles her mother a great deal, and Patricia so far is undamaged by the dirtiness she has to pass through if she is going to keep living in New Orleans without the means to shield herself. That is what Vendetta once was. For the first time Lennon looks at Vendetta as a woman that men wanted, and he hopes she can't see that right now he feels terribly sad for her. All she has right now is her wisdom. And she's probably thinking that right now all he has is what he's gotten from books. "You not a bad-looking man," Vendetta says absentmindedly in the same light from the neighbor's window, and Lennon breathes a huge sigh of relief.

He stays for a Coke because he doesn't think he's a whole lot closer to figuring out what he wants to do with himself, aside from not punishing Ciana. "Baby, you asking the wrong person," Vendetta says. "I'm hoping this mean Ciana done wrote up Maureen opening late all the time, and that's why Maureen ass on the line. That cow try to get me in big trouble, you know I want her setting down on St. Claude Avenue."

"So Ciana and I work alternate days and never see each other." He doesn't mention that little competitive thing they would have, orderliness and productivity and flawless performance. For all he knows, Maureen is a perfectly decent person who has had to be demonized because there has been no other choice.

"Absent make the heart grow fonder," Vendetta says.

Lennon considers this. But the twelve hours between nine P.M. and nine A.M. are not enough. He has had all the hours between nine A.M. and nine P.M., and then he has wanted more. He considers St. Claude Avenue. He feels homesick just thinking about being that far downtown. He thinks about the job at Rite-Aid. Certainly N.O. Drugs is not a religion or a tribe, but he's not sure he wants to give up what have become traditions, the three different windows, the screw caps that flip, the "Hi, I'm Lennon" on the receipt. "I know I'm not going to Memphis," he says.

"You know, this not your mama fault," Vendetta says.

Patricia walks into the kitchen just at this point, and Lennon thinks he is never going to find out *why*, but Vendetta is not like his mother; circumspection at the table is not a particular virtue. Vendetta is an old hand at euphemisms, but often as not sees no need for them; it's easier just to talk fast. She has been talking over little heads ever since the first time she had a little person on her lap. Patricia sits on her lap now and strains her ears for clues. The child knows that the day is going to come when she's going to put it all together, and this could very well be the day. "Your mama done nothing but be herself," Vendetta says. Lennon nods. "Matter of fact, them twins done nothing but be theyselves, which is two ho's." Patricia wriggles, just to let her mother know she's no dummy. "Now your mama, she *wrong*, but she not mean, know what I'm saying?" Vendetta doesn't stop for Lennon's response. "And them twins, all they doing, they trying to get something out you. They doing it out of greediness, not meanness, not really."

"You can be mad at somebody who's greedy," Patricia says.

Lennon wants to ask if the child can sit on his lap so he can squeeze her silly, but everybody in the world already thinks he has social problems, so he doesn't.

"We talking about fault, baby," Vendetta says. "Lennon got to find out who at fault."

Lennon tells Patricia that he's going to find out right now who's at fault. Otherwise Vendetta would turn this into a bedtime story. For all three of them.

"You need to kick Diane fat ass," she says.

Diana's skinny backside. Lennon shudders at the thought, and then he knows Vendetta is right. Diana learned the word *gay* in about third grade, learned its pejorative power, channeled all of her intelligence into correlating it with what she knew about her slightly ruined brother, and then she set about ruining him completely. By the time the Hollingsworth twins were toddling down the block, Diana was probably already teaching them to taunt Lennon. But they were not enough. Diana had an entire school full of children on whom to use innuendo. She never came right out with her meanness; she whispered. Her parents reveled in her normalcy. Her brother's near-perfection as a student was a given. A disappointment almost.

"Diana's in Paris," Lennon says.

"She not on the *moon*," Vendetta says.

Patricia is excited when Lennon goes on about it being the middle of the night in Paris; just today they have studied time zones, but her chauvinistic teacher has told them there are four time zones, and the middle of the night is somewhere that Patricia cannot understand. Lennon can hardly understand it, either. He is tempted to phone Diana right this very second, to wake her up as long as he is paying a lot of money; never mind that she will think someone is dead. Vendetta wants him to stay with her until it is morning in Paris. Not for Diana's sake, but for her own. "Late as you staying up, *I'm* staying up," Patricia says, and she wriggles deep into Vendetta's lap, just in case Lennon has designs on her mother. Lennon can't think of a better reason to leave right now.

Diana picks up the phone and says, "Allo?" with a perfect French accent. Lennon identifies himself through the gritted teeth of a person who can't stand a French accent on an American, even one living in Paris, especially one at whom he is furious. "What's going on?" Diana says with true indifference, even though it is three o'clock in Paris, even though they have not spoken since her last visit to the States, whenever that was. Lennon has forgotten that Diana doesn't have a neurotic bone in her body. "I just realized you screwed up my life, and I felt like telling you while I was in the mood," he says.

"Well, I'm kind of pissed at you, too."

Lennon hasn't had time to expect much, but he definitely didn't expect this. "Hold on," he says, "you're not going to do that. First tell me why everybody thinks I'm gay. I go to Memphis, and I come back with even my girlfriend thinking maybe I'm gay."

"That's really your girlfriend?"

"How do you know I brought somebody to Memphis?" He's paying thirty-seven cents a minute for this call. His parents are too wealthy to pay for calls like this. They wouldn't have called her.

"E-mail, stupid. I know everything. That's what I'm trying to tell you."

She is not going to sidetrack him. "Yes, that's my girlfriend. I take her to church, and everybody's praying for my damned soul because you've got every goddamn Baptist in Memphis believing I'm gay. Not to mention half the actual gays in New Orleans."

"Well, you'll be glad to know you won't have to worry about New Orleans anymore," Diana says. "Fine help you turned out to be. All anybody asked you to do was look out for Andrea and Antonia while they got adjusted. You'll be glad they're not coming back. You're just lucky they're not fucking dead."

A frisson of fear runs through Lennon until he remembers that it's only been a few days since he saw the twins far too alive at church. If anything has happened to them, it has happened in Memphis, under the watchful eye of their mother. "Okay, I'll bite," he says.

"Their mother found a coke stash in Andrea's laundry," Diana says. "She figures Antonia's into it, too. So she drags them kicking and screaming to a lab, and of course neither one comes up clean, and last thing I heard they're sitting up in that house like they're practically in prison."

"That's funny," Lennon says. "I thought they liked painkillers."

Diana has nothing to say to that.

"I saw more of them than you thought I did," he says after a good piece of thirty-seven cents' worth.

"I actually know what you're talking about," Diana says.

"You know, I called to ask you what you have against me," Lennon says.

"I just hate you, that's all," Diana says. "I mean, you're my brother, so I love you, but basically I hate you."

Lennon doesn't react. It's not as if this is news to him. "You want to be a little more specific?"

"Look, "Diana says, "I was set up not to like you. They named you Lennon, for Chrissakes, and then all of a sudden by the time I'm born their shit doesn't stink. You were born to a nice normal couple; I was born to a pair of born-again Christian Caucasian-wannabe right-wingers. Of course I would hate you."

"Cut out the psychoanalytic stuff," Lennon says.

"But I had reasons, too. Remember my frogs?"

Lennon remembers her frogs. He's surprised it's taken Diana all these years to mention her frogs. When Diana was in fifth grade she raised three frogs from tadpoles, a fairly miraculous feat in Lennon's opinion. Lana, Rana, and Dana. Naming them was fairly terrific, too, he discovered a year later when he saw *rana pipiens* in a children's biography of Linnaeus. To their father, though, they were Diana's silly pets, and when it came time for the science fair, he appropriated them for the project he wanted to do for Lennon, injecting epinephrine and ACTH and making them change colors. Lennon took first prize, and the frogs died. Diana never said a word beyond excessive grief, but he's sure that she, too, at some point heard her father say girls' brains are wired for some nice things but not some complicated things. "I'm sorry about your frogs," Lennon says.

"They'd be dead by now anyway," Diana says. "What you ought to be sorry about is that you ruined my life. If they hadn't had a boy, a girl would have been enough."

She is doing it again, turning herself into his victim while he is paying for it. "I called because you're ruining *my* life," he says.

"What do you say we call it a draw," Diana says. "I don't get to be the boy everybody wants, but you don't, either."

32

BURGER KING is a strange place to be thinking about how useless it is to accumulate knowledge, but lately Lennon has been thinking in a lot of strange places. That might have to do with his having to study in a lot of strange places. The exam is next week, and he pulls out his notes whenever he can. At red lights. In line at the grocery. No sooner does he have the notes in front of him than his mind wanders. Right now his mind is wandering to the value of *knowing*.

It has nothing to do with material for the exam and everything to do with Vendetta's fine mood today. He's on a thirty-minute break, and she's across the street in the pharmacy proselytizing about how wonderful it is to *know* a fact even if she never has to do anything with that fact. Vendetta knows all she has to do is call a real estate agent and tell her that by law she can force her sisters out of the house, so please come over now, and she is empowered by that one piece of information. It's all it takes for Vendetta to shut them out. She doesn't have to tell them; she doesn't have to use her fact. She just has to have it.

Lennon certainly knows that's true about ninety percent of what he's studying; that's what school is all about. Learn it for the test. Never use it again. Why else did he learn the plots of nineteenth-century British novels? But schooling isn't what he's extrapolating to. He calls the personal line in the pharmacy on his cell and asks Ciana if he can have an extra hour. Of course she is amenable. Ciana will do anything between now and the test if it helps. She is more rattled by it than he is. And he knows very well that she wasn't rattled when she took it. He likes to think that she has more at stake this time.

He doesn't phone before he goes over to Corinne's house. He has a little of the contagion of Vendetta's fine mood. Which comes from knowing something. On his way he stops by his house and picks up that leather binder that holds all the photocopied papers full of facts that point at other facts. They are circumstantial evidence of what he wants, at least that's what he will tell Corinne, and she is surely more ignorant of the law than he is.

He stands squarely in front of the beveled glass and grins broadly so Corinne will be hard-pressed to see him and turn away. When she comes through the door from her kitchen and sees him, she hesitates in her step, and he grins more broadly, giving Corinne no choice but to come forward and answer to his presence. "What do you want?" she says through the closed door.

"I strongly suggest you talk to me," Lennon says. He holds up the binder.

Corinne opens the door about six inches, then fills those six inches with herself.

Lennon folds his arms and bounces on the balls of his feet. "We can have this conversation with me standing here for everyone to wonder about, or you can let me in and I'll be discreet."

"Or we can not have it at all," Corinne says.

"I don't think so," Lennon says. He doesn't move a muscle, because Corinne is just the type to scream "rape." He stays where he is and stares at her. He'll stay as long as it takes.

She opens the door the rest of the way and lets him in. She leads him into the kitchen, and he knows that in her house this is not because he is a good family friend. It is because he is her mother-in-law's groundskeeper. She doesn't offer him anything to drink, but if she did he wouldn't accept it. He knows she would give him a paper cup.

"So," Lennon says cheerfully, "how does your husband think his mother fell?" There is no sense building up with informal chitchat.

"You know what he thinks."

"Standing doing nothing in a store that was actually closed?"

"No, in FAO Schwartz." Corinne enunciates each initial distinctly.

"FAO Schwartz is closed right now because it's in Chapter 11. That FAO Schwartz?"

"Oh, fuck," Corinne says.

"Look, I'll come right out with it," he says. "I'm going to blackmail you, but not the way you think."

Corinne goes to the refrigerator and takes out a Diet Coke, which she proceeds to prepare for herself in a glass filled with ice cubes. Lennon hopes she thinks it bothers him. "I told you if you ever wanted to take me up on my offer just to call," Corinne says.

"I want something better than money," he says, and he lets her stew over that for a moment. "Not jewelry. Not that grandfather clock."

Corinne does some voluntary stewing. "This better not be about sex."

"What?" he says. He thought he knew what to expect, but Corinne has caught him completely off guard. The anecdotal value of this moment is priceless. "Hell, no," he says.

Corinne carries her thorough humiliation better than any woman Lennon has ever seen. "Now how would *I* know?" she says, making him sound like the disgusting one.

"Here's what I want from you, Corinne," he says. "All you have to do is cut the crap. You tell me what happened on those rocks, and you back off on Ciana, and I'll leave you alone."

"What do you mean, what happened on those rocks?"

"Ciana wants to believe her mother fell. I think you pushed her."

"What do you mean, 'on those rocks'?"

Lennon figures it out: this woman has no recollection of having let the sedative loosen up the truth when she was in the hospital. Maybe he doesn't need for her to know she's her own source. "The rocks in Central Park. In New York. You and Mrs. Jambon were on top. And you were furious at her. Suddenly she was at ground level. I know that. Ciana knows that. So far nobody else does. Want to make the connection for me, or should I make it myself?"

Corinne suddenly is terribly interested in the ice in her glass. "You're probably wearing a wire."

This is another surprise, but it pleases Lennon because he can force Corinne to deal with him physically. He stands up and removes his jacket, spreads his arms, his legs.

"You think I'm not going to check, don't you?" she says, and she comes around the table. With her fingernails she goes over the entire surface of his chest, raking by quadrants.

"You wouldn't believe the millions of bacteria that accumulate under a person's fingernails," Lennon says.

"I'm sure your hygiene is fine," Corinne says, and she goes back over the upper left quadrant to be sure the seam of his undershirt is the same as what she just felt in the upper right quadrant. "All right," she says.

"Recording this conversation makes no difference either way," Lennon says, and he thinks about knowledge again but decides not to share what he knows about knowledge with her.

"If you get me in some kind of trouble, you wreck up things for my kids, and if you wreck things up for my kids you make Ciana really unhappy," Corinne says.

"You mean if I tell the police?"

Corinne nods. "Even though I didn't do anything."

"Telling the police is an extreme measure," Lennon says, and Corinne looks up at him, actually looks him straight in the eye, as if for one second, but just one second, he might be worth considering as a person. "But what about telling your husband?" Lennon says.

Corinne doesn't need time to process that possibility. She's considered it for quite a while. "The same thing, only different, probably. Maybe ruinous, maybe not. Sometimes I think he'd tell you to go to hell because he knows me and knows I wouldn't hurt anybody, but sometimes I think he'd forget that I'm not the only one who's pissed off at his family, and then he'd think I did something wrong. Which I didn't. I did not push that lady down those stupid rocks."

"Maybe I have evidence to the contrary," Lennon says. He holds up the folio of papers. In it is the autopsy report that of course cannot prove that one woman's hands pressed heavily and relentlessly against another woman's body, causing her to stumble and fall a few weeks before she died. Also in the folio is the name and phone number of the emergency room nurse who was alone with Mrs. Jambon at Roosevelt Hospital whenever Corinne scurried off to a pay phone. For all Lennon knows, Mrs. Jambon whispered to the nurse that Corinne pushed her. For all Corinne knows, Mrs. Jambon whispered that very thing to that very person. For all anyone knows, it actually happened.

"Your mother-in-law did speak when she was in the hospital in New York," Lennon says. That much is the truth.

"What. So we had a fight. An *argument.* She gives me that piece of shit, Burberry knockoff for Lord's sake, seven dollars from a street vendor, and she takes it back when I complain, and I pull on it, trying to get it back, trying to be a good sport. But that's pulling, that's not pushing. On a thing, not a person. She's pulling, I'm pulling. We're up on that rock, it just so happens, and it's like this stupid tug-of-war. Pulling on the ends of this cheap scarf."

Lennon has the picture now. Corinne let go.

He lets silence lie between them for a while.

"Not to speak ill of the dead, but if Mrs. Jambon said I dragged her up there and pushed her, she was lying," Corinne says.

"I'm sure that's true," Lennon says. "Though I can't imagine why she'd want to do such a thing."

Corinne doesn't hear the irony in his voice, and she's so happy that she offers him a Coke in a real glass with real ice that has her personal fingerprints all over it. Corinne tips her Diet Coke glass in Lennon's direction in a mock toast. She has a load off her mind.

The phone rings, and Lennon sees no harm in Corinne's taking a glance at Caller ID to be sure it's not her children's school. "Oh!" she says. "It's Celeste." As if this explains everything. She doesn't consider for a second letting the voice mail pick up. Instead she answers with her voice pitched just high enough that Lennon is tempted to feel sorry for her.

Corinne takes the phone into the next room, and she talks in phrases that are coded to make Celeste do all the exciting work of the conversation. After she has said, “Remember when my sister-in-law was at the house with that woman she works with?” it’s only a matter of time before she can hint at her current situation by saying cryptically, “Yes, the *other* one.” Corinne gets muffled a few times when she is covering the mouthpiece and whispering, and then he hears her say, “I know, can you believe she’s trying to get away with that?” Corinne wants to be Celeste. Celeste does nothing all day but talk. Celeste will get yeast infections forever, but Celeste never will get a job. Corinne comes back from this phone call simply crazy about her own illusions.

As soon as he’s had enough Coke to make his particular glass contaminated forever in the Geoffrey Jambon household, Lennon says, “You know, whatever caused the fall isn’t what caused the death.”

Lennon could swear Corinne is looking at him as if he is getting ready to betray Ciana to her. Corinne is not a woman who ever has had to practice the subtle arts of seduction. And she surely is not a woman who has had to fend off the attentions of strange men. But right now she is doing her level best with her posture to remind him that she is better than Ciana, more attractive than Ciana because she is slight, more innocent than Ciana because Lennon is too carried away to think otherwise. "I won't tell," she says softly. He's sure she has pale pink visions of stargazer lilies in her head. She might even be having olfactory hallucinations.

"It's in the autopsy report, and no one knows besides me," Lennon says.

Corinne nods.

"Well, I'll tell you first that she had a skull fracture, and nobody ever would have known because you said she fell at ground level. And she had respiratory distress, so without the autopsy, everybody would have thought she died of pneumonia."

Corinne's eyes are wide, her breath bated: she is full of lilies; the next sentence from Lennon is sure to be about lilies.

"Okay," Lennon says, aware he has used the last of his compassion, "she died of an embolus to the lung. It was a piece of adipose tissue. Fat. And do you know why she had an embolus to the lung?"

Corinne shakes her head, no, and Lennon can almost see her thought process because it has to be so terribly simple, trying to reconcile the evaporating molecules on a flower with the fat droplets in a woman's veins. It won't work, and it especially won't work for someone like Corinne, who thinks of fat only as immense, as killing someone in a huge suffocating mass around the heart. "I don't get it," she says finally.

"It killed her because it escaped from the bone marrow when the bone wasn't set immediately after it broke, because she had to come back to New Orleans."

Corinne looks at him with the hope that he doesn't

remember whose idea it was to come back to New Orleans. He remembers.

"I think Geoffrey would understand," Corinne says.

"Then why don't you tell him?"

Corinne falls silent.

Lennon sits and listens to the silence of heat blowing through the house and absorbs his newest piece of knowledge. Of all the knowledge he has taken in this afternoon, most has come from Celeste Waters's call. Corinne might say that telling Geoffrey will ruin her children and in turn will ruin Ciana. But the truth is that telling Geoffrey will ruin Corinne. Not because she'll be in trouble with the law. Not because she'll be a sinner in the eyes of God and her husband. But because she'll have to go out and get a job. She will never be Celeste. If any of the science he needs for the NAPLEX has been edged out this afternoon for this fact, it is all right with him.

"What do you want from me?" Corinne says finally.

"You give Ciana her due," Lennon says. "Whatever you took when her mother died, hand it over. And lay off. You see this face?"

Lennon leans across the table and gets his face too close to Corinne's for her comfort.

Corinne nods.

"Well, it's not going anywhere," Lennon says. "Get over it."